Soulship: First Orbit

By Nathan Thompson

Chapter 1

"I am sorry," the woman in front of me wept. "But this can't be your family anymore."

I nodded sadly. The news had not surprised me. And I could not find it in my heart to hate the only woman who had tried to be my mother.

"I tried," she said, still covering her face. "Please know I wanted to keep you. We all wanted to keep you. You're a good boy. You don't deserve this."

"I know, Mother Anne," I said calmly, biting back resentment over her use of the word 'boy.' My malnourished state still led people to believe I was far younger than I looked. "I am grateful for all of the years you kept me safe and warm. I am of age, now. You have done all you legally can."

"It's not right," she insisted, still weeping, her dark hair falling in front of her face. I winced as I noticed the gray that had not been there before she had chosen to take me in. "You should not have to pay for your parents' sins."

I wanted to laugh darkly, and quote one of the many sayings about the sins of the fathers passing on to their children. But that would be suicide, of course, because it would mark me as possessing the same dangerous knowledge that had led to my own parents' executions so long ago.

And had I been a year older at the time of their deaths, and a hair less careful, I would have certainly shared their fate.

"I am not paying for anything, Mother Anne," I said instead. "I am the surviving child of the last two terrorists ever to threaten the Global Republic. I am grateful for the mercy that the Glorious State has shown me all these years. As I know you also are."

Mother Anne bit her lip.

"Yes, of course," she said, frowning bitterly as she swallowed. "The Glorious State has liberated us all and kept us safe. Of course they would never make you pay for your parents' sins. I only wish more could be done for you… all hail the Global Republic," she added, in a tone that said she had just lost something important.

"All hail the Global Republic," I echoed easily. Because I had already lost everything.

Awaken, the heretically English words said as they suddenly appeared before my eyes. *For you are the hope of the night sky.*

I did my best not to react as the words vanished from my eyes a split-second later. But before I even had time to wonder who had just tried to kill me by forcing me to read an illegal language, they reappeared the very next moment, the exact same phrase now written in Spanish. Then French. Then Mandarin. Then Japanese. Then in a dozen more scripts, many from languages my parents never had time to teach me before their deaths. I kept my face as neutral as possible through all of them, for possessing literacy in any single one of them was enough to brand me as an educational terrorist, as the last, and greatest, living enemy to the Global Republic and its Glorious State.

"What was that?" Mother Anne asked as she blinked rapidly.

I nearly sighed in relief, realizing that I wasn't the only one to have suddenly seen a hundred illegal scripts. But that very well could have been the second trap, and so I acted oblivious.

"What do you mean, Mother Anne?" I asked, sounding confused.

"Nothing," she said, wiping her face. "Just saw a string of gibberish before my eyes. Probably just the stress," she added. "But enough of that. I can pack some rations for you, at least."

My stomach shamed me as it groaned in response.

"There is not much to spare, Mother Anne," I made myself say. "Won't the other orphans need meals as well today?"

"You know very well that it has been far easier to gain food credits for them than it has been for you, and that the others would never forgive me for letting you leave empty-handed. They're just as heartbroken over losing you as I am. Wait here. I will be right back."

Mother Anne brushed her long skirt as she rose and hustled off to the nearby kitchen. I remained seated, torn between constant hunger and constant shame. This woman had sacrificed much for me, allowing me to have a full meal almost every day. My being a non-citizen had made my rations increasingly expensive to acquire, and now it had come to choosing between providing my own rations or that of three other orphans here. It would not have come to that, if a certain party had not made sure that the rules regarding the higher expense were viciously enforced.

That certain party was now outside. I could hear his heavy footsteps as he walked toward the door to our orphanage. He opened it without knocking, and walked through the building like he owned the place. Because, as far as our Glorious State was concerned, he did.

"Greetings, Director Jones," I said, standing respectfully. The large man shot me an annoyed look.

"Why are you still here?" he demanded angrily. "Ms. Anne was supposed to have evicted you by now."

"Director Jones, she has just delivered the news to me. Mother Anne has given me a moment to process the news while she makes sure everything is in order for me to leave."

"What's there to make sure of?" he growled, taking a step toward me. "You broke the law, like the terrorist-spawn you are. You should already be outside, waiting for them to take you to the processing center."

"I assure you I will leave shortly, Director Jones," I replied, lowering my head and doing my best to remain respectful. "I merely wish to say one final goodbye to my former family. Please grant us this small mercy."

He growled, and did his best to loom over me. It was an easy accomplishment for him. My growth had been stunted from malnourishment, while Director Jones was naturally tall and had a body that was somehow overfed, despite the fact that the Glorious State had certainly eliminated unequal access to food with their careful and wise regulations. He could break my body in half, and that was no exaggeration.

But I did not leave yet. Because I knew that by law, I could still remain here for a few moments longer.

And because I knew he wanted to spend time alone with Mother Anne, and I still did not care for the way he looked at her.

Mother Anne walked back into the room then, a small parcel of food in her hands. She had already wiped the tears from her face, and now wore a brave expression, probably on my behalf. But the beautiful middle-aged woman froze at the sight of the man who had total control over her orphanage.

"Director Jones," she said in a quiet voice. "I did not expect your arrival today."

"You should have," the director snorted, smiling darkly at her. "A crime happened here on my watch. Should I not give due diligence? Should I not make sure more children here do not go astray, and wind up evicted as well?"

He made no effort to hide the threat at the end of the speech, and Mother Anne's eyes widened when she heard it.

"And what's this?" he gloated as his eyes lowered almost enough to look at the bag in her hands. "Is the boy stealing food again? Or are you helping him, Mother Anne? Surely you would do no such thing. You are a better citizen than that, are you not?"

"I…" the poor woman began helplessly. But there was nothing she could say that would help her right now, and we all knew it.

"Don't worry, Mother Anne," the director gloated, chuckling at the sight of her face. "This is why I will be spending more time here. Your burden for these children is too great. You need my guidance, to keep them from manipulating you. Or should I report that another ration crime just happened this very moment?"

"You are mistaken, honored director," I said, bowing slightly from where I stood. "What you are seeing is no crime at all. Mother Anne has just now shown me the error of my ways. She has informed me that all food in the orphanage will be secured now, even when taken out of the building. She has only left my presence just now to secure said food, and was packing her own lunch, in case a change of plans occurred and she was ordered to escort me to the processing center herself."

"That's ridiculous," the large man snapped as he rounded on me. "Don't insult my intelligence! Even I know you aren't too stupid to untie a ration parcel!"

"I dare not question your wisdom, honored director," I replied calmly. "But your work is important, and your burden is no lighter than Mother Anne's. Had you more time, you would have noticed that the esteemed Mother tied the rations securely, with many layers of packaging. Such layers would easily be removed by a strong man like yourself, but it would no doubt cost my weakened body as many calories as the rations inside would provide. By the time I finally opened the last of the wrappings, I doubt I would even have enough energy to take a single bite."

That was an exaggeration, to be sure. But my own words were close enough to the truth that they shamed me nonetheless. Mother Anne had wrapped the food so that it would last me as long as possible, but it would have taken my feeble arms an embarrassingly long time to get through all the parceling. Another glance from the director showed that he believed me, that he truly thought I was that weak.

"Whatever," the man snapped, turning back to sneer at the orphanage's mother. "But you're not going anywhere, Anne. That agent is stopping by to pick him up. You and I are going to discuss the future for this place."

The woman who had tried to be my mother shuddered at his words, and I could no longer bear it. I stepped forward and fell on my knees, kowtowing to the man in front of us.

"What are you doing?" the director shouted in disgust. "Get away from me, you disgusting, bony thing!"

"Director, please allow me to present my gratitude," I said, keeping my head low. "You have been responsible for the upkeep of this home. It is thanks to your generosity that I have had a place to stay all of these years. It is thanks to your generosity that I have been fed, and clothed, and dry. I accept the consequences of my actions," I said with as straight a face I could muster. "But know that I will never forget your many acts of kindness. I promise to write to you often, so that I may show proper gratitude," I said, raising my head to look him in the eye. "Even if I must write such letters by hand."

The lecherous tyrant blinked as he processed my words. Then he paled as he recognized my threat.

Literacy in the Sanctioned Language was still legal, but non-digital writing was highly discouraged. For if the person could put words of one language on paper, might that mean that he or she had seen written paper before? And if they had seen one language on paper, might they have seen other languages, languages full of all manner of false knowledge, also on paper?

As a non-citizen, I was already under constant surveillance. This confession could not make my life any more difficult. But Director Jones had far more to lose.

"You wouldn't dare," he whispered quietly, trying to hide his own fear. For there was little he could do to keep me from writing a letter addressed to him, and we both knew that.

"I swear to you, honored director," I answered him levelly, "that I will write to you every time I think of you, and Mother Anne, and the other children of this place."

"Get out," he hissed at me, scuttling away from me as if I were one of the diseases the Glorious State had already vanquished. "Get out of here, now."

But he did not dare to do so much as glance in Mother Anne's direction. I knew then that I would take at least one small victory with me, terrorist's child or no.

"Mother Anne, I will now take my leave," I said, rising to my feet without taking my eyes off the director. "Know that you have my gratitude as well."

And that was all I dared to say to her. I walked outside as quickly as I could. If I looked back at Mother

Anne I knew I would stare at the parcel of food she still held, and I did not wish to follow my greatest accomplishment with another defeat.

I left the building and began walking to the nearby street corner, where I could await the agent's arrival. Behind me, I heard shouting, and then the door to the orphanage slammed open, with Director Jones' heavy footsteps trailing off into the distance. I wanted to sigh in relief, but a nearby garbage dispenser caught my eye. I saw it, froze, then hated myself for freezing.

The director's steps had long trailed off. No one else was outside right now, as it was not time for a scheduled break. If I were to dig for food, would anyone know?

And if I did not dig for food, when would my next meal come?

And what if there would be no next meal? What if I had already eaten my last ration, and now other people's waste was my only source of food?

There probably wasn't going to be the remains of any prepared meals, but people threw away plants and leather. I had eaten those before, and survived. But what if people suspected I was able to do so because of the heretical knowledge my parents had taught me?

Another woman's voice soon saved me from my fearful thoughts.

"Jasper! What are you doing out here?"

I recognized the voice, and dared to hope.

"You shouldn't be outside yet!" the blonde uniformed woman told me. "You were supposed to wait inside the orphanage until I came to pick you up!"

"Apologies, Lieutenant Sells," I told the young lady, a talented individual that had already managed to find employment directly within the Glorious State, despite being even younger than myself.

"Don't 'Lieutenant Sells' me," she snapped. "It's 'Nova' to you. I didn't forget where I came from just because I grew up and started working!" Then her face softened. "I just want to make sure you stay safe. There's no telling what could happen to you if you went somewhere alone."

I nodded and chose not to mention that I had spent many nights alone before Mother Anne had been able to take me in, and that I would likely spend many more now that she had been forced to throw me out.

"Sorry, Nova," I said, relaxing and speaking less formally to the girl who had been my closest friend over the years. "Director Jones showed up. He threw me out early."

"What?" she said, startled. "Why?"

"The same reason he was so vigilant with me to begin with," I said as we both began to walk to the processing center. "To spend more time with Mother Anne."

"What do you mean, 'to spend more time with Mother Anne'?" Nova demanded in a shocked tone. My friend was two years older than me, and had graduated from the orphanage before Director Jones' tenure had begun there. She did not know the man like I did, and hadn't had the chance to come by her old home within the past year.

I looked around, wondering just how much surveillance I was under. The truth was that I had long lost all faith in the Glorious State and the Global Republic it governed, but speaking against its officials was still dangerous. But Nova was an official herself now, a rising star, much like the heretical translation of her name, lost to all but time and terrorists. Could she somehow help protect Mother Anne?

Blast it all, I decided, and spoke up.

"I mean, his intentions are less than honorable," I said quietly, but firmly. "She is uncomfortable with his presence, and he does not care for her wishes. I threatened to write to him."

She blinked for a moment, before she began clenching her fists.

"I can't believe it," she growled. "No, I *can* believe it. I can easily believe it. But thank you for telling me, Jasper. And thank you for trying to protect her," she added softly. "You're far braver than you get credit for. I hope you know I see it in you."

"Thank you," I muttered, not meeting her eyes.

It was hard to handle Nova's affection for me. She was a striking woman, with bright blue eyes, golden hair, tanned skin, and finely-shaped features. Beyond all of that, she was passionate, smart, and capable. Her competence and charisma had overcome her own orphan background and allowed her to shoot up through the ranks of State service, making her one of the youngest lieutenants ever to be promoted. Most of the time, I was able to classify her care for me as the platonic love it almost certainly was. But every now and then, my heart shamed me by wanting more from her, despite the fact that I was a half-finished young man with no future of his own, without even the ability to purchase his own food or clothes. The comparison between us always depressed me, so I doggedly reminded myself that I was lucky to have her friendship and smothered any thoughts that ever went further than that.

"I mean it, Jasper," my friend insisted. "I haven't forgotten you, and I never will. I came out here to make sure you'd be taken care of. The treatment you've received ever since your parents' death isn't right. Our new world is supposed to be better than this. I signed up for this job because too many people have forgotten that you have to work to maintain a new world. Our Republic really can be glorious, if enough people just keep fighting for it."

"We know that, Nova," I soothed. "We are told to remain vigilant at all times. In case a new terrorist should one day appear."

If she sensed the irony of my words, she didn't show it. Instead, she kept right on speaking.

"And that's wrong," my gorgeous friend insisted passionately. "We don't need people just being vigilant. We need them active. Asking themselves how they can make this a better world. Helping their neighbor. Having high standards for their leaders. Becoming leaders themselves, wherever possible. I know people get scared sometimes, but if an orphan like me can find a job helping the Republic, anyone can! Just watch, Jasper. Maybe I can't fix everything myself, but I can make things better, even if it's just enough to cause one more person to try, and then they can make a difference, too! And that's what I'm going to do right now. Come on." She grabbed my hand and took me to a side street, leading me away from the processing center.

"Nova, where are we going?" I asked, looking around worriedly. I knew this could end badly. There had to be at least ten surveillance devices monitoring me right now.

"You have to be starving, so I'm buying you some food," my bold friend said stubbornly. "And before you start arguing, yes, I can in fact do that. I have the clearance to procure a handful of rations as I see fit. After that, we're going to the processing center, where I can argue your case for you and work out the bureaucratic nonsense that keeps getting in the way of your getting a basic citizen's rights. These things aren't supposed to happen to you, Jasper. And I finally have the power to do something about it, or at least part of it."

Awaken, the words flashed in front of my eyes again. *For you are the hope of the night sky.*

Again, I did not react, save to let go of the hope that Nova's passion had just instilled in me.

"Jasper," Nova said, blinking. "Did you just see something?"

"What do you mean?" I controlled my tone carefully.

"Don't get paranoid on me right now, Jasper," my friend answered impatiently. "This is serious. I think we might be under a terrorist attack."

"Then you should understand why I'd be paranoid, Nova," I answered back. "I have no idea what is going on either, but I will be the first person everyone suspects."

"You're right," she said. "Let's go to the processing center, just to be safe. Then we can figure out if we're the only ones seeing this weird, illegible script."

Just then, an alarm sounded, followed by a message from the official speaker devices that could always be found nearby, no matter where one happened to be.

"Attention, citizens. The Republic has detected signs of a possible terrorist attack on the public's morals. Stay inside your buildings and do not attempt to read any foreign script. If you accidentally read it and suspect you can understand it, report to the nearest processing center for a moral examination. That is all."

"Everyone's seeing it then," Nova said. "I had thought it to be a coincidence when I saw it earlier. This is bad news. Let's get you somewhere safe, Jas."

That will not be the processing center, I wanted to tell her, but I knew she would not listen, and I did not have nearly enough muscle to pull myself out of her grip. Her feet moved quickly, and I stumbled along after her.

Hurry, awaken, the words said again in every old language. *For you are needed, oh hope of the night sky.*

Nova shook her head.

"It's back again," she grumbled. "This doesn't make any sense. Why would a terrorist send everyone a threat in a language we can't even read? It wouldn't cause nearly as much panic as it would if they were using State Script. All they're doing is announcing their presence. State Surveillance will be able to find them if this keeps up."

"Could it be a test?" I asked, hoping that my curiosity wouldn't earn me any extra scrutiny. "An attempt to catch anyone familiar with the illegal languages?"

That idea made the most sense to me, but Nova shook her head.

"If surveillance could just make words appear before everyone's eyes, they wouldn't do it to everyone all at once. That would just make their jobs harder. This is something else, and we need to figure out what."

I beg you, the words continued. *Hear me, my Beacon, and awaken. You are needed in the night sky above. Why have you not answered?*

I tripped over my own two feet. Nova's swift reaction kept me from crashing face-first into concrete.

"Jas!" she said worriedly as she drew up beside me. "Are you alright?"

"Yes, sorry," I said, rapidly spinning a lie I that could bear to tell my best friend. "Haven't eaten yet today."

It was true, even if it was not the reason for my fall.

"Right, I'll be more careful," she said compassionately. "And I promise I'll get you fed as soon as I'm sure we're safe. Can you keep up if we go this pace?" she asked as she switched to a brisk walk.

I nodded, and I reminded myself that I had no time to feel shame. We walked a few more steps before the dangerous words returned again.

You... the words said in every language but Sanctioned Script. To my horror, Nova did not react in the slightest, not even shaking her head like she had the last time the words had appeared.

You... noticed, the writing declared, appearing slowly, as if it was making sure I could follow along. Again, Nova did not seem to notice, and I realized that the words were speaking to me directly.

Can you... read me? the terrifying script ran before my eyes. *Please... answer... urgent... danger... coming...*

I realized I now had two choices. I could answer the script, and risk my very life—if what I had could still qualify as one. Or I could believe that I must now hide from a foe that could speak to my very mind, and see how long it took me to finally go mad.

Yes, I finally dared to think, but no response came. So I made the words appear in my mind as script in English, my once-native language. *Yes.*

Why? the words asked me next. *Why... only... you?*

As if the writer did not know that their chosen languages were no longer legal.

The Glorious State and its Global Republic had existed for a little over two decades, though I suspected it would soon teach otherwise. According to what we were taught, the new government encompassed the entire planet. For the writer to not know his or her words were dangerous would mean that they had lived in the most remote of places since before I was born. Assuming, of course, that this was not a trap.

These scripts are forbidden, I thought back hesitantly. *You endanger me by using them.*

What? the mysterious writer replied. *All... planet's... tongues? Why?*

Who are you? I asked instead, angry at the other's ignorance. *Who are you that you do not know this? Why did you risk exposing me, instead of using the Sanctioned Script, the only legal language for the last two decades?*

Sanctioned? the stranger asked me. *What is...no... out... of time. Must write quickly. You are holding my body's hand.*

I somehow managed to keep myself from once again tripping in surprise.

"Nova," I asked very quietly. "Did you just try to speak to me?"

"No, Jas," my friend replied, still holding my hand and walking quickly. "Why?"

"I must be panicking then," I replied. "Let's keep going."

And so you lie, I accused the mysterious words. *Who are you, truly?*

I am the part of her that flies through your night sky above, the suspicious script replied. *And were you not standing within daylight, I swear you would see me. There is no time to explain. They are coming for you all. But they will come for her first.*

Who? I demanded, now far more concerned than I was a moment ago. *Who is coming for her?*

"Hang in there, Jas," Nova said as we walked. "Almost there."

The monsters that your ancestors put to memory and books, the messenger replied. *Time and time again.*

Specify, blast it! I thought furiously to the entity claiming to be a woman as I struggled to watch where Nova was pulling me. *There were a million different nightmares written within my parents' burned books! You could be referring to any one of them, and I would never know before I met them! If your use of illegal language does not kill me, the vagueness of your warnings will! Write clearly, or else depart and stop risking my life!*

I, the other being began writing, and then stopped. I waited as patiently as I could, finally deciding that the other was too ignorant to be my surveillance or a supposed terrorist themselves. They had something they needed me to know, yet they lacked all knowledge of my world's present. *So much has changed since I left my body here. The safeguards have all been undone. Never mind. Do not go where she is taking you. Her hunters are already waiting for her there.*

I wanted to scream that the stranger should be able to talk to Nova herself, if they truly had a connection to her. But we were mere minutes away from the processing center, and I could even see the ugly building looming in the distance.

"Nova," I said, pulling on my friend's arm, wishing I was stronger and better fed. "Wait."

"What is it?" She turned to look at me with concern. "Do you need to rest, Jas?"

Why can you not speak to her yourself? I wrote in my mind. *Is she not your body?*

My first message should have awakened her genetic memories, but she was never taught any of your planet's old languages, and I know no other written words. She must read them, so that they can burn into her mind.

That was a frustrating complication, but after a moment, it was easily circumvented.

"Nova," I said, "your communicator."

"What about it?" she asked. The State frowned on communication devices being overused, especially government ones, but as long as Nova was willing to put up with giving a report for this unscheduled communication, she would be fine.

"I need it, and cannot explain why. Please trust me. Just this once," I begged.

Over our heads, the government speakers repeated the warning to stay inside, and not read anything. Nova hesitated, then frowned.

"What do you mean, 'just this once'? Here. Hurry," she said, slapping the communicator into my hand. "Although I can't imagine why you would need it."

Nova had already turned the handheld device on when she handed it to me. I quickly activated the keyscript function and began typing words in Sanctioned Script as fast as I could.

"Jasper, I'll get in trouble if you send anyone a message," my government friend warned me, but I shook my head, thrusting the device back into her hands as soon as I had finished writing.

"Read it," I said, hoping I was not making a terrible mistake by believing the unseen stranger. "Quickly."

My friend impatiently humored me as her eyes scanned the short message I had typed on her pad.

Awaken, I had translated. *For you are the hope of the night sky.*

Her bright blue eyes flashed.

It was almost imperceptible. But I got the impression that a thousand lights had just turned on in my friend's mind.

Once again, I wondered what I had done.

"Nova?" I asked my fellow orphan.

"I'm here, Jas," she said, blinking. "More than I ever have been. You may have just saved the entire planet." She looked up and around, as if seeing everything for the first time. "If it hasn't already ended itself."

What did you just do? I sent to the hidden stranger.

"She woke me up, Jas," Nova answered, looking at me sadly and guessing my thoughts. "She made me realize why I've always wanted to make the world a better place. It's my purpose." She looked away. "We need to leave, now that I know the processing center's not safe. Let's go."

She began pulling me down another street, though clean alleys surrounded by crumbling buildings.

"Where are we going?" I asked the woman that I hoped I still knew.

"The State's broadcasting waves are jamming most of her signal," Nova replied. "But it can't reach every part of every city. If I can get somewhere clear of the waves, she can reach me, and bring me back aboard. Then I can awaken her in turn, energize a few of her systems, and we can stop the invasion."

She shook her head as we walked. "I can't believe it came to this. None of this was supposed to be necessary. Language wasn't supposed to become illegal. There wasn't supposed to be a 'Glorious State.'" She turned her head to face me, catching my eyes with her own. "And I wasn't supposed to wind up an orphan, with no one to protect me except for a kind orphanage mother, and a young boy smart enough to keep me safe before that. I mean it, Jas. The only reason this world has a chance at survival was because you made sure I had one myself. Thank you. I'll never say that enough."

Then she turned her head forward again, and we kept walking.

"Attention, Lieutenant Sells," the State speakers said over our heads. "Your presence is requested at the nearest processing center. Report in and stand by for further instruction."

That was rather obvious of them, but Nova did nothing but hiss.

"Spent the best years of my life trying to fix this place, only for it all to turn on me," my blonde friend grumbled. "Stay close to me, Jas," she added unnecessarily, because I still was not strong enough to pull my way out of her grip.

Protect her, the word-person sent to me. *Please. She is the hope of the night sky. Protect her, until I can take her back and save you all. I promise I will find a way to reward you for it.*

"Can you see the messages your friend in the sky is sending me?" I asked Nova, trying to keep the annoyance out of my voice. The idea of me, a stunted, malnourished boy, protecting anyone was a mockery I was unwilling to appreciate.

"No, Jas," Nova replied. "I have a loose connection with her, and it didn't activate until you wrote that note. She's probably talking so much because most of her senses are jammed. She can't even make out our figures clearly. So don't worry too much about what she says anymore. You've done your part. I'll take it from here."

The speakers blared their command again, and Nova began to pull me faster. I noticed that the Glorious State's messages were becoming more distant. I recognized the area we were crossing into. It was one of the 'less equal' districts, one where I had often taken Nova to forage for food before Mother Anne had found us and taken us in. The lack of surveillance made it much safer, at least for people like me, than the more heavily patrolled areas were.

You are almost there, the invisible woman messaged me. *Just keep her safe a little longer, I beg you. Then I will record your heroism for all the ages to come.*

You offer me lies, I thought back bitterly. *All records can be burned. But I will do what I can nonetheless.*

The stranger in the night sky made no reply. I turned my attention to the streets we were traveling, to try and help Nova navigate.

"There," I said, pointing with my free arm to another alley three blocks down. "There are no recording devices down there. That was always the best spot to find food or supplies."

She nodded, and broke into a jog.

"Sorry, Jas," she said as she continued to drag me along. "We have to hurry. They're closing in."

Before I could ask how she knew, I heard something hiss from three or four streets behind us.

My blood went cold. I had enough forbidden knowledge to remember that there was no natural creature on this part of the world that could hiss like that.

"Nova," I huffed as I struggled to keep up with her. Her pace was already tiring me, and I knew I was slowing her down. "They are only after you. You should leave me behind."

"Don't be ridiculous, Jas," she snapped without looking at me. "They wish to capture me. But they will kill you. Now hold on. We're almost there."

The alley was just one street over now. We would be there in moments, despite my body's miserable speed and endurance, and Nova's stubborn insistence in protecting me.

Another hiss sounded, no further away than it had been moments ago.

"Lieutenant Sells," the speakers sounded out. "Be advised that you are currently in danger. Stay where you are, so that other agents may come to your assistance."

"Not even bothering to pretend anymore," my beautiful friend snarled. "Figures. They don't really need to now."

We crossed into the alley. I recognized the spot—the large, outdated garbage bin. There were no cameras here, no recording devices. This was a corner that the Glorious State had long forgotten it owned.

I can reach her now! the woman in the stars above shouted in script. *You have done it! You have saved your world!*

"Brace yourself, Jas," Nova panted in a determined tone. "She's about to take us somewhere else. It will be good, though," she insisted, staring at me. "She can take care of you. Help your body recover from all the neglect you've suffered."

Then she suddenly winced, looking uncharacteristically self-conscious.

"Not that there's anything wrong with the way you look now," she said quickly. "I didn't mean…"

"I am not offended, Nova," I said patiently. "I am aware of my body's condition. If your magic sky-woman can somehow fix it and keep me fed, that will be all I need from her. I am surprised she has not already offered."

"She… doesn't know," Nova said, biting her lip. "She can't see much of you. And she didn't believe me when I told her. But I wouldn't have either, if I was her. Anyway, we just need to wait for a few more moments, and we'll be safe."

I nodded, still wondering why she was acting so strange. But the next moment, I heard a chuckling hiss echo all around us.

"Safe," a sibilant voice mocked. "The little boat thinks she will be safe."

And with that, one of the monsters the stranger had failed to warn me about stepped into view.

Its body was completely black, from its face and foreclaws all the way to the tip of its restless tail. Had it stood on its hind legs, it would have towered over us, but as it was, it slunk low over the ground on all four limbs. Two smoky wings billowed on its back like shrouds, concealing the details of its form, save for its glowing purple eyes.

"But you are not safe, little boat," the monster chuckled. "You have walked into a trap. One that we spent decades in the making."

"You haven't caught me yet," my friend growled, pulling out the baton strapped to her leg. "And you won't."

"Oh, we will, little boat," the monster replied unworriedly. I wracked my brain to try and figure which legend, which myth might name him best. But there were none specific enough. "The rest of you thought to arrive here in time to thwart us, but the truth is that we have been here all along. Waiting to catch you, the last Soulship. So that we can finally own the night sky of every world. But go ahead and try to escape. I'd love to see you fail."

He snorted in contempt, and purple smoke rolled out of his nostrils.

I reached back into my myths, and named him.

"Dragon?" I said, disbelief locking my body down for a moment. "You are a *dragon?* Dragons are *real?*"

He snorted again, and ignored me. My deduction had not impressed him.

"Yes, Jas," Nova said, baton still held ready. "Dragons are real, and come in many kinds. But the very worst race among them all has blinded the minds of your world's leaders. And done so when I had least expected it. I'm sorry, Jas. I messed up." Her voice shook for just a moment. But then she was back to the brave, strong woman I had always known. "But don't give up, yet. I can probably take him, now that some of my power has awakened."

I wanted to sigh in relief over her words. The longer the dragon-man stood there without acting, the more time Nova's friend in the sky had to rescue us. We needed him to forget that.

Hurry, I typed in my mind. *We are found.*

I know, she typed back quickly, and then went silent. I tried to think of ways to further distract our would-be captor. But the dragon-thing merely sighed at us, making more wisps of smoke.

"You could not battle me, little boat," the dragon-thing hissed. "My kind was hatched specifically to defeat your little flesh-bodies. Now come quietly, and I will spare the manchild you insist on protecting."

"Liar," my friend spat. "You will kill him for sport, if nothing else."

"So?" the monster replied. "At least you will not see him die painfully. But you have no other options. He cannot aid you in fighting me, and you cannot defeat me on your own. My patience is growing thin. Submit, or I will force you to, and punish you for your resistance."

"Very well, then," I said, stepping forward. "We submit. But give us a few moments to say our goodbyes."

"What?" Nova shouted, staring at me in shock.

"Time is short," the shadowy dragon hissed. "And you are in no position to bargain."

"If your words were true," I argued, "you would not bother with demanding surrender at all. You would have overpowered us, and left nothing to chance. You do not wish to risk combat, and we do not wish to risk death. But this woman is my closest friend. We have known each other for most of our lives. I beg for time to say goodbye."

"What are you doing, Jas?" Nova whispered. "This is unnecessary."

"Are you truly confident that you can beat him?" I whispered back. "Or should you risk fighting him at all?"

Her hesitance was all the answer I needed.

"Very well, then," the shadowy drake rumbled. "You have one minute."

With that, he relaxed, moving to squat in a sitting position with his hindlegs.

I could not believe it. One minute should be more than enough time, if Nova's mysterious friend could be trusted at all. If it was not enough time, then we were doomed to begin with.

But Nova did not share my optimism, and that worried me.

She glanced back at the monster before us, then back at me. Then she dropped her baton and took my hands.

"Okay, Jas," she said. "We'll go ahead and say our goodbyes. Thank you for getting this time for us."

She spoke in a defeated tone. Not as someone going along with my plan.

"I'll go first. I want you to know that it wasn't your fault this all didn't work out. It's not mine, either. Maybe you can blame it on the part of myself flying over our heads. No, that's not fair either. Blame it on my fighting too many monsters, for too long, without rest. She's been trying to fix everything that's gone wrong, and she can't. But no one else is trying, anymore. Does that make sense?"

Her eyes searched my own. I could tell she was hunting for validation.

"No, Nova," I answered honestly. "But that's okay. I believe this isn't your fault. But tell me why you refer to the other person talking to us as another part of yourself, and why the dragon creature is calling you a boat."

"A boatling," the monster corrected arrogantly. "And I'm calling her that because she is small, and because she is effectively a boat that floats through space."

"How supremely helpful," I said, my sarcasm overcoming what fear I had of the monstrosity. I would probably be much more afraid later, but for now, I needed to help my friend.

"No, Jas," Nova said sadly. "It would take far too long to explain all the things you don't understand right now. But I want you to know this much. I'm still the same Nova you knew before. Even though I'm not really human. Even though I have a whole host of power and memories I wish I had more time to share with you. But the most important thing I need you to know, Jas, is that I'm the same girl you can't ever see clearly."

I tensed, because her words offended me.

"I know, I *know,* Jas," she said stubbornly. "You knew I was special. So you saw that, instead of a scared, hungry girl that didn't know the streets like you did, and took me under your wing. You made sure I always got fed, even if you had to suffer for it, because you saw great things in me. You saw a little girl worth protecting, worth holding when she cried, and worth encouraging when she felt scared and overwhelmed. You saw only greatness in me. You didn't see the small, lonely side of me, that had fallen in love with the boy who had been her hero all of her childhood. Goodbye, Jas. Live as long as you can. I wish I could do more in return for all you have done for me."

Brace yourself, the stranger from the sky said. *I'm teleporting you both now.*

Nova's words were senseless. There was no way I was leaving without her and it would have defeated the purpose anyway, but it no longer mattered. The distraction had worked after all.

Our bodies began to fade. I felt the strange sensation of ceasing to be in one place and starting to feel sensations somewhere else, as if I were touching, smelling, and hearing things much farther away.

But then the dragon near us suddenly exhaled. An invisible presence wrapped around me, smothering me. I saw a black shadow wash over myself and Nova, preventing us from escaping into the sky above. Only the thin edge of it chose to entangle me, but it wrapped around Nova in layers.

Foolish little boat, the shadowy dragon's voice hissed all around us in the darkness. *Did you really think you could escape from a Chain Dragon's brood?*

I did not, Nova said back without her mouth. *But I know I can at least save him.*

A blue light shined out from the darkness that had wrapped around my friend. It burned as a small sphere, originating between her chest and stomach. Two lines traveled out from it, racing up her shoulders, down her arms, and into the hands she still gripped my own with. The blue light blasted out as it left her palms, burning away the much-thinner shroud trying to smother me. Then her hands opened and shoved me away.

Goodbye, Jasper Cloud, Nova's voice said in my mind, echoing through my brain as it moved across time and space, *I love you.*

As I screamed in impotent rage, my body vanished from the face of the planet.

Chapter 2

I landed, still screaming. The ground beneath my body was cold and metallic.

I shuddered from the impact, but my landing was gentle enough even for my feeble bones. It did not make my throat any less raw. I stopped shrieking Nova's name long enough to rise to my feet, looking around at the place her sacrifice had sent me to. Darkness and steel were the only things my eyes could find.

"Nova!" I cried out again. *Maybe I was wrong*, I thought. Maybe she had managed to escape herself, at the last moment, with that strange power that had flowed out of her core. Maybe she would appear any moment now, or had already arrived somewhere else in this strange place.

I waited for another minute, but my beautiful friend remained absent. I cursed as I replayed her final words, her confession to me, one I had never expected. *Why?* I asked myself. Why had she chosen me, of all people? She was a star plucked out of the night sky, and I was a hunger-weakened wretch with no future whatsoever.

"It should have been you," I muttered. "You should have been the one to escape." And I was right. What was I supposed to do now?

Come… here, the mysterious stranger typed. *Follow… blue…line.*

A small line lit up on the floor, the same color as Nova's strange energy. It traced off into the distance, like a vein or a wire current.

I followed it, like the stranger requested. There was nothing else for me to do. Unless I wanted to try and forage for food here, in this giant cage of shadow and steel.

Be… careful, the messenger sent to me. *Not… safe.*

Then why did you seek to bring us here? I thought angrily. She did not answer.

I heard something bang in the distance, and decided not to test her further. I walked directly on top of the glowing line, gaining enough illumination to see that I was navigating through corridors of dark, narrow hallways. They were metal, like everything else in this frigid, dark place, but here and there, I saw small patches of rust. Again, I heard something bang in the far distance. The sounds filled me with a level of dread I had not felt even in the streets back home, where one small mistake would have earned me a beating and the loss of every morsel of food I had scrounged up. I contemplated searching for food here, learning how to survive in this new place of cold iron and dark tunnels, where something I could not see bumped about in the dark.

"It should not have been me," I muttered again under my breath. Then, remembering Nova, I mustered up my last shred of courage and walked forward, stepping out of the narrow halls and into a wider, brighter room.

Here, the entire floor was lit with blue lines. They trailed along square tiles in circuits, lining each edge and congregating in the very center of the room around a large, horizontal capsule that was nearly waist-high. The blue lines flickered briefly, draping darkness over the entire room for a moment.

"You… are… here," a young woman's voice called out tiredly from the tube.

I followed the voice. It reminded me of Nova's somehow, compelling me to walk closer as I tried to figure out how.

"No…" she said suddenly. "Don't… need… closer."

Her voice strained to reach me, and yet it requested me to keep my distance.

"You told me to come into this room, and then tell me to stay at the very edge of it?" I asked, suspicious. This woman had knocked over what was left of my world with her messages. She had yet to earn my full trust. So I kept walking forward. "I thought I was supposed to come here because it was safe. Why should I linger at the edge of the room?"

I heard a ragged sigh come from the capsule, and I could not help but wince in pity as I heard it.

I had not yet begun to trust this woman, but I could tell she was suffering, and tired, and hungry. Her anguish made my heart twitch in empathy.

"Fine…" her weak voice somehow strained its way across the room. "Didn't… want… see me...but...wanted… see you… anyway."

Her sorrow compelled me. I kept walking closer. The blue light flickered directly under my feet as I crossed the tiles. Here and there, I began to see more devices inside the room. Large black screens that resembled ancient televisions, so common before the time of the Glorious State. Small pedestals with buttons lining their topmost surfaces. Occasionally, the blue light tried to flow into channels carved inside the devices, but dried up halfway through, leaving the rest of the mechanism dark. In other places, I could tell that the channels for the light had been damaged, making the light pop through the air in sparks.

"Don't… touch… sparks," the woman called out tiredly, as if I might not have considered them dangerous.

But I was not interested in them. I was interested in the voice that reminded me of Nova. I was interested in seeing the woman who sounded just as frail as I was.

I kept walking closer. I still wanted answers from this place that resembled the ruins of the fabled starships my parents had told me illegal stories about. I wanted to know who this person was, why she had dared to warn us, and if there was any way that Nova could still be saved.

And finally, in spite of all my caution and confusion, I wished to see if this woman could be saved herself. Her pain was too familiar for me not to try.

Finally, after another minute of walking through the room of shadow, steel, and blue light, I was close enough to see the top of the human-sized capsule that the woman had been speaking from.

I was not surprised to find that the very top was open, or that a young woman was inside of it. But I was very surprised by her appearance. Her skin was an ethereal gray, with just a faint trace of blue, the same shade that I had seen in Nova's hands and on this strange ship's floor, coloring her like blush. Her shoulder-length hair was straight and dark, splaying limply over the padding around her head and neck. Her body looked tired and frail, and I could see her straining through every small movement , from breathing to shifting slightly in her padded bed. Her eyes were also gray-blue, and as she blinked at me, I saw their dark pupils sparkling in the dim light, with an intensity that reminded me of Nova's own gaze and drowned out all the pain and weariness the rest of her body was projecting.

She was beautiful. Her fragile state, and my own lingering suspicion, did nothing to keep me from noticing that about her.

"Hello there," the woman said sadly. Her voice had a faint rasp to it. It reminded me of a well-crafted instrument that had been forced to play constantly while being scratched and struck, and never getting the maintenance it needed. "Thank you for coming closer. It is so much easier to speak at this distance." Her bright eyes glanced downward, as if she was trying to look at herself. "But forgive my appearance. I have been… damaged... for some time."

"Until I find it displeasing, I will do no such thing," I said firmly, unable to take my eyes off of her own. They glinted as if they were a gray sea under the sun, and I had no defense against them. "Now, tell me who you are, how I can help you, how you are connected to Nova, and how we can still save her."

The tired woman gave me a smile that was nearly as bright as her eyes.

"I see," she said simply. "So that was why she loved you." Then her pupils tracked along my body, as if she finally took in more than my face. "Wait. You helped her in your current condition? What happened to you?"

"A starvation so ancient, it is not relevant right now," I said impatiently, trying not to snap at a woman that looked as deprived as I did. "How can we save her? And do we need to save you as well?"

But the woman in the capsule did not seem to hear me.

"I don't understand," she said softly. "How were you able to protect her? And why did you bother?" She looked away for a moment. "She said she loved you… yet she let you suffer like this?"

"She didn't *let* me suffer like this," I growled in frustration. Memories of Nova's confession banged against too many corners of my brain. "The rulers of my world forbade that I be fed and sheltered. There was little she could have done for me, and she always dared to do far more than she ever should have. And I didn't protect her either, because in the end, she threw away her own worthy life for reasons that wound my mind. Now tell me how we can save her."

"You can't," the encapsulated woman said bitterly. "I have failed you all." She turned her head back to me, and now her eyes flashed instead of glistened. "Will you accept this apology, man whom Nova loved? Please? I am sorry. I tried to save all of your people. But I failed long before I even arrived. Will you please believe that? That I am sorry I failed?"

"You say we are doomed?" I asked, trying to get my emotions under control. Even with everything that had just happened, it was hard to maintain my anger at a woman who looked so broken, and so tired. "My entire world? Nova included? And that nothing can be done?"

"Yes," she whispered in a small voice. "Your world. My other body. This broken body. And even yourself. All of us are doomed. I have made too many mistakes."

I heard another banging noise in the distance. This one sounded louder, and closer.

"Tell me your connection to Nova, why you are doomed yourself, and why you bothered to save me if I will still die here," I said, forcing myself to remain patient. The frightened back corner of my mind was insisting we did not have much time left.

"I am Nova, and Nova is myself," the woman answered. "And I am also the vessel you are inside of. I am a Soulship, a friend to all forms of life that carry hope. This body's name is Vessa, as is the ship you are standing in. May I know your name, man who cared for Nova? So that I can thank you properly, and then continue with your questions?"

"Jasper Cloud," I said quickly. "Please continue your explanation."

"Thank you, Jasper Cloud," Vessa said. "Thank you for the love you have shown my other body, and for risking yourself so freely. I would praise you to your family or clan, if there was still time."

"I have no clan," I said, still listening for whatever it was that still clattered in the distant dark. "And my entire family lies dead, murdered by righteous-sounding men. There is no one, other than Nova and a small orphanage, that would care for any deeds I performed. Please, explain why we are doomed, and why you still bothered to call me here."

"She made me," Vessa replied. "She wanted you to be safe, to live as long as possible. She believed that as long as you escaped, you would thrive. She did not believe me when I said I would be taken as well. The thing you hear in the shadows beyond is coming for me. It has entered my shell through the wounds I sustained earlier. It will take this current body, and then drain the last Soulship of her power. Before then, it will find you and kill you too, unless you are somehow able to hide."

No, I thought. *I forbid it.*

I had just escaped the monsters that ruled my own world. I refused to die here, when I had just found a way to the stars.

And I refused to mark as lost the woman I loved.

"But I can do one thing for you, Jasper Cloud, who loved Nova well," Vessa continued. She closed her eyes and waved a slender hand. Blue light traveled from her capsule to one of the half-lit devices, causing the light to travel all the way up and reveal something that looked a good bit like a small rectangular chest. "I can honor her request that you be cared for. You have been deprived of much. Food and medicine are within this casket. It will all go a long way in undoing the neglect that others have inflicted on you. I only wish you had more time to take advantage of it."

The top of the chest opened. Mist rolled out, as if it were a cooler of some sort. Inside were pouches, much like the rations issued throughout the Global Republic. They looked easy enough to open, and were in such quantity that they probably would have fed me for a whole year, even if I chose to eat as many as three a day.

I wanted further answers, but Vessa appeared unwilling to talk more until she fulfilled her obligation. And, truth be told, I was always hungry. So I grabbed a packet, opened the top, and put it to my mouth.

The contents were mostly liquid. It tasted, for lack of a better word, healthy. As it went down my throat, it felt like it was providing nutrients that my body had been craving for years. I felt my mind sharpen, my muscles pulse with energy. The constant pain in my belly vanished almost instantly, and just from this one packet, I felt more nourished than I had even when Mother Anne had been able to get me two meals in the same day. My back creaked, and it became much easier to stand straighter. It was almost as if my body was returning to the state it held before my parents had been killed, when I had been well-fed and constantly full of energy.

"Do you feel better, Jasper Cloud?" Vessa asked with a sad, tired smile. "This food is meant to counter planet-wide famines. One meal can bring a starved person back from the cusp of death. One meal a day can bring that person back to normal health in less than a month. If I had that long, we could restore the vitality that your body has long been denied. You would have a stronger, healthier form, one that would better match your handsome face."

Then, of all things, she looked away, as if in embarrassment.

"Forgive me," she said to the inside of the capsule. "I had forgotten my own broken appearance when I praised you."

With the constant, nagging hunger gone from my mind, I was able to hear her self-deprecation clearly. I focused on how tired, hurting, and unhealthy she looked, and how damaged this ship also appeared, and how she had called the ship a part of herself as well.

And as I looked closer, I noticed that her body looked even more starved than my own. I had been drawn in by her sparkling eyes and her ethereal beauty, but the truth was that her limbs and torso looked painfully frail.

"Your body," I said, as my brain became increasingly clear. "Your physical one, not this ship itself.

Does it require food? Or is it somehow tied to the state of this ship?"

"Both," she answered, turning her head back to look at me. "Though sometimes, one can strengthen the other, if it is in very good condition. But right now, you behold me in a twice-wrecked state, with a flesh-body not even strong enough to leave this bed. I would have given anything not to have been seen like this."

"Do you require food?" I repeated, looking again at her weakened form, and pulling out a second bag of super-nutrients. "Are you hungry? Will one of these packets help you at all?"

The tired woman turned her beautiful eyes away again.

"Nothing can help me," she whispered under her breath. But I saw the hand closest to me suddenly twitch.

I brought the packet over to her, noticing how much easier it was for me to walk now. In fact, I no longer felt tired at all.

"It will not matter in the end," she insisted, still not looking at me. I quietly opened the packet and put it down next to her open hand, and then backed away to give her space. Her eyes turned just enough to see me, and I recognized the hungry, desperate shame she felt. I had not wanted an audience when I had been that starving, either, so I turned away and did what I could to grant her privacy. Hopefully, she was strong enough to lift the packet on her own, but I knew from experience that she needed dignity as much as she did physical help. I would not offer unless she clearly could not succeed on her own. Fortunately, it proved unnecessary.

"Thank you," Vessa said after a few moments. I turned around and saw that she had finished the pouch, clutching it tightly in her hand, as if she was unsure it was real. "You did not have to be so kind to me. Let me answer what questions we have time for."

She sighed, sounding a little more relaxed, if not happier.

"I come from a race of people who bonded themselves into the greatest of vessels that ever sailed through the night sky—the name for what you call the universe. We have forgotten whether we are truly flesh or truly machine, but we remember our mission. Our race's purpose is to ensure that hope remains among the younger tribes nestled between the darkness and stars. Too many races had been on the verge of extinction, to the point where this galaxy risked going dark for good. So we were created, ships that could love, care, and protect. We were shelters, protectors, providers, at least until the peoples could curb their destructive impulses long enough to master whatever source of power gave life to their world." She looked away wistfully, as if she was recalling a fond memory instead of the current devastation that grieved her so much. "Under our care, they flourished, and began learning how to advance their bodies and minds beyond the frail forms they had been born with. Some races mastered the various elements and began to work miracles among their worlds. Others formed bonds with mighty beasts, strengthening both their bodies and the harmony of their world. Finally, some were able to tap into the energy of the galaxy itself, the power that moves creation forward. In time, each of these races curbed their tendencies to war among themselves, and took their places among the night sky. They began to aid us in driving away the cold that tried to smother the night sky, allowing our reach to expand, and to protect more worlds, let more races grow in spite of the perils that sought to smother them. Soon the number of thriving systems became greater than the number of Soulships able to take care of them.

"So we split off small pieces of our consciousness and wrapped bodies of flesh around them, so that they could grow into our avatars that would watch the worlds in our absence. Nova is one such part of me, a Beacon. She was meant to be received by a caring family that would shelter her until more of her mind grew. But something must have gone wrong."

"The family likely met the same fate as my own," I said grimly. "Murdered by the forces that destroyed all the records of my world. Who, and what, are they? And how can I rescue Nova from them? And how can I stop them from hurting Mother Anne, and other orphans like me?"

Vessa paused her narrative as she looked up at me.

"Tell me, Jasper Cloud," she pleaded. "Tell me, I beg you. Who taught you how to always be brave?"

"I am not brave," I answered. "I am starving. If I wish to survive, I must protect what little I have that gives me life."

Her eyes glittered at my response.

"I see. Know that there are many forces that seek to smother, devour, or enslave. If they are allowed to do as they please, all of life would have long since crumbled, including their own. Your world once held the greatest library containing knowledge of their names and how to fight them all. That place was destroyed long ago, yet your people saved the legends inside of it."

"Is that why they killed my parents?" I asked. "Is that why my world has no more books and stories?"

"Your stories were preserved," Vessa answered me. "I made copies, and rescued what original works I could long ago. They are elsewhere on this vessel, within the libraries I built inside myself. I had hoped to go through them with Nova when she came here. If I had managed to merge with her again, your world might have been saved. I am sorry."

"Who is our doom?" I insisted. "What creatures are going to kill us? Is it the dragons lurking on my world? And tell me, how can Nova be saved?"

"She can be saved if someone strong enough were to rescue her from the Drake that is encaging her. If I were a little healthier, I could have done it myself. If another Soulship had survived the last great war, they could have helped in my stead. Or if a being had awakened the power of their planet, they might have been strong enough. The Cage Dragons are built for capture, not battle. At the Drake stage, they are not very strong. But I have no contact with any awakened beings, and my enemies now corner me. You have heard the closest one just now, the one I do not have the power to keep at bay. It is among the weakest of hunter-beasts, but it is enough to ensure my death. So, you see, Jasper Cloud, every single thing has happened that was needed to doom us all. My brothers and sisters were all destroyed or taken in the earlier wars. I have become too damaged to continue their duties for them. Your world grew a cancer under my nose that thwarted my plan to use Nova to save it. Finally, enough of my enemies have succeeded in tracking me down, in confining me to this distant corner of the galaxy, in apparent tandem with the monsters ready to enslave and devour your own world. I wish one single thing had not gone wrong, so that we would all live."

More banging sounded out. The blue lights all flickered for a moment, and then I heard something rattle and crash.

"It is coming now," the tired woman said sadly. "My end is here. Thank you for speaking with me, Jasper Cloud. I wish I could live, and spend more time knowing you."

"What is the thing that is coming?" I asked. Time was short. But one sentence still stood out from Vessa's speech.

If a single thing had not gone wrong…

"It is the weakest of eaters," the ship-woman answered. "A type of vermin, one that I could have slain in this current body, had I but one extra day of strength. Even your people could be a match for one, if they were armed with their guns of powder and fire. Any strong source of heat is lethal to them."

As I listened to her, the nearby sparks falling from broken devices caught my eye. I looked back at Vessa's frail form, and tried to imagine what she would look like if she'd had one extra day of food and rest.

I did not think her body would look too different than my own.

"Please," she asked of me. "Do not fight it. It will still kill you. You are unarmed, and your people cannot draw from a Source. It has fangs and claws, and has already stolen power from me. You might be able to hide from it, if you are careful. You could take what food you could carry, and then hide in my husk for as long as there is still air to breathe. I do not know how long that will be. All I know is that I must beg you for one final kindness."

A crystal tear trailed down from one of Vessa's eyes.

"Please kill me, Jasper Cloud. I do not wish to die feeling the eaterling's teeth on my flesh-body. It has already harmed me greatly by ravaging the insides of my ship. Please put your hands around my throat, and save me from one last painful indignity."

I stared at her, briefly overwhelmed by this woman's despair. What little frustration I still felt toward her immediately evaporated.

Who was I to judge her for her brokenness?

She had been alone, for far longer than I had. Been hungrier, for far longer than I had. And she claimed, in spite of all that, to have tried to help far more people than I had ever dared to care about, and to do so for ages upon ages of time.

"Please, Jasper Cloud," she begged again. "I am sorry I cannot offer you anything in return. I have no power left to share. But my ghost will be forever grateful, if you would but do this for me."

The banging continued to advance on our current position. The creature hunting this woman was no longer bothering to hide. It would be here very soon.

"You say heat is lethal to this thing," I repeated, thinking quickly, and counting the number of devices spitting dangerous sparks into the room.

"Had you but a burning stick, you could have saved us both," Vessa spoke in a trembling voice. "But salvation has already been forbidden for me over a hundred times. Please, Jasper Cloud. Put your hands around my throat, and grant me final rest. Then hide. It will be too busy consuming my flesh-body's corpse to notice you."

Another banging noise interrupted our conversation. This time, it was followed by a wet, exultant rasp, and by rapid patters of feet.

"Too late," the ship-woman said in a stricken voice, eyes going wider. "You no longer have time to strangle me, Jasper Cloud. I beg you," she said, desperation making her voice shake. "The loose, unlit tile on the floor. It will come free easily. Please strike my temple with it, and then go hide. Hurry."

The thing was moving quickly now. It would be here in minutes. But it did not sound like it was any larger than myself.

I had already moved to the tile Vessa had indicated. It came free easily, despite the fact that my body was still frail. The tile was light and strong. It would serve well for ending a life.

"I will help you," I promised as I hefted the metal tile in both hands. "You will not feel this thing's teeth on you."

Then I crouched behind the largest, darkest pedestal in the room.

I peeked around the edge and watched. Vessa had sighed and closed her eyes at my words, and I thought I saw another tear sparkle down her face. She waited for a few moments, then opened her eyes again.

"Jasper?" she asked fearfully. "Jasper Cloud? Are you still there?"

I forced myself to remain silent. I even began to hold my breath.

"Jasper Cloud?" she said again. "If you do not kill me soon, the eaterling will be able to catch you before you can hide again. Please hurry. This…" Her voice quivered with grief. "This is already very hard."

My heart broke. But I thought of Nova, on Earth and endangered, and hardened it again.

The pattering footsteps grew louder. Hungry, excited rasping accompanied them.

"Jasper?" Vessa begged again, her voice going high and cracked. When I did not answer again, she let out a strangled sob. "I…" she began, then swallowed. "I understand. I forgive you. Thank you for feeding me. Run far. Live well. I…" She swallowed again. "I will try to be brave."

Then she closed her raining eyes, and began muttering. The blue light along the tile floor suddenly went dim, except for the damaged devices, which began throwing out even more sparks.

A distraction, I realized. *She is making one final attempt to hide me from the thing. Even though she thinks I left her.*

The pattering came to a screeching stop as the unseen creature reached our room. I heard the thing exhale, then let out a grating laugh. It said something in a language I did not understand, and then it stepped into the room.

The chamber was much darker now, and my hiding place did not grant the best view. But I could still make out a tailed, bipedal shape that made hesitant steps into the room, dipping and raising its head after every advance. From the sounds it was making, I realized it was sniffing at the ground with its nose and tasting the air with a wet tongue.

That was not only gross, it was problematic. If the monster could find my scent, Vessa and I were doomed.

And so was Nova.

The eaterling finally creeped into view, stopping just as I was able to make out the details of its form. Nature or madmen had apparently thought it wise to mix the traits of a rat and lizard into a humanoid form. Fur and scale traded places at random all over its body, giving the monster a diseased look, its yellow, rolling eyes reinforcing my disgust. Its long tail resembled that of a rat's, but its face resembled a lizard's, with fleshy whiskers covering the snout. They writhed through the air as the monster sniffed again, and I suppressed another shudder of disgust.

I gripped the tile tighter. Vessa's pleas made far more sense to me now.

"Human?" the monster rasped, in English. It hissed the word again, in a few more languages, until I saw the monster shrug.

"It does not matter. If they were your Beacon, they would have driven me off by now. You brought a stray on board, ship-woman. How amusing. Did you want someone to hold your hand while you died? It's too bad they ran off."

The monster chuckled again, and I parsed through its words. It still spoke in English, yet it said I was no longer here. Did that mean it somehow lost my scent? But why would it announce that in English, if it was not trying to trick me?

"Let's test and see if the human is still here, ship-woman. I hereby promise to leave the Soulship's body, and seek food elsewhere, if the human will come out and reveal themselves in the next ten seconds. Ten… nine…”

The monster counted down. Since I was not stupid, I ignored its empty promise. But why would it need to test at all? Had it truly lost my scent?

As I gripped the tile tightly, I realized the square had a faint metallic scent of its own, and so did the wide pedestal I was hiding behind. Perhaps it really could not smell me. Or perhaps it was merely sadistic.

Either way, I had nothing to gain by answering its lie. I remained silent, breathing as quietly as I could. The creature counted deliberately, chuckling again as it finished.

“No answer,” the monster rasped with another laugh. “The little human has abandoned you, ship-wench. What a pity. They would have had a fighting chance at me, but they still did not even dare. Tell me how that feels, ship-wench?” The eaterling took another step forward. “How does it feel to be abandoned by one of the races you supposedly worked so hard to enlighten? Meanwhile,” the rat-lizard added with a snarl, “you label my own kind monsters. Condemn us for seeking the best and fastest paths for advancement. Force us to consume only animals, plants, and the dead. You compelled my kind to look on as the brightest and most fulfilling sources of sustenance flourished unhunted, oblivious even to our existence, until they were strong enough to hunt us in turn. Tell me how it feels, ship-wench?” the monster rasped again. “Tell me how it feels to become my food in their stead? Without any of them so much as lifting a naked finger in your defense?”

The monster paced forward, its breathing becoming heavier. Its yellow eyes stopped rolling about and locked onto the capsule containing Vessa’s human form. Obsession writ itself over the monster’s entire body.

“I am going to consume you, ship-wench,” the monster rasped. “I am going to devour your flesh-body.

Then I will rest here until I am finished digesting you and absorbing the power of the last Soulship. Then when I have finished Advancing from devouring the greatest of preys, I will hunt the human down and consume them as well. Then I will be strong enough to consume all of the other hunters who are still looking for you, which means the power they have already claimed from you will become mine as well. Then after I have picked your metal body clean, I will make this place my personal nest and sail through the night sky, free to devour whatever else I wish."

The disgusting creature's breathing grew even more ragged as it crept closer to Vessa's capsule.

"Because no one will be able to stop me, ship-wench," the monster gloated, panting heavily as it reached the capsule. "How could they, when I had already devoured the last goddess guarding the night sky? I, an existence you thought yourself so far above, will be greater than anything else alive, after reducing you to rat food. I—"

My tile took it on the side of the head.

The eaterling staggered away then, realizing too late that there had been someone else in this room, and that its obsession with Vessa had enabled an enemy to creep up on it easily. At least I thought it might have realized by then. I was too busy striking it a second time to tell or care.

Finally, it whirled on me and hissed threateningly, baring its claws as it sized up the being that had come to challenge its claim over Vessa as prey.

And as it postured, I struck it a third time, directly on its tendril-covered snout.

The monster screeched in pain, for the edge of my tile had sliced off one of its tendrils. Its tail writhed angrily behind it as its legs coiled and vaulted its hideous bulkdirectly into me.

I was already falling before it reached me.

I had spent the last ten years never speaking a word about my parents, except to condemn their crimes as educational terrorists, so that I would not share their fates. But the painful truth was that I had always been profoundly grateful to them. They had taught me science. That the lights in the night sky were stars and worlds beyond my own. That my own world had over a hundred thousand stories, with a secret inside every one.

The greatest secret, though, was that they had taught me war.

They had taught me that sometimes, the weak can stand against the strong, and that the strength of the powerful can be used against them.

As Vessa had warned, the eaterling was indeed stronger than me. It had already gained power from somehow devouring energy from her metal body. And even then my body was still very weakened. My blows had been little more than an annoyance, save for the one that had actually severed a tendril.

But there were a dozen different defensive arts on Earth that taught how to redirect an attacker's force away from a would-be victim's body. Before the rise of the Glorious State, my parents had found just enough time to teach me the basics of several of them. I used one now, pushing with both my feet and the tile I still held to launch the monster behind me.

The eaterling cried out in rage as it flipped through the air. The monster was agile, and had a tail for extra balance. It had recovered in time to land on its feet, snarling at me and lashing its tail with unsuppressed hate.

It should have shown more self-control. I had thrown it directly into the midst of Vessa's malfunctioning devices.

Its naked tail struck the surface of the smallest sparking console. Tiny motes of fire blackened the hairless, ratlike appendage and began spreading outward, eating away at the limb as if it were papyrus. The eaterling yelped in horror and pain as it realized its foolish mistake, hopping and turning and desperately yanking its tail away from the sizzling device in order to beat it against the floor.

And once again, it displayed a failure to multitask, turning its back on me in its pained frenzy.

I had continued to roll after throwing the monster. It was painful, as I was out of practice with such movements and my body was still in very poor shape. But I was able to regain my footing in time to charge the giant vermin. I slammed the tile into the eaterling's unbalanced torso with all the force my weakened body could bring to bear. It flailed its claws all about and managed to land a painful scratch on my shoulder, but I had caught the thing in mid-air. I launched it onto the top of the largest broken console, where it landed back-first in the middle of glowing wires.

"It burns!" the wretched thing screeched as its back arched and its fur and scale caught fire. "It burns-it burns-it—"

I did my best to drown out its awful cries by swinging the tile into its head over and over, until its throat was bare, and I was able to swing the tile edge-first directly into its neck. It was gruesome, exhausting work, and I tired out before I could finish severing the creature's head, but it stopped moving just before the metal square fell from my exhausted hands. It just lay there with its mouth open and its thick, forked tongue hanging out, as blood dripped from its throat onto the metal floor beneath my feet.

As the blood struck the tiles, blue light leaked from inside of it, flowing into the channels around them, as if it was power returning to its original source. When I looked back up, I saw a cloud full of multicolored threads drift from the eaterling's corpse and into me.

My insides stirred about as the vapors burrowed into me. I felt them pass through channels I had never known my body had. New urges and senses awakened in me, as if some slumbering beast had suddenly stirred, invigorating my muscles. My mind became sharper, opening to some new science I had never heard of before.

And a new, energizing sensation began to circulate through my entire body, making me feel as if I had just gained a second set of veins to power my once-frail form. I stood even straighter, feeling all of my fatigue vanish. I even felt my height change ever so slightly, making me look just a little less like a half-grown child.

The new blue light raced over to Vessa's enclosure, making the capsule flare brightly for a moment. I heard the ship-woman gasp in surprise as her own body began to creak and change.

"Jasper?" she asked out loud. "Jasper Cloud? You are still here?"

"Yes," I said, dropping the tile and walking over to the cooler that contained the food. I had become hungry again, so I grabbed two pouches before I walked back over to Vessa. "I am still here. The eaterling is dead. Are you alright?"

"I am alive," she said, no longer sounding tired. "Alive, instead of eaten and shamed. And I am… better. A small part of myself has returned to me. I can think more clearly now." There was a pause, as if she was still considering something. "And I am hungry."

"Here," I said as I reached her capsule. As I leaned over it, I noticed that her body had filled out ever so slightly, gaining just a hint of muscle definition back. Her face glowed with new health, and as I held out the pouch, she reached up and snatched it out of my grasp.

"Thank you," she said quickly, as if she had remembered her manners at the last moment. Then, just before she started tearing the packet open with her teeth, she looked back up at me.

"You took power as well," she said, narrowing her eyes as she examined me.

"Explain what has happened to me," I insisted. "Please," I added, remembering my own manners.

"The easiest way for a being to gain more power from their Source is to slay another creature. All three beings release a little bit of the three Sources when they die: mana, essence, and qi. A practitioner of any one Source can seize some of that energy and use it to augment themselves. If they are a bond-user, they can draw the essence, if they are a magic user, they can draw the mana, and if they are a cultivator, they may draw the qi. Each Source can help them advance in their chosen discipline. You…" She trailed off, her eyes widening. "You drew in all three Sources when you killed the eaterling."

"How could I have done that?" I asked. "I thought you said my race was unable to draw from a Source."

"I will explain," she answered quickly, and there was now a fierce sparkle in her eyes. "But first, we will eat. Then, after I have satisfied enough of your questions, we will embark on a plan to save your friend, and my Beacon."

Chapter 3

"Compared to the rest of the night sky and especially inside my ship-body, time passes very slowly on Earth," Vessa said as she tossed away the second package and wiped her face with her sleeve. Her former embarrassment over eating had vanished, evicted by her restored vitality and sense of purpose. "Every day here is but a moment back on Earth. That still does not give us as much time as I would want to have, but it will be sufficient nonetheless," she said fiercely. "I have given you a brief explanation over the different Sources, and how they can empower a person. Essence is the power that lets practitioners form pacts with beasts. It is the power constantly present in the environment, and perhaps the most stable of the three Sources. It is the greatest source for directly empowering one's body and mind, as well as the easiest to directly absorb, but it grants almost no special powers by itself, unless one makes some sort of pact with another creature, or constantly slays other living beings, thereby gaining a small portion of their traits. You probably noticed your own senses sharpen after killing the eaterling."

"I did," I said dryly, "though I am surprised to discover that, considering how unobservant the stupid thing was."

"Its senses and wits were clouded by its desire to consume me," Vessa replied without hesitating. "Later, when we have more time, we will discuss an appropriate payment for your act of saving a Soulship's life, but for now, we must focus on getting you strong enough to save Nova and the rest of the night sky."

I desired little more than just that, but now was not the time to say so.

"Now, back to the lesson. We only have a limited number of days, so I must speak quickly, and you must comprehend as rapidly and completely as you can. Essence, to quickly repeat, will directly strengthen your natural abilities to a greater extent than qi, and especially mana, ever will, but it will be the most difficult to use for special abilities. Forming pacts will help, but each pact will still only provide narrow benefits. What few abilities essence does grant are commonly referred to as *charms*. Now for mana," she continued, lifting a second finger. "mana is the most malleable of the three Sources, the one directly dependent on physical and natural laws. It can be used to enhance any activity and perform all manner of techniques, but it is the hardest Source for your body to directly absorb over time. Where essence users gain impressive physiques and sharp minds, but limited means to bring more power to bear, mana users will be able to quickly summon impressive amounts of power to perform supernatural feats, but afterwards, their bodies will only be slightly stronger than the average non-practitioner, unless they have advanced many times. Mana practitioners are the ones who must study and practice constantly to learn new techniques or advance themselves to the next stage. They call their special powers *spells.*

"Qi users are the final group. They draw power from the energy that is constantly flowing through the entire universe. They are the most balanced of the three types of practitioners, as qi can be used to both refine the body and to power special abilities that they call *techniques*. But those same benefits require qi users to balance their methods in extracting from their Source. They must meditate and battle like essence users, and study, practice and experiment like mana users, though not to the same degree of either group.

"So as you can see, each Source has its own strengths, drawbacks, and requirements for progression.

Drawing from any of them is an arduous but rewarding task that will grant longevity, increased chances of survival, and the ability to move one's very civilization forward, as Source practitioners are often the only ones that stand between their worlds and the things that crawl through the night sky. One of the most important tasks of any Soulship has been to guard and cultivate a new world until enough Source practitioners emerge to defend it.

"Your ability to draw power from all three Sources is an anomaly, theoretically possible but never proven to exist beyond my own race. It is all but unheard of for a practitioner to use even two Sources, and fewer still choose to develop both at once. Advancement takes time and resources. Most dual-practitioners simply specialize in one, and count it to be a blessing whenever they can slay an opponent or otherwise add power to their second Source. I will have to check my records, but as far as I know, no non-Soulship practitioner has ever drawn power from all three Sources as the result of a kill. We have time for a single question," she said firmly, as she caught my inquisitive expression.

"Please explain to me how you were able to raise up so many civilizations when killing another practitioner was the fastest track to power," I said after a moment's consideration. "But before you do that, are you sure you are well? You were—" I struggled to think of a tactful way to phrase my concern— "not very well a short time ago."

"That was two questions," Vessa sighed, closing her eyes for a moment. "One of which you already asked me a few minutes ago."

"Yes," I said awkwardly, reflecting on the change in both of our moods. Now that the threat of horrible death and starvation had passed, the ship-woman had gone from despair to utter confidence, speaking without hesitation. I, meanwhile, had lost much of my confidence now that everyone was safe and fed. My body's renewed health and vitality were pleasant sensations, but my inexperience with them made me uncomfortable. "But since the first question was phrased as a request, I have technically complied with your demands. Please assure me that you are well, and then educate me on the matter of drawing from my Sources through the death of another."

"Fine," Vessa sighed again, rubbing her temple. It did not escape my notice that, despite my concerns, she was now strong enough to lift her arms without noticeable effort. "And I should be the one who is sorry. I have done nothing but ask of you from the very moment I have contacted you. Yet you have taken every new experience in stride, risking your life several times over with no promise of reward. I apologize for having to rush this knowledge, and for not giving you more time to rest and recover. And yes… I am not well. I do not yet know how unwell I am, and will need more time to comprehend just how badly I fell into despair, but know that I no longer wish for death. I no longer want you to kill me, and I am grateful you did not listen when I asked. Thank you again. I will get better with time, and it is all your doing."

Her sparkling gray eyes fastened on mine as she spoke. I reminded myself of Nova, and told my heart to stop falling into them. But the gray-hued woman did not seem to notice, and continued her lecture.

"As to your 'official' question," Vessa said with a smirk, "recall I told you that drawing the Source out of the newly dead was the *fastest* way to grow, not the best. Drawing from each Source in its unique fashion will provide a greater, and safer, amount of power over long periods of time than you would gain by slaughtering every person you meet. Still, though, it was a temptation we had to take note of, as it was one of the easiest ways for a race to wipe itself out. And not every practitioner allowed us to educate them," she continued sadly. "Now that my race is almost extinct, I do not know how many keep to the old laws we worked so hard to pass down. That is why, in exchange for the knowledge I am about to teach you, I must ask you to hold to certain oaths. For starters, I must ask you to never harm or slay another being without absolute necessity, especially one who is innocent."

That sounded an easy thing to agree to. Combat on the streets of the Republic had always been a massive risk for one such as myself. But I still stopped myself from nodding in agreement.

"Denied," I found myself saying instead. "Instead, I pledge to slay or save anyone I must, as my conscience directs, especially in regards to protecting Nova."

"That was basically the same thing I just asked of you," Vessa said with a frown. But I shook my head.

"I have witnessed my world doom itself by listening to the wrong elders as they commanded us whom to kill, and whom to spare. The first acts they demanded were to spare and ignore those who were gaining power for their own means, and to hunt and slay those who could teach us how to guard ourselves from further lies. And you just asked me to take an innocent life no more than an hour ago," I reminded her.

"Very well," Vessa said from her bed, closing her eyes patiently. "Your conscience has proven sufficient so far. And until either of my bodies recover, you are my only tool. The night sky will burn if we cannot cooperate. But if you abuse these powers, I will no longer teach you to wield them. I cannot compromise on that."

"For now, that will do," I agreed softly, noting that the ship-woman's fatigue had begun to reappear on her face. I reminded myself that, despite her improved appearance, she was still not strong enough to leave the confines of her flesh-body's bed, or to turn on the rest of the lights in her ship-body. Then I reminded myself that we had little time for pointless arguing, and forced myself to relax.

"To return to our conversation," the ship-woman continued, "you can Draw from all three Sources, which is the best and worst blessing one could possibly ask for. You will be able to make the absolute most out of any opportunity for advancement, because you can take advantage of anything that benefits at least one of the Sources. But at the same time, every single practitioner or predator will have a reason to seek your life, and as you become stronger, that will only become more true. Those that sought to claim Soulships will seek to claim you as the next-best prey, the next-best fruit for their own advancement."

"So in other words," I reflected, "I have much to gain by appearing weak, and not worth killing."

"Or by appearing so strong that you are a threat," the ship-woman countered. Then she sighed again. "By telling you of this, I have given you another incentive to take the shorter road, and begin ending many lives."

"Will the shorter road help me save Nova?" I asked the Soulship.

"From the first threat? Yes," she admitted. "But from the stronger, second line of hunters? Not hardly."

"Then I still have no incentive to take the shorter road," I spoke firmly. "Teach me how I can grow strong enough to ensure she is always safe."

Vessa smiled at me, then suddenly looked away.

"I can do so, but you must stop interrupting me," she grumbled. "To finish, I must teach you the basics of Drawing from each Source. Pay close attention, because not only will you have three times as many opportunities as the average Source practitioner, but you will also have to work three times as hard. Most Source practitioners start Drawing far earlier in life than you have, and they had the advantage of letting their Source shape their body's growth. Most practitioners your age or younger will have far more experience and natural strength than you do, no matter what Source they draw from."

I nodded grimly. Even after slaying the eaterling and consuming Vessa's miracle food, my body was still not even as strong as an average Earth person of my same age.

"But do not despair," Vessa added, watching my troubled face with concern. "You have proven yourself able to overcome difficult odds, and your body's condition is correctable. If you are willing to perform the labor, I can teach you a way to Draw from each Source in such a fashion that will completely reverse the damage that your malnutrition has caused, making your potential to be no less than any other practitioner beneath the night sky. From there, we will work on making you strong enough to overcome Nova's captor and enable her transport to my ship-body."

I still wanted to ask her a dozen questions about whether such a feat was truly possible, but I had already interrupted her enough. I paid as close attention as I could to her next words.

"I will now teach you to Draw from a Source. There are many methods, and many schools have been founded to espouse one method over the others, but for now, kneel on the floor in the most comfortable position possible."

I did as Vessa instructed, finding a spot not too far from her capsule that was free of debris.

"This process will loosely resemble a dozen different meditative traditions you no doubt remember from Earth, though it will not be identical to any of them. The goal, though, is not to attain any special form of enlightenment or inner peace. You are merely redirecting your attention away from your current distractions and focusing it on the Sources present in your environment. This is ideally done when your body and mind are already giving you as few distractions as possible, which is why I encourage practitioners to be at their peak physical and mental health when they attempt to Draw from a Source. You should always try to eat a balanced meal and get a good night's sleep whenever possible, as well as find a person with whom you can discuss any concerns that are giving you worry or anxiety. But for now, close your eyes, and let go of the worry you feel for the people on your planet, for Nova… and apparently, for me."

She sounded odd as she finished speaking, but I followed her directions and did my best to put them out of my mind, to turn my thoughts away from the fact that my best friend was still in danger right now, and that she had confessed her love to me while paying no heed to my malnourished and unattractive form. I also tried to forget that I had just discovered monsters were real, that they were apparently about to devour everyone I cared about, that they were probably responsible for the deaths of my family, and that an hour ago, a woman with the most beautiful gray eyes I had ever seen had just asked me to put my hands around her throat and murder her, and that instead of complying, I had killed another living creature by bashing its head in and slicing its throat.

Such thoughts proved surprisingly difficult to ignore.

"Right," Vessa said from her tube. "I had forgotten that such directions sound wise until students attempt to enact them. If everyone could let go of their worries so easily, the night sky would never be threatened again, because there would be mighty heroes roaming across every corner of every planet. Let me help you, Jasper Cloud. Know that Nova will be safe. She is strong and will endure, and you will be back in that alley before her captors will have time to even lay a claw on her body. You will be strong. You already have what it takes to be strong. You have already used what strength you have to act wisely. Relax. You are capable and have been victorious against danger before. Relax so that you can see how your accomplishments can grow. Let go of your worries to see what you can gain."

That did it. That last advice worked for me.

The more I tried not to think about my worries, the larger they grew in my heart and mind. I focused on my opportunities instead, the fact that my body could be restored, that Nova could still be saved, that I was currently inside an actual starship, one that could travel through the night sky. All I needed to do was pay attention to what Vessa was trying to show me.

As soon as I realized that, my mind went still. I became aware of several different substances thrumming around me.

The first was a thick fog of power. It was always resting, always hovering, always present. It moved slowly, and tried to soak and permeate through everything it touched. It wanted to enrich its surroundings in the way that nutrients enriched soil, letting things grow a little larger, denser, and more powerful. It wanted to expand and fortify me, strengthen my muscles and organs, reinforce my skin and bones, sharpen my mind and senses. All I needed to do was give it permission to soak into me, so I did, and it methodically began its work. The sensation was odd, though. I felt stronger, healthier, more energized, but nothing more. Beyond making my body stronger and my mind sharper, the fog had no motivation beyond that, and its apathy was noticeable and unsettling.

The second substance was a current of power that traveled through the air, darting about and never staying in one place. It wished to enter me, then exit just as quickly once its work was done. But it would wish to enter again the very next instant, bouncing back and forth rapidly. I realized it wanted me to do the same, that it wished to teach me, and have me act on its instructions, so that it could teach me further. To do that, I had to reflect on whatever lesson its presence taught me in that moment, and then contemplate the next step. As I did so, the presence felt pleased, giving my muscles and organs tiny bits of instruction on which way to continue growing. I felt every action become just a bit easier, as if I was consciously and subconsciously discovering little shortcuts to make life easier. This Source wished me to excel at each and every task I performed, and to discover new ones I had never known I could do. But it required far more mental effort than the previous Source had.

The third Source was at once the easiest and hardest of the three. Its presence felt thick, but not still. It was constantly moving, ever so slowly, as if it were carefully pushing everything in existence around, moving it just enough to correct its balance. It wanted to flow into me, slowly and deliberately, thoroughly examining me, but only through invisible, and somehow proper, channels. It was patient like the first Source and insistent like the second, determined to balance me, to soothe the overworked portions and gently nudge the stagnant areas of my being. It felt the most alive and compassionate of the three Sources, and felt curious over the effects that the other two were having on me. I felt it attempt to further refine their benefits, making sure no portion of me became too large or too strained.

The three Sources conflicted a bit, as each found themselves wandering into each other's way, and the final Source wished to influence the work of the other two. But as I kept myself relaxed, and focused on my appreciation for the benefits of each of them, they stopped opposing one another. They came to some form of agreement, as if they were the only three settlers in an unpopulated planet, or three healers working on a patient covered head-to-toe in wounds. There was enough for each of them to do in my body without getting in each other's way, and the challenge of fixing all the damage that my malnutrition and neglect had caused would require them to occasionally work together to achieve their directives. They came to some sort of pseudo-sentient understanding, and compromised. The first Source, essence, was allowed to augment and fortify whatever it wished, but it could not do so in a way that would completely undo the instructions or balance provided by the other two Sources, or at least not without giving the other two time to make corrections afterwards. The second Source, mana, would provide as much instruction as possible, but it must wait until essence had finished enhancing my being, and it must allow qi, the final source, to focus its instructions into aligned goals. Finally, qi was to give the other Sources plenty of room and time to work, and to keep its circulations slow, so that mana and essence could adjust easily to its presence while still fulfilling their own directives.

When the three Sources had worked out their peace, they began to settle, flow, and circulate, respectively. It was as if there was a new world forming inside my body, with the essence forming the crust and mantle, the mana forming the atmosphere, and the qi forming the oceans and seas. The planet was tiny, though, and lacked detail. It also felt barren, as if many pieces of it were still missing.

I inhaled, finding I could take a deeper breath than ever before. As I exhaled, it felt as if a host of impurities were exiting my body.

"Well done," Vessa said from her padded capsule bed. "You are now a Tri-practitioner. One who Draws from all three Sources."

"Thank you," I replied, taking another breath, and finding it still more beneficial than the last. "And thank you for your help, as well." After a moment, I added, "And I suspect you did more than relax and encourage me."

"You are welcome, and correct," the ship-woman admitted from her repository. "As a living ship, I am both an environment and a living being, so I can regulate the Sources inside of me to a degree. When more of my ship-body has been reclaimed and repaired, it will be more useful to Draw from the Sources inside of me. But for now, I was able to shepherd your three Sources into a direction that would be harmonious. The result was beautiful," she added softly. "The image you saw in your body was your Soulscape, the form the Sources take inside of you. It reflects a key aspect of your nature, and will gain more detail as you Advance. In time, you may be able to project the image outward, or gain special abilities derived from it. I have seen some Soulscapes take the forms of animals, and weapons, or large structures, but I have never seen one take the form of an entire planet. I would call it a good omen, if I could be more sure that our fortunes have finally turned."

"I will hope for you then," I surprised myself by saying as I rose to my feet. For the third time today, I felt even stronger, healthier, more whole. My body filled out yet again, making my arms look well proportioned while still extremely thin, instead of sticks that were about to break. I had also grown taller. Just how much, I was not sure, but I was probably approaching the average height of a young man my age. "Why is the world inside me so empty?"

"I do not know," Vessa answered me. "But perhaps you are meant to fill it."

It was entirely possible she meant that my Soulscape planet would gain more rivers, mountains, and life as I Advanced. But on a whim, I walked over to the food storage unit and drew another pouch.

"Are you hungry again?" Vessa asked, slightly concerned. I did not blame her. Right now this was possibly our only source of food. "You may eat if you need to, but the changes should not have caused you to feel hungry this time."

"Merely curious about something," I said as I shook my head. "You said my Soulscape could grant me abilities? And that I should fill it?"

"Yes," she replied cautiously. "But please do not try to swallow the pouch itself. That will go badly."

I grinned, and nodded. Then I closed my eyes, and turned my attention back inside myself, to the empty parts I felt in the spectral world. I felt them reach out for something, yearning to be filled. I concentrated on the sensation in my hands, the feeling of the pouch inside my palms.

The planet inside my soul suddenly *pulled*, yanking on the pouch of food in my hand as if it hoped to swallow it through my palm. The pouch pressed directly and alarmingly into my skin, but caught on something, as if it were trying to fit into a hole that was far too small. My Soulscape seemed to give up on devouring, and the ration relaxed against my hand.

"What just happened?" I asked, surprised.

"You impulsively attempted to activate an ability you did not fully understand," Vessa said wryly. She now had enough strength to raise her head to look at me, and was wearing something of an amused expression on her face. "It is something every new practitioner unfortunately does, despite the inherent danger. Feel free to consult with me in the future if you ever feel a new power start to develop. I will most likely be able to walk you through its use in a safe and convenient fashion."

"Thank you," I said as I swallowed my newly discovered pride. "I will keep such knowledge in mind. Since you witnessed my fumbled technique, do you know what it was that I just tried to do?"

"I applaud you for immediately applying what you have just learned," the ship-woman said in what I chose to believe was sincere approval. "From what I can tell, your Soulscape attempted to store the item in your hand within itself, and probably in a way that would help it learn its properties and effects. You have a more beneficial version of the extradimensional storage ability, with the caveat that you are currently able to store nothing larger than a pebble, or perhaps a ring. But it will most likely grow in size and utility as you Advance. In the future, this will be an extremely convenient ability."

"But not now," I noted, "since pebbles are easy things to carry, and I still have at least ten free fingers for dealing with any random rings I find."

"Then it seems I must wait for you to find your eleventh ring before your spirits will lift," she teased. "But do not discount this discovery. Spatial power is rare among all three Sources, and often must be achieved with the use of a wondrous item. And since your Soulscape actively desires to store and transport things, you will likely obtain some extra benefit from doing so. Continue to practice this power on any item you find small enough to transport. It should be safe, as long as it is not a lit flame or an open container of poison."

"I'll be sure to watch out for those." I grinned. "But I suppose you wish to begin the next lesson."

"I wish to sleep, frankly," the woman replied, letting her mask of wry calm slip off her face. "And then leave my capsule. And then bathe, and wear clean clothing. But we do not have time to do the first yet, and my flesh-body is still not strong enough to take care of its own needs outside its current confines. The fastest way to accomplish those things is to continue what training we can still do here, and then send you on your first mission. Since there is little I can teach you until we both recover more, that means you will be leaving in about fifteen minutes."

"How exactly will I be leaving?" I asked, curious. "And where will I be going?"

"Your destruction of the eaterling has given me enough power to reactivate the transportation array," Vessa answered me, composed once more. "I will be able to send you further out, to a location where no hunters will be able to find you. There, you will be able to Draw from the Sources that still linger on that world, and scavenge for a few resources that will help me recover and assist you in Advancing to the first stage of a true practitioner. The cultivation of each Source has its separate stage, and each will grant you different benefits, but we will go over them in detail after you return from your mission. For now, though, I will teach you the most basic skills that even children learn, and then hope it will be enough for you to survive for a few hours. You will be going to a dead world, one my race was unable to keep from destruction. There should be little treasure left there, but even fewer treasure hunters, so it should be safe for you to acquire the materials I need."

"What am I collecting for you?" I asked, feeling apprehensive about going into danger once again, and so soon. "And what dangers should I be on guard for?"

"You should be on guard for anything more dangerous than a surprised eaterling standing next to a fire. Which is to say you should be on guard for everything. Avoid any kind of contact with anything that can move on its own, be it a large carnivore or a small winged insect. But the biggest danger will be from any practitioner capable of traveling between worlds, any of whom will easily be powerful enough to slay you, and have no likely reason to help you. But none of this should be a concern. This ruined world was picked clean long ago. No one should have any reason to remain there, and all I need you to collect are some soil samples. If I can just get those, I will be able to convert them into usable material for us both. Now, again, we are short on time, so listen carefully as I teach you what techniques your body can handle. Also—" she closed her eyes, and another column lit up all the way, opening on its side— "I can provide you more suitable clothing. It will protect you somewhat from the environment and allow Source energy to channel out of your body just a little easier when you use your techniques. There will also be a large satchel to carry material, though your spatial ability already helps with such things."

The new clothing looked nothing like the special starship suits I read about in my safer childhood. In fact, it was nothing except for plain shoes, loose linen pants, a white linen shirt and a gray leather belt, as well as a shoulder-belt with the satchel attached to it. I supposed it was meant to help me blend in, or at least blend in better than the supposed spacesuits would.

I was about to step somewhere to give myself a small bit of privacy, but then a thought occurred to me.

"Would you like me to hand you a change of clothes as well?" I asked the ship-woman, who had been confined to her bed for an unknown length of time.

"I am not strong enough to change my own clothing," Vessa replied with a frown. "And I am not yet desperate enough to allow you to change me. Bring back the soil, and I will be able to do just a little more for myself. Please," she begged bitterly.

"As you wish," I said with a nod, putting the suit back. I thought to offer to find something warm to cover her with, but then realized my offer would probably only embarrass her further. I did not feel cold, so she probably did not either. "I am ready to begin learning, if you would teach me now."

"I will," she said quietly. "And I apologize for not responding better to your kindness. Please know I am already far more grateful than I am able to show. But here is your first lesson. We will begin with qi, and how you can use it for a technique that coats your body with a thin shield…"

To my surprise, the lessons were quite easy. I learned to perform a number of tiny miracles that made me feel immensely proud, until Vessa reminded me that small children were also taught these same techniques. When she was satisfied with my ability to conceal my presence, hurl tiny darts of energy, and coat my body in a thin layer of qi, she directed me to take one more food pouch and to stand near another half-lit pedestal.

"I am sending you away now, Jasper Cloud," Vessa called from her capsule bed. "Good luck. And remember, be safe. Nova and the rest of the night sky depend upon your returning alive."

Then the nearby pedestal flared, and I vanished from this world of darkness and glowing steel.

Chapter 4

I was still unused to interplanetary travel, so I stumbled as I stepped into my new world, landing with a crouch onto the rust-red dust. A quick glance revealed no creatures were visible near my location, so I stopped myself from inhaling just long enough to summon a protective layer of qi around my body. The blue-white Source was no thicker than my thinnest fingernail, but it would work to protect my still-frail constitution from any harmful impurities in the air and ensure I could breathe safely for at least a few hours. Then I worked to make my inner essence hover tightly around my other Sources, blanketing them and making all three Sources harder to sense from other practitioners and mystic beasts. Then, and only then, did I turn my attention back outward. I noticed that the air felt arid, warm, and dry. I looked up to see a smog-colored sky roll about my head, churning constantly with dirty-orange clouds. Dusty plains surrounded me for as far as my eyes could see, with the only real landmark being a haze-covered collection of rubble and towers to my north. There was no nearby cover except for some large boulders and the petrified remains of broken tree trunks.

I took a careful step forward, testing the gravity of this new place and finding it to be no different from my own world. That final question answered, I knelt back down on the ground and removed one of the small glass vials Vessa had given me to collect samples. Remembering her instructions, I carefully waved it over a particularly dusty patch of ground, injecting my mana into the vial with the mental commands 'open' and 'collect.' The thin, plastic film over the top of the small container vanished as it began to suck up a small amount of the brown-red dust, sealing again when it had collected the appropriate amount. I put the vial back into my satchel, sighing in relief as I realized that a third of my task was already done.

Then, after another thought occurred to me, I stretched out my palm over the rest of the dust and reached for my Soulscape.

The spectral planet inside my soul stirred, projecting its own senses outward. It seemed satisfied with the dust, and carefully sucked up a few motes of dirt up through my palm, leaving whatever impurities it deemed harmful on the outside of my qi shield. The rest flowed through invisible pathways in my body into my Soulscape, settling onto a microscopic location of my tiny world. The translucent planet ceased its pull through my hand and gave me a satisfied pulse, as if it wanted me to know that it needed no more dirt for now.

I respected its wish, but then looked up, waving my hand through the air and sending another query to my Soulscape. The ghostly planet woke back up, regarding whatever particles it could sense in the arid air, and accepted them with an indiscriminate appetite. Oxygen and other elements flowed into my Soulscape until it once again decided it had its fill and turned its attention away, with another pulse commanding me not to wake it up again for a while. But it seemed to glow just a little more brightly, leading me to believe it had benefited from my small test.

I looked around again, remembering that I was still on a foreign world with any number of unknown dangers. The streets of my homeworld had already taught me that inattention could be deadly. I still saw nothing dangerous in sight, and I still found that far more troubling than knowing where something dangerous actually was. But I needed to finish collecting Vessa's samples, so I began walking toward the broken city off in the distance, not having any other landmark to investigate.

As I walked, I went over the mental list Vessa had given me. I specifically needed to find red clay, brown dirt, and silt, along with anything else that might be useful, such as organic material or any mystic treasures that had somehow escaped the notice of every scavenger before me. She had not expected me to find that last class of item, but she said I would be able to sense any mystic object by the special traces of essence, mana, or qi it would produce. But I began to suspect any such items would have already been noticed and picked clean, because this world felt almost completely bare of the three Sources. It gave off only the tiniest wisps of essence, the qi flow felt like a dripping faucet, and I could not sense any mana at all. So I turned most of my efforts toward finding the other two soil samples.

After about half an hour, I noticed a dip in the terrain to my left. I veered off in that direction, walking slowly and carefully, vigilantly searching for any signs of movement or unusual sounds. Nothing swooped out of the air or rose up from the ground to eat me, and I began to suspect that Vessa had truly tried to send me to a place that would not result in my instant death. Then I reminded myself that she only had to be wrong once for it to matter, and went back to being hyper-vigilant.

The dip proved to be a large trench, that had probably once been the bed of a mighty river. To my dubious fortune, a small stream was still flowing in the middle of it, no wider than the width of my hand. The dampened ground nearest the water's edge qualified as the silt Vessa had requested me to obtain. Upon collecting it, I would be two-thirds of the way done with this mission and one step closer to finding a way to save Nova back on Earth.

That did not negate the fact that this was possibly the most dangerous location on the entire planet. Water was a requirement for life. If there was any kind of predator left in the area, this spot would have to be one of its favorite locations. In fact, in this barren place, the most effective way for it to hunt would be to linger close by the stream and wait for some other creature to come by for a drink.

I scanned the trench as thoroughly as my improved senses would let me. Nothing seemed out of place, not that I had any idea what the life of this world would even look like. I couldn't detect any lingering traces of any Source either, which was also no guarantee of safety. Powerful practitioners or mystic beasts contained more Source energy, but they also had more ability to hide it, and they would be better at sensing its presence than I would be. I remembered that particular lesson from Vessa quite clearly. I also remembered picturing a giant evil god sleeping right under me without my knowledge, waking up long enough to kill me and devour my Source energy, and then going back to sleep, the whole time Vessa had been talking. In the end, I had decided that such fear was useless and paralyzing, so I did my best to ignore it.

But I was unable to do so right now. With every step, I imagined some kind of giant winged beast or massive sand worm swooping out of nowhere and devouring me in a single bite. I gritted my teeth, thought of Nova, and forced myself to think of something other than my newfound lack of power and knowledge.

Nothing ate me by the time I reached the stream bed. I removed another vial and carefully knelt next to the wet silt, looking all around as I instructed my mana to activate the device. But the vial sucked up the silt without any trouble, and nothing bothered me as I absorbed a few particles of the wet dirt into my Soulscape. Then, after carefully examining the clear, empty water, I carefully waved my hand over it and let my spectral planet greedily take a drinking-glass-sized bite out of the stream, showing more enthusiasm for the water than it ever did the air or dirt. Once again, nothing leaped out to swallow me whole.

I sighed in relief. So far, I had managed to collect two-thirds of the needed materials in less than an hour. If this kept up, I would be done and gone long before whatever slumbering dragon, mindless army of shambling undead, or gang of men on motorbikes would notice I was ever here. I looked back at the water, wondering if I should put it in a spare container as well, but the food pouches hydrated me as well as they fed, and Vessa had a dispenser for water that she was bringing back online. I gave one last glance to determine if there was anything else useful down here, and it was then that I heard a small squeak to my right.

I froze immediately, turning my head just enough to spot the first living creature I had seen on this dead world. I saw a red-furred mouse, about the same color as the red clay covering the ground, crawling toward me curiously. It was half a stone's throw away from me, and small enough to fit in my palm, despite how adorably fluffy it was, including its long, brush-tipped tail. But before it came any closer, it froze itself, becoming as still as a statue. Then it slowly pointed its nose off to my right, sniffed once, then froze again.

It had made noise, as if to alert me of its presence, then went perfectly still, as if it had just spotted danger, then tilted its head in a certain direction, as if to indicate where the danger was.

In other words, the danger was less than a foot to my right.

Qi, essence, and mana surged their power into my legs, in whatever capacity they could. I leaped as quickly, as high, and as far to the left as I could, twisting to look at whatever threat had crept up on me without my notice.

I spotted the offending target, a brown rock roughly the size of my head.

With eight legs.

I began backing away hurriedly, bringing my right hand up as I worked to remember the only active defense technique Vessa had taught me so far. The rock tensed suddenly, and four eyes on top of the smaller rock right in front of it suddenly blinked. A spider. The two rocks were a spider, one probably large enough to wrap its legs all around my torso and plunge its fangs directly into one of my vital organs. However, it was clearly a stalking predator, and since I was over three times its size and now aware of its presence, I was no longer possible prey, and it knew that.

But then it shifted its attention to the little mouse that had inexplicably chosen to save my life and revealed itself with its squeak. The rodent twitched, and then with a lash of its fluffy tail, it sped down the riverbed toward the ruined city in the distance. The rock-skinned arachnid reared up, spread its fangs and pedipalps, and fired a thin strand of webbing from somewhere under its mouth. The thread hit the little mouse in its back right leg, and the small animal let out a squeak as it was yanked backward. The spider then began to scuttle in reverse, retreating somewhere to devour its prey in private.

By then, I had finished my technique.

Vessa had instructed me to run at the first sign of danger, but I found that, despite several years as an orphan on the streets of the Glorious State, my instincts regarding an arachnid sneaking up to me were no different than the average person's. I immediately leaped away, panicked, and tried to kill the thing from as far away as possible. I traced my mana-infused hand through the air, mentally incanted the proper formula in my mind, and fired a bolt of mana through my finger at the dog-sized arachnid.

The spider was scrambling away rapidly, but the mana spell aimed with the mind, not the eyes. It flew unerringly to wherever my intent directed, and my intent directed the burning blue arrow straight into the frightful thing's head. The spell would completely bypass the monster's carapace but be stopped by most Source protection. Apparently, the creature did not yet qualify as a Sourcebeast, so my bolt blasted right through its thin Source protection and burrowed into its brain. The monstrous thing jerked and crumpled onto its side, legs twitching into the air as it went into death throes. A faint bit of the three Source energies hummed through the air, some of it settling into me but providing nowhere near the benefit that the eaterling's death had. My skin did feel a tiny degree harder, however, possibly allowing me to resist the next papercut.

I turned my attention to the small mouse that revealed the spider's presence in the first place. The tiny creature was still struggling to free its leg from the webbing, but the silk was not strong enough to be an issue for my much larger body. As soon as I removed it, though, the red little mouse immediately darted away from me, vanishing from view in a few breaths. I could not find it until I heard another squeak from farther away.

It stood on its hind legs, staring at me with twitching whiskers. It was clearly interested in me, yet it seemed ready to bolt if I made the slightest sudden movement.

Also, its fur had changed color again, blending in perfectly with the brown riverbed. It had not done that when I had first seen it. The only purpose I could conjecture for doing so now was to draw attention to the fact that it wanted me to notice what it could do. Which meant it wanted my attention, wanted me to be impressed with it on some level, and was intelligent enough to plan. It was also clearly intelligent enough to communicate with, and it wanted me to know that.

I slowly opened my mouth.

"Can you speak?" I asked, keeping my voice low.

It did not answer me. I reminded myself that it was a mouse, and that I was currently talking to said mouse out loud. I tried not to feel stupid. But then the little animal closed its eyes, and a handful of essence motes shook loose of its body.

Safe-safe?

It was not a voice, just an impression of a voice that I felt through my own essence. But once it sensed the communication, my own essence stirred ever so slightly in response. Loose motes, like the cast-off cells of my own skin, shook off.

Yes, I somehow knew how to say. *Can you hear me?*

The little mouse nodded, lashing its furry, fluff-ended tail.

Help-help? it asked next. *Leave-leave?*

You and me leave? I asked, clarify. The tiny creature nodded again.

Help-help. You-me. Stay-safe. Leave-then?

The impressions were weak and barely understandable.

You helped me back there, I sent next. *On purpose?*

Yes-yes. Me-helped. You-helped. Made-safe.

I thought I understood. Not only had I protected the mouse in turn, I had slain its hunter. No matter what, there was one less predator for the creature to fear now.

I need brown dirt, I told the little mouse. *Then I will go. And you can come with me to somewhere else.*

Else-else? the little mouse asked. *More-food? More-safe?*

Yes, I said. The statement about more food at least, was certainly true. And the mouse had already proven willing to work together for mutual benefit. There would be safety in numbers, at least.

Unless the magical creature had more of its kind around.

Are you alone? I asked the little mouse. *Do you have friends or family?*

Friends-gone. Dead-dead. Bad-bad. Hide-much.

Are there other hunters? More spiders?

Worse-worse. Big-big. Much-hide. Leave-soon?

Soon, I promised. *I just need some brown dirt. Then we can leave.*

Help-find, the little mouse sent as it turned around. *Lead-lead.*

Thank you, I told the creature, and it ran a small distance away before turning its head to look back at me.

Bond-bond? If-help?

Vessa's lesson about essence users and mystic beasts returned to my mind. Under the right circumstances, both practitioner and beast would benefit from a formed pact. But the essence practitioner had to be strong enough by themselves to be useful to a mystic beast. An extremely powerful creature would get absolutely no benefit from bonding with me and might eat or slay me just for proposing the idea.

But this little mouse was both intelligent and weak enough, or just desperate enough, to benefit in some way by forming a bond. That was probably why it had risked revealing itself, and why it had bothered to warn me about the rock spider sneaking up on me. I would have to bring this matter up with Vessa to make sure, but this was either a horrible idea that would end very badly or be a fantastic benefit to begin my first Advancement, for both the little creature and myself.

Do you have a name? I sent the now-silt-colored mouse. But I received an impression that it didn't understand the question yet, which suggested it had not Advanced very far itself, despite its impressive speed and talents for camouflage. I counted myself fortunate that we could understand each other at all and continued following the creature as quickly and quietly as I could. As I watched it scurry ahead, I tried to think of a name for the little creature brave enough to risk friendship in this barren, hateful wasteland of a world.

The little mouse led me down the side of the riverbed, high enough to be far from the water but low enough to still be able to use the trench as a bit of cover. I followed its pattern of moving quickly, becoming absolutely still, then moving quickly again until we reached a certain spot.

It was using a map, I finally realized. The little mouse was having me race to hiding spots it had frequented in the past, then checking to make sure it was safe to race to the next familiar place of cover. Once it was there, it would look to make sure the sky and earth were clear to run to the next spot, and that the next location with cover was still vacant enough to be safe itself.

It was a far more efficient way to travel than what I had done before, walking around while trying to watch every direction at once. I knew how to survive on the streets of the Global Republic's cities, but out here in the wild, my fluffy little friend had much to teach me.

My survival depended on learning as much as I could from the creature, and as quickly as possible.

After about an hour of running and resting, the shadow of the ruined city draped over the ground in front of us. The water in the riverbed had risen considerably, tripling in width. A new impression from my fluffy friend told me that the water was no longer safe to be near.

Leave-leave, the tiny rodent told me. *Not-good. Bad-bad.*

That explained why the rodent bothered to travel all the way to the middle of nowhere to get a drink in the first place.

After a brief rest, we began dashing to new spots of cover, large rocks at first, then rusted pieces of rubble and shattered remains of buildings. If I could, I'd have asked the little mouse what had happened here. I was familiar with the signs of decay. Many districts in the Glorious State had buildings that were falling apart from neglect. Those not taken over by gangs often made good hiding places, where I could store what little possessions I had. Judging by how familiar the mouse seemed with this city, I began to suspect it was taking me to a little treasure-spot of its own.

But the highest buildings far in the distance had clearly been much taller, and from the wreckage at their tops, I could tell that it was not time that had brought their zeniths tumbling down.

As we paused behind another rubbled wall, I saw my furry companion look up and sniff the air.

Night-soon. Bad-bad.

We had apparently been taking longer resting between runs than was safe. That was my fault. My body had been drastically augmented, but my endurance was still far below that of a normal human's, and most people I knew would have had trouble racing across distances this great anyway. But I forced myself to focus on the task at hand. I took out another food pouch for energy, draining most of it, letting a tiny portion travel to my Soulscape instead of my stomach, and then leaving the remainder for the tiny creature to eat. My new friend perked up immediately, surprised at how delicious and nourishing the meal had been to it.

More-more? it asked hopefully, though I got the sense it was also full.

Back home, I promised. *Plenty to still eat there.*

It lashed its brush-tipped tail in excitement.

Quick-then. Night-bad.

The smog-colored sky had gained the briefest tinge of red to itself. I did my best to take the mystic beast's warning seriously.

We began to risk more speed, resting less between sprints. The ruined buildings grew larger and more frequent in appearance, and I finally saw the remains of wrecked pavement appear on the ground, larger chunks that had not fully crumbled with age.

Which meant once again that the passing of this great city had been more violent than simple neglect.

Now we were creeping along the sides of what looked to be former apartments, meant to house large numbers of people. The little beast impressed that I should keep my body as low as possible down the walls and avoid lingering near any windows. Then it began to scan ruined alleyways, and it moved twice as quickly through this area as it had through the cover just outside the city limits.

But I could keep up easily now, because I was familiar with moving quickly through the terrain of failed civilization. I began to privately suspect that the cities of my own world would not have too long before they shared this one's fate.

But what if Nova and I could prevent that?

I owed the land of my birth close to nothing, but one of the sayings I had treasured reading stated that the best revenge was living well. What could be better living than turning my former home into a lush, tyrant-free paradise?

I reminded myself to save such thoughts for later, and to focus on acquiring what I needed so that my new friend and I could quickly leave this place.

The little mouse suddenly paused again, even though we had just exited the cover of the nearest alley. I clamped down on the urge to ask why and mimicked its behavior, which was absolutely not moving at all. Not even a twitch.

Danger-danger, the tiny creature projected. A moment later, I heard something cry out. It was a curious squawk, possibly some form of carrion eater. A moment later, the squawking became surprised and anguished.

Dead-trick, the little mouse impressed upon me. *Run-now. Quick-quick.*

The tiny creature zoomed forward. I did my best to keep up.

For the first time, the little mouse took me directly inside a ruined building. It hesitated right at the entrance just long enough to sniff cautiously.

Safe-safe, the mystic beast told me, darting quickly inside. *Go-go.*

I stepped into the ruined building, which was either an old store or one of the larger apartments, by my best estimation. The floor was full of rubble, but this very well may have been the first building with all four walls intact. My furry friend ran up the crumbling stairway in the corner of the room. Since the steps were made of concrete and not rotting wood, I followed him. I found the little mouse perched on a window in the nearest hallway, waiting for me.

Come-come, its mind sent impatiently. *Look-look.*

I carefully peeked out the window to see what it was that had the small creature so excited. I saw nothing near our building, but further down the street, a figure swayed into view.

It was male, and he had clothing somewhat similar to mine, save that he was also wearing an opened, tattered white robe. He swayed and shambled almost aimlessly, dragging a rusted, blunt, and pitted sword along the ground. His chest and face were covered with blood, and several black feathers stuck out of his mouth. Patches of skin were missing on his face and hands. His dark hair was completely unkempt, and his eyes resembled two orbs of dead glass, taking in nothing, as he stumbled down the street.

Man-thing, the little rat sent to me. *New-thing. Here-came. Dead-now. Still-hunts.*

I worked out that the decomposing-but-somehow-still-moving figure was a practitioner that my tiny friend had seen arrive on this world, possibly one of the treasure hunters Vessa had said I might encounter. But something had slain him and then animated his corpse, turning him into one of the walking dead that had once been so prevalent in the old fiction of my world. Judging by the blood and feathers covering him, he was responsible for the death of whatever avian had squawked earlier.

What made him like this? I asked my guide.

Night-thing. Huge-strong. Hide-must. Kills-all. Show-soon. Leave-then?

If we need to see it at all, I replied cautiously.

It felt as if the little mouse wanted to agree with me, but it still nodded its head furiously. That was rather odd, considering how cautious the creature had been. But it had also been willing to risk itself in order to reveal danger I would not have noticed otherwise. Maybe there was some reason I needed to see whatever creature was raising the dead in this former metropolis.

Dirt-now? the mystic beast asked me, and when I returned my gaze to it, I found that its fur had changed to white.

Please lead the way, I sent to the little creature, and it scampered off to the room at the end of the hallway. I followed it into what looked to have once been a family's living space. Trash, dust, and debris still littered the floor, but the familiar sounds of running water drew my attention toward the remains of a kitchen sink.

The little mouse was already waiting for me as I approached the ruined countertop with a pipe dangling brokenly below it, somehow still letting out tiny, intermittent drops of water from a leak in it. Could the water plant of this city still be working? Had their technology been far beyond that of my world?

At any rate, there was a little den stuck just beneath the leaking pipe, stacked full of random knick-knacks that reminded me of a classic packrat's den. Little bits of cotton or lint, that had somehow survived through the ages, formed what could have been a tiny bed. Next to it was a pile of metal, containing a few old screws and nails, a couple of different-sized coins, and a ring that looked surprisingly pristine.

But what caught my attention the most was the clay bowl directly under the leaking pipe. It was filled completely with the black soil that Vessa had wanted me to find, but growing out of it was a wilting flower with gray petals, that hung limp and downward. One of its leaves appeared to have been carefully nibbled on, but the rest of the plant was in much better condition, even though it clearly wasn't getting enough nutrients. I tried to recall all the different species of plants I had read about so long ago, before I realized I was on another planet and that I should count myself lucky enough to have plants, flowers, and mice to begin with, instead of more alien lifeforms.

The little mouse hopped over to the wilting plant and stuck its paws into the fur covering its stomach. To my surprise, it pulled a tiny vial, an eyedropper full of the creek water, straight from its belly, as if it had a pouch there like a kangaroo. Then it delicately lifted the dropper to hover near the plant's stem and began squeezing out the water in it onto the soil covering the plant's roots.

My tiny little packrat of a friend was trying to be a gardener.

Why are you doing this? I asked the mystic beast. *Is it because you need the plant for food?* But somehow I doubted it. The mouse had been far too careful of its nibblings on the single leaf, and I had seen just enough of this place to suspect that it could find other material to eat if it really had to.

Life-life, the little creature sent me as an impression. *Care-care.*

What? I asked, confused. *Your species cares for plants? Why?*

Care-plants, the little rodent answered me as it kept carefully squeezing out tiny droplets of water onto the soil under the sickly flower. *Care-life. Care-you. Form-bond?* it ended hopefully.

I still didn't understand. Most species on Earth were not particularly charitable. If they cared for another organism, it was usually out of some form of self-preservation, or mutual benefit, such as a bird eating the bugs off of a cow's back. The only possible exceptions I remembered reading about were the friendliness of dolphins to humans and certain species of whales that would protect other fish and people from aquatic predators.

Care-life, the little mouse repeated as it finished watering its plant. It brought its whiskers next to the wilting flower, nuzzling it almost affectionately. *Care-you. Care-growth. Form bond?*

Care-growth…

I replied that last phrase to see if it would help me understand. The little mouse hadn't been bothered by my killing of the rock spider earlier, and it clearly knew that other creatures were being eaten by the practitioner zombies roaming the place. But it had gone out of its way to ensure that both myself and this plant would survive… and grow.

I knelt down and attempted to sense any lingering Source energy. I still sensed essence energy emanating from the mystic mouse, a few flecks of essence that occasionally shook free from its furry body. But when I focused harder, I began to notice faint trails of both essence and qi emanating from the potted plant.

"Source energy," I whispered quietly. *You guard Source creatures… why?*

Was it trying to Advance using the plant's essence?

But that didn't make any sense. The plant wasn't getting any stronger. If anything, it was getting weaker every day. The mystic mouse's best hope for Advancement was to consume the wilting flower right now, instead of feeding it a handful of drops every time it went to the riverbed.

Care-life, the little mouse repeated. *Form-bond?*

Not here, I decided. *Not safe. When we leave.*

Plant-come? the mystic animal asked, and I felt a strong pulse of hope accompany that impression.

It truly wanted to save the flower's life, and my own. For whatever reason, this tiny creature that should focus exclusively on its own survival was trying to take others under its wing, at risk to itself.

I didn't understand it. Why would something so small and weak protect anything else? Help anything else grow? What good could possibly come to the little creature for helping other beings work past their troubles? Would they even be able to repay its kindness? The plant certainly couldn't, and most other creatures probably wouldn't bother.

It was madness, I knew. The little mouse was endangering itself foolishly, and would meet a horrible end if it kept this up, one that could have been avoided if it just kept its head down and worried about its own problems.

I'd have to look after it, I decided. At least until it Advanced enough to be wiser and more careful. I owed it that much, anyway.

Yes, I promised the little mouse, because the plant would die on its own out here, too, and for all I knew, Vessa would have a way to save it and make use of its Source energy. *But I'm going to need some of its soil. Can it live if I take this much?* I asked as I held out a small vial. The mystic mouse nodded.

Yes-yes. Spare-spare.

I scooped up a small vial full, letting a few crumbs of soil clinging to my finger pass straight into my Soulscape. The spectral planet jerked awake, sensed the wilting flower, and pulled hard at it, despite it being far too large to fit inside the opening to its realm. I jerked my hand away from the plant. Storing lifeless objects was one thing, but putting a living being, however harmless, inside a realm linked to my inner being could easily end badly for myself or for said creature. I remembered Vessa's earlier warning and resolved to discuss the matter with her first.

So I put the potted plant into the large satchel attached to my shoulder, along with the scavenged pile of treasure the little rodent had collected, because for all I knew the items could have been mystical hidden treasures containing the secret to immortality itself. That was unlikely, but the mouse had bothered to collect them and it would be no trouble for me to bring the items along in my satchel. Judging by the little beast's excited hops, it appreciated the gesture.

If that's it, we can leave, I told the creature. *You'll need to stay close to me to be able to come with me.*

Part of the reason Vessa had considered this world so safe for me to visit was because the Soulship would be able to transport me back no matter where I stood on the planet. This dying world possessed neither the technological interference of Earth nor disrupting amounts of Source energy. I literally could leave this world whenever I wanted to. But the little mouse shook its head.

Wait-wait. See-thing.

The little mouse took me to another window. As I looked outside, I realized that the sky was losing the last of its red light. The sun somehow set completely in another fifteen minutes, though I never saw it in the sky to begin with.

As the last of the light left, a starless night sky fell over our heads.

And something on top of the largest, tallest tower rumbled.

The mouse had brought me to a good vantage point, and while I had to crane my neck uncomfortably upward, I still could see part of a massive wing unfurl atop the tower, dark and membraned. The shadow-shrouded owner of the giant wing sighed, as if it were sucking in a great breath. Source energy all around floated up, in such density that I could see it from my own vision. I heard something from the streets below groan, and as I looked downward, I saw the practitioner zombie from earlier suddenly collapse, with polluted strands of all three Source energies trailing out of its mouth like filthy smoke.

The strands curled upward, to the top of the broken tower, and it was impossible for me to miss overwhelming strength radiating from a being that clearly did not fear a single creature on this entire world.

I backed away from the window in a hurry, shrouding my own feeble energy with every single trick Vessa had taught me. But the little mouse by the window seemed unconcerned.

Too-small, the mystic creature assured me. *Can't-sense.*

That flew in the face of all the warnings Vessa had burned into my mind earlier, but I reflected on the fact that the winged creature atop its roost was unable to remove power from us in the same way it had absorbed the zombie's Source energy, and it seemed unwilling to move from where it was.

It still felt like a terrifyingly unnecessary risk. The power rolling off the giant sky-beast was more than enough to make all my insides tremble. It was rather embarrassing to see that the tiny rodent next to me was unaffected. Perhaps handling the presence of a powerful mystic beast or practitioner was a skill I could practice over time.

Why did you show me this thing? I asked the little mouse.

Bad-thing, it answered as it stared out the window. *Big-threat. Kill-much. Hurt-more.*

Everything here is already dead, I answered the little mouse. *Unless there is someone else you think we can save. Is there?*

No-no. All-dead.

Then why care? I asked suspiciously. Did it delay our departure just so it could terrify me?

Beast-grow, the Sourcebeast impressed into my mind urgently. *Beast-leave. Kill-more. Kill-more,* the little rodent repeated, pleading with me to understand it, and see the relevance of its warning.

It's like a practitioner, I realized. *If it gets powerful enough, it will leave this place and threaten another world. Assuming it's not already strong enough now, and is just being lazy.*

Yes-yes, the rodent nodded. *Big-threat. Kill-much. Hurt-more.*

I still didn't understand why the little creature cared so much about lives not its own, and I worried for it all the more because it did. But regardless of how powerful and threatening the giant Sourcebeast in the distance was, it would not be able to stop me from returning to Vessa's ship-body. There was nothing left to do but return to the Soulship with the gathered materials and see if she knew what to make of my new companion's warning.

Alright, I have a friend who might know how to stop the creature, I told the overly compassionate rodent. *But there is another I must help first, who will be in danger very soon if we are not able to help her.*

The little Sourcebeast straightened immediately, and began bouncing where it stood.

Go-then! it insisted, even though it didn't even know Nova's name yet. *Help-help!*

Alright, I sighed, worried that someday the little creature would try to help someone and get used horribly for it. *I can take you and your leafy friend with me, but you both have to be on my body or clothes. Hop onto my hand and we can leave.*

I knelt down, and the creature leaped into my palm with an excited lash of its furry tail. I covered the tiny thing carefully with my other hand and sent the small bit of mana needed to link my body back to Vessa's ship-body.

The world shimmered, and my body faded back into the night sky.

Chapter 5

Darkness, metal, and faint blue light greeted my eyes the next minute. A quick look down told me the transfer had been successful. I had appeared directly on the ground this time, I wasn't missing any body parts, and the little mouse was still tucked safely between my hands. It squeaked curiously at the sight of its strange new world, crawling up my shoulder to get a better look at the place.

"You're back," Vessa said weakly from her capsule, and my new friend squeaked when it heard her voice. "And with a new friend, apparently. I thought I told you to run from anything you saw?" The little beast I still desperately needed to name squeaked again, and I saw Vessa tilt her head up to get a look.

Friend-friend? the fluffy little thing asked me. I nodded, and the next thing I knew, it had darted halfway across the deck. It climbed up onto Vessa's capsule-bed a moment later and began sniffing at her from the edge. The ship-woman crooned in awe.

"A lifemouse," she said softly as I walked over to her. "You managed to find a lifemouse. How? How was that even possible?"

"I wouldn't know," I answered, reaching for the satchel holding everything I had brought with me. "I wasn't the one who did the finding. I brought the samples you asked for, as well as a few odds and ends. But what can you tell me about our new little friend?"

"They are supposed to be no more," the ship-woman breathed, still transfixed in amazement over the tiny thing squeaking above her. "They are seekers, scavengers, and protectors. It should be no surprise that it would find you, but I hadn't known them to still exist under the night sky. They have been gone for ages. Few even remember them." She blinked as she spoke. "This…

this proves it. Not everything is lost from the worlds that my kind once failed to protect." She turned her head to look at me, eyes shining with hope and hesitation. "When we rescue Nova, Jasper Cloud, I may have another favor to ask of you. Will you permit me to plead with you again, when that time comes?"

"Help me rescue Nova, and I promise to hear you speak as long as you wish," I answered firmly, though her hesitance was odd. If she asked me to travel the stars and find wonders with her, I would take it as a boon to myself, not a favor for her.

She looked away from me for some reason, and I began to feel as if I had said something foolish. "The lifemouse asked to bond with me," I said hurriedly, hoping to change the subject. "Is that wise?"

"Wise?" Her head snapped back toward me. "It's the wisest course of action possible. One you should begin immediately, in fact. Bonding with a lifemouse is possibly the most incredible boon you could ask for as a new practitioner. You will begin gaining a Sourcebeast's benefits right from the beginning, and they will only grow over time. You will acquire sharpened senses, faster reflexes, and an increased ability to hide in any environment. Beyond that, you will gain an instinct for finding resources and noticing danger. It will not strengthen your body like another Sourcebeast would—not until it advances and takes on new powers, at least—but it will do more for your long-term growth and survival than any beast I can think of. Even finding a hatchling dragon would not be so fortunate for you right now. Though I suspect this little mouse will help you find other mystic beasts as well, when the time comes."

We-here, the little beast spoke up. *Bond-now?*

Yes, I answered the mouse. *Though just to be clear, there will probably be other beasts I bond with as well. Is that okay?*

Yes-yes! the creature squeaked, adorably excited and clearly a social animal to the core. *New-pack! Good-good!*

"I can hear it," Vessa said, giggling from her bed. It was a nice sound that reminded me of Nova's laughter when I had tried to cheer her up back on the Republic's streets. "It's just impressions of speech, but it's intense, and passionate. I can't wait for it to be able to actually speak one day. And it's so fluffy!" she added, reaching up to pat the whiskered ball with legs. The thing actually purred as it nuzzled Vessa's hand. "You and I get to be friends, even though you're bonding with him, okay?" She turned her eyes back over to me. "Sorry for ignoring you in favor of the adorable new mouse. How did the rest of the trip go? You said you found the samples?"

"I did," I replied. "The three types of dirt, as well as some odds and ends our little friend had stashed away. I've been trying to think of a name for him, by the way…"

"Nestor," Vessa said, still petting the little mouse. "It means Voyager in one of your planet's languages. You have to let me name it, since you're already going to get more time with it," she commanded.

"That is no issue," I replied, a little surprised at how easily my little stowaway had wormed his way into the ship-woman's heart. "Nestor, it is."

Nestor, I impressed back into the little mouse. *She has named you Nestor.*

Nes-tor? the newly-named Sourcebeast tested curiously. Somehow, I realized the creature was male when he responded to the name. He tilted his head for a moment, then bobbed it up and down. *Nestor. Yes-yes. Nestor. Bond-now?* he asked hopefully.

Yes, I replied. *Bond now. Pay attention to what the woman in the tube tells us.*

Can-do. Hear-her, the little mouse said as he jumped down, his fur becoming blue as he ran across the lit tiles. As Nestor scurried up to me, I set the pack to the side, since Vessa was insistent upon us forming the bond this very moment, without waiting any longer.

"Alright, Jasper Cloud," Vessa said as Nestor stopped in front of me. "Reach out with your essence again, like you first did when you tried to communicate with our friend. As you do so, agitate every Source energy you have, while concentrating on every charm, art, and spell you know. Your potential bondmate will do the same, and then, if you both agree with what you find, the two of you will slowly merge your Source energies. Creating the pact will leave you both vulnerable until it finishes, though, so it typically should only be done in a safe location, preferably surrounded by allies who will guard either of you if something goes wrong. But this is the best we can do for now. Go ahead, Jasper Cloud."

I knelt down in front of my fluffy new friend and reached out with my Source energy. I relaxed my essence and let my other Source energies move about unrestricted in my body, bringing to mind the handful of techniques I knew. Flakes of essence, threads of qi, and droplets of mana all floated off my body and meandered to meet Nestor's own Source energy as it drifted toward me.

Time flashed once, and in that brief flash, I knew all of my new friend. It was so much knowledge that it overwhelmed me, and I could not focus on more than a handful of details.

He was a survivor, and had been for some time.

He had lost count of the times he had almost died, and did his best to learn from each one.

He had seen others die, of his family and those he felt an instinct to save.

He had tried to save them.

He had failed.

He wanted to try again.

Would I let him try with me?

There were other hints of knowledge, special powers he was born with and would develop over time, but at the forefront was Nestor's desire to save and provide for a new packmate, to have as many other packmates as he could get away with having, and a desire to let me do the same with him.

I refused.

I brought to the front of my mind the knowledge that his goals would kill him. He had survived until now, but all it would take would be for one other creature to take Nestor's aid for granted, to put their needs above his own when his life was in danger, and he would die. His dreams could not, and should not be realized, not as he saw them now.

I offered him a new dream.

As you care for me, I will care for you, I sent back. *We will protect each other, and grow together. If we find others who we can risk showing weakness to, we will protect them as well. But I will do all I can to stop others from using you for their own gain, at your expense.*

Nestor found the concept foreign. Why would those who did not wish to use him for food still mean him harm?

Anything can use you for food, I told him firmly. *Anything can spend part of you as fuel for something else. Not just for the meat in your body or the Source energy within your spirit. If we truly do travel together, we will probably find many who will decide they can gain much by causing us harm. And I will do my best to protect you from them.*

The little mouse was still confused. But when I offered to protect him from such hunters, he relaxed immediately, letting his essence connect against my own without any further reservations.

His acceptance pained me. It reminded me of the way I once saw the world, before men in nobly-named offices sentenced my parents to death for the breaking of yet-unwritten laws.

I hoped that Nestor's eventual loss of innocence would be less brutal than my own.

The next moment though, I was swept away by the sensations of the bond completing. Flecks of Nestor's essence mingled with mine in a cloud that spread out to envelop us both. The lifemouse's essence entered my body at the same time my own entered his.

My Soulscape twitched awake, and began spinning.

Nestor's ears flicked, and his eyes widened in amazement.

Think, the tiny Sourcebeast sent, and this time I felt something a little stronger than a neutral impression. *Think-think. More-clear. Can...* He paused and closed his eyes, the fur around his face wrinkling slightly, as if he were concentrating. *Can... talk-close. Talk-soon,* he finally sent, and this time I felt the hint of a child's voice, instead of a neutral impression. *Talk-soon,* he repeated. *More-clear. Thank-you.*

I could not relate.

My senses had become uncomfortably sharp. The shadows inside this place were thinner now. I could see further into the blackness everywhere. Sounds were also more acute, as every hum from a nearby device became a little more than just faint background noise. My nose had to adjust to every smell becoming more intense, and to the ability to notice subtler smells, like dirt on Nestor's fur and the faint fragrance coming from the flower in the open satchel. Then my mind began to filter my senses in a way that my mind could tolerate. Except for one thing.

I could tell for a fact now that there was absolutely no danger lurking by, and I was unprepared for the sensation. It was too new, too raw, too strange. It tore apart the cloak of fear I always wrapped myself in, the warning that there was always a chance something was hiding in the shadows nearby. It was that fear that had kept me sharp all those years at the orphanage, that allowed me to be ready when the day of my eviction finally came. But now, I could no longer maintain that edge, not when I could enter a room and know with total certainty that nothing else was in there with me.

That was not true, I told myself, desperate to keep that part of me, no matter how fearful and mad it was. I had seen magic now, I reminded myself. There could always be danger that my senses could not detect. Hadn't that danger been behind all the prestigious powers of my former home?

Or you could just learn to accept that sometimes you will be safe, a voice whispered in my mind, and I shuddered when I heard it. I was not ready to think such things, I decided. Best to move on, and ignore such fears. Best to keep doing as I had before.

Nestor squeaked again, reminding me that there were others in the room. I rose back to my feet, letting him scamper about and explore his new environment.

Do not wander too far, I told him. *Not much beyond this room is safe.*

He projected that he was happy to obey, and then began sniffing at the tiles on the floor, following the trails of blue light running between them. I turned my attention back over to Vessa, and saw that she was smiling at me.

"Congratulations, Jasper Cloud," she said warmly. "You are now a pactmaker. One of the youngest ever to have achieved such a feat, and certainly the first to have ever done so before Advancing at all."

"Thank you," I said, walking over to her. I was able to see her features in greater detail now. Her skin was still gray with a faint blue blush, and it still looked just a bit healthier than it had when I first saw her, thanks to the food packets she had consumed. But the fatigue was back in her eyes. I could tell that transporting me to and from another world had exhausted her. She still had a long way to go before she was truly healthy again, just like myself. "Here is the bag of everything I could find on the planet below, including the soil samples you asked for. By the way," I said as I put the bag next to her. "That dead world you sent me to. What was its name?"

I had not needed to know the name of the place at the time of my visit, and had not even thought to ask. Now, though, I was curious. I had seen the ruins, as well as the beast that had made them its lair.

"I honestly don't remember," Vessa answered. "Not its original name, at least. There are far too many worlds for me to remember every single name, at least in my weakened state. I do remember that it was a fringe world, one I wasn't responsible for until all of my brothers and sisters fell. The people of that world swore fealty to practitioners on another planet, as their people chose to advance technologically, instead of through Source energy. They thought they could achieve many of the same benefits as the practitioners did through improvements in medicine or engineering, all without relying on Source energy and spending lifetimes cultivating it. I named the world Techne because of that, when it came under my care. But when it came under assault, I was too far away, and the practitioners responsible for it never came to its aid. I was never able to learn the details of what ended it, but the world was stripped barren of almost all life by the time I was able to reach it, and I had no time to examine the world for smaller Sourcebeasts such as the lifemouse."

"There was a larger one still on the planet," I said grimly. "All I could see of it were massive wings, and the Source energy it drained from the walking dead."

"The dead walk?" the ship-woman said as she sat up sharply, intensity replacing the fatigue on her face. "Explain."

"I would not know how," I admitted, shrugging my shoulders. "I saw the corpse of what was likely a former practitioner stumble through the city's streets with the remains of a dead bird clenched in its mouth. When night fell, a great winged beast atop the highest broken skyscraper drained it of its Source energy, causing it to collapse to the ground. Nestor believes the creature is gathering power to leave the planet, though I would not know how."

"A deathbeast," Vessa sighed as she covered her face. "A being that can absorb more Source energy from a kill than other beasts, and from a much greater distance. They can Advance easily compared to most other Sourcebeasts, although Advancing in this fashion twists them, eventually making most either insane or undead themselves. If they become strong enough, they can contaminate an entire world, which is why most other Sourcebeasts and practitioners will band together to destroy one. If this one ever grows strong enough to leave Techne under its own power, it will be a great threat to any planet it invades. And right now, there is absolutely nothing we can do about it, because neither of us are powerful enough to confront it, and I don't trust any tribe, sect, or guild with knowledge of our existence at the moment. And even then, there are far greater threats among the night sky right now."

"After we save Nova, I will have you tell me of them," I said quietly.

"Even if we save Nova, I will have to rely on you for a little longer, Jasper Cloud," Vessa said tiredly. "Until I recover more of my power, there is no other practitioner I can trust with knowledge of my existence. So I will share all of the knowledge you are willing to bear, until I no longer need you and you can finally stop risking your life on behalf of all the worlds under the night sky."

"That would be an uncomfortable change of pace," I replied grimly. "My life has been at risk ever since the death of my parents. But perhaps you can tell me of these other items Nestor and I recovered?"

"Certainly. One moment," Vessa said as she touched a button on the side of her capsule bed. The side of the tube adjusted to create three curved, half-funnel openings. "Place each sample down one of these holes, and then show me what you and your new friend have brought back."

I complied, setting the items out to where she could see them and pouring the vials one by one into the appropriate slots while Vessa commented on my other treasures.

"Oh, my," she said, eyes widening. "Well, we'll start with the unimportant items first. The lint and cotton won't be good for much more than a bed for Nestor, which I imagine is what the little mouse already used it for. The nails are of good metal work, even if some are rather rusted, and we could perhaps use them for more resources, or find a collector for them, if you are ever able to trade without revealing my identity. The coins will be even more valuable as antiques. The ring, however, you can use to store one type of Source energy. I recommend you use mana, but feel free to experiment with it. It can't store much now, but as it gets used to your specific energy its capacity will increase. Finally," she said as her eyes fell on the wilted flower, "you have, somehow, recovered what may have been the last Sourceplant on Techne. Though it was likely one of the last plants there to begin with, and a Sourceplant will have a slightly easier time surviving in a harsh environment than a normal plant would, especially if a lifemouse has taken it under its care. Still, this is an extremely lucky find. In a hundred years or so, this plant may be able to start helping you acquire and refine Source energy. Possibly sooner, if we can cultivate it well."

"A hundred…" I began to say, and then trailed off. "I think you are misinformed as to how long people of my race normally live. Even if you somehow manage to improve my health, I will likely be dead in a hundred years, or close enough to it that it will not matter how much I Advance."

"It's more the fact that I've forgotten how little you've been taught about Drawing from a Source." Vessa turned her head to answer me. "Even the early stages of cultivation can advance your lifespan by years, in the case of mana users, or decades, in the case of essence and qi users. Later stages will advance your lifespan by centuries, and it is not unheard of for the more advanced practitioners to live even longer."

"In that case," I said slowly, "wouldn't everyone try to Advance? Especially if all it takes is Drawing from one of the three Sources?"

"Almost everyone tries," Vessa acknowledged. "But everyone's talent and opportunities differ. And for even the most talented and wealthy, Drawing is difficult, arduous work, and the higher you Advance, the more benefit that killing you provides to another practitioner. Many people find it unsafe, and look for other ways to extend their lifespan, such as through technology, like your world and Techne did. And this is especially true now that my kind is no longer around to provide mentoring and protection. With me, Jasper Cloud, your Advancement will be both safer and faster, which is why I offer my patronage for the danger I must now put you through."

"Very well," I replied, not quite knowing how to thank the woman, as I was still having trouble wrapping my mind around the possibility of living for hundreds and hundreds of years. "We will cross that bridge when the time comes. This plant, though, what is it exactly? Can it help those others than myself Advance?"

"It can," Vessa said with a nod. "This is a blossom fruit tree. Not the rarest of finds, but useful all the same. Its fruit and petals can both be beneficial to acquiring Source energy, and it can raise one's talent for Drawing ever so slightly, which is still a huge boon for those with low to no talent at all. But it will provide blossoms and fruit rarely, even when it matures, and the more quickly you harvest them, the slower new ones will grow. But when it reaches full maturity, its Source energy will spill into the nearby environment, making it more beneficial to Draw the respective Source energy in that location. So it will not help us immediately, but it's definitely worth investing in. Especially as we are now, needing every scrap of power we can get our hands on."

My Soulscape stirred again. I could feel it hunger for the blossom fruit plant, even though its opening was still not large enough to store it. The tiny planet itself was still positioning the dirt and water I had stored in it before, merging with it somehow, as if it was trying to become something more than an image.

"Vessa?" I asked, still thinking. "We spoke of placing things inside my Soulscape…"

"We did." The ship-woman nodded. "I was just thinking of that. I see you've already placed some things inside of it. They appear to be benefiting you ever so slightly. You're wondering if something bad will happen if you place the plant in there."

"I was curious if the act would kill either of us, yes," I admitted.

"You'd be fine, but the plant wouldn't have enough soil, water, or air to survive. Not yet, anyway. But it's still fascinating. It's as if your Soulscape wants to become a planet itself. Don't give it anything toxic, but keep feeding it anything that isn't alive. It's trying to grow, and this could help your own progression greatly. In fact," she said as her eyes narrowed in thought, "you may wish to consider putting the ring inside of it. I can study what happens if you do.”

“You are sure I will be fine?” I asked, hesitating slightly, because absorbing trace amounts of water, soil, and food had seemed far more harmless than sucking a ring into my soul.

“My professional opinion is that you will be completely fine,” Vessa assured me. “Now hurry up and swallow that ring.”

Putting my reservations aside, I slowly injected a bit of my mana into the piece of jewelry, and then opened it up to my Soulscape. My internal spectral planet sucked it in greedily. Then it laid the ring next to the soil, water, and nutrient paste and began pulling the mana out of it, spreading the energy throughout itself. When it was finished, it knocked the ring to the most forgotten corner on its landscape, as if to indicate to me that it no longer wanted it.

“Fascinating,” Vessa said as she watched me.

“Yes,” I said dryly. “It appears my Soulscape is a housecat pretending to be a planet.”

“What?” she blinked as she asked, before finally cracking a smile. “Oh. I get it. You told a joke,” she said, grinning. “Right. Very funny. Ha ha.”

I suppressed a wince. I could not tell if she was making fun of me or trying to pretend to find me funny. *Perhaps she was trying to do both,* I thought.

“But yes, it really is fascinating,” the ship-woman continued. “Your Soulscape isn’t just storing objects. It’s absorbing properties of them, adding them to itself while preserving the original. Well, except for the Source energy. It’s sucking every bit of that dry. Try recalling the ring.”

I wasn’t sure how to do what Vessa was directing, but I projected my desire to have my ring returned into hand from my Soulscape. The illusory planet shifted apathetically, and released its hold over my new item. The plain piece of jewelry appeared in my palm a moment later.

"It seems I was right," the Soulship woman said. "You can recover the item if you desire."

"I hope so," I said as I stared at the plain ring, slipping it onto my palm. "My Soulscape seems alive. As if it has a mind of its own."

"It doesn't," Vessa clarified. "It has desires, but not a mind itself. Soulscapes are both pieces and reflections of your own mind, your own desires."

"I am afraid I do not believe you," I said slowly, "as I have no desire to swallow random bits of dirt."

"Neither does it," Vessa rebutted. "I'm sure you noticed. It has a purpose for everything it's swallowed so far. You can see it moving the mana you put into it right now, whirling it into clouds above its surface. It wants things because it has some kind of plan in store for them. It's trying to build something, Jasper Cloud. Which means you are as well, even if you don't know it yet."

That made no sense to me. For the last ten years, I had no purpose beyond surviving the current day, lasting long enough to make it to my next meal. Trying to plan beyond that would be suicide. The people around me would assume I was carrying out some dark plot left behind by my parents, tear down everything I had tried to build, and then execute me on account of educational terrorism.

I shook my head to clear away such thoughts. It wasn't important for now. I'd learn more about the strange planet in due time.

"What should we do with the plant and other materials?" I asked next, moving my hand over to them. This time, I began filling my ring with spare essence, although I was running dangerously low on all of my Source energy, after battling that rock spider and completing my earlier mission. I would have to Draw more energy soon, and probably rest so that I could recover my body's more mundane forms of energy.

"For now, nothing," Vessa answered me. "We can't use them yet, so you can just put everything but the plant inside your special storage world. When you've done that, take the plant over to the device a few feet away. Stick it inside the largest depression, then hit the button to the right to activate the water dispenser. If you're ever thirsty yourself, you can hit the button above it to have it work like one of your world's water fountains."

"You have a large number of devices responsible for emergency supplies in here," I noted as I sent the metal items into my Soulscape and picked up the potted plant. "Is this one of the ship's storage spaces?"

"You could describe it as such if you wished," Vessa answered as I walked to the water dispenser. "It's actually an emergency command room. This was where myself and any officers present would try to get my ship-body to safety while any other survivors slept in suspension centers."

"So you had a crew at one point?" I asked as I gently positioned the plant inside the exotic pillar. I had just enough experience with water dispensers to know that they often sprayed water in a completely unexpected direction. Vessa paused before answering me.

"We all had crews at one point. Practitioners, doctors, experts in various crafts. They helped us maintain peace and growth, to keep the night sky clean of things that wanted to swallow up all its lights. Our captains and admirals were those we trusted the most, for they bonded with our systems as well, and helped us be even more effective. But it was not enough in the end. We lost the war, and now, we have been hunted to extinction by foes I cannot even bear to name. My main officers were killed before they reached this room, and if any crew made it to the life support pods, they are surely dead by now." She turned her head away from me, staring at the side of the tube. "It has been so long, I am afraid I have forgotten most of their faces, and all of their names."

"Suppose I can repair and power more of your ship," I asked, changing the subject for her just as I finally got the water to work right. The clear liquid sparkled in the dim light, making me feel like I was watering this plant with tiny diamonds. "Would that make it easier for you to think? And would it help your body recover enough to walk about?"

"It would help immensely," Vessa replied, turning her head back to me, seeming grateful to be talking about an objective instead of a painful memory. "My flesh and metal are linked. Repairing one will help me better take care of the other. It will take some time before either body is completely healed, but if we were to start recovering my rooms from their invaders and restoring power to them, I could remember more techniques to teach you. And I'd probably be healthy enough to dress myself," she added with a grimace, gripping the sides of her bed experimentally, and seeming disappointed at the result. "But you are not strong enough for that yet. Powerful creatures lurk in many places here. They cannot currently approach this sanctuary, but you will need to become stronger before you can leave the safety of this room."

"Good to know, I suppose," I replied, removing the plant from the water dispenser and setting it on a dark pedestal next to Vessa's tube bed. "Is this a good place for it?" I asked, feeling supremely foolish. Vessa had insisted that she was linked to Nova, and Nova had always been fascinated by flowers. Whenever she had gotten sick at the orphanage and been forced to lie in bed all day, a colorful plant had done wonders for her. But right now, I was acting in ignorance. I still had no idea what Vessa meant when she called Nova her Beacon, and for all I knew, having a wilted, dimly colored plant just out of her reach would be an irritation for her. But she smiled at me, then quickly looked away.

"Yes, that will do marvelously. Thank you. It is an unnecessary gesture… but very appreciated."

She turned back to stare at the distant ceiling, and I realized her gray eyes were glowing ever so faintly. "It's working. The soil is already helping. I had forgotten how badly I've needed it all these years."

She must have caught my confused expression, because she turned her head to look at me directly. "Soulships draw power from planets themselves, from the air, dirt, and life in them. I don't know if that was by design or accident, but it gave us another reason to care for the night sky's worlds. Ideally, we orbit around a planet just low enough to absorb trace elements of its atmosphere for a day, and that will power our ship-bodies' main systems enough to operate indefinitely. If we ever needed to travel quickly, or to multiple locations, taking in passengers would do wonders. They would carry all sorts of elements on them—the soil on their feet, the fibers on their clothes, and even the air they exhaled would help power and maintain our outer bodies. Now, though, I am far too damaged to be able to process such elements except through this emergency capsule, and I can only handle them in small amounts. Feeding my ship-body in this fashion would be like receiving nutrients or blood intravenously for your own fleshly body: it has to have a specific amount and a specific type of nutrients or it will do more harm than good. But now, I can perform a number of vital tasks, such as cycling the air in this place, increasing the Source energy I produce naturally, and ensuring that the dangerous parts of my ship-body remain sealed. I will be able to send you to a place to collect the next bit of ingredients I need, but for now, I must finish adjusting to the nutrients. You should take the time to Draw from the Source energy present, and we should all take some time to rest." She blanched for a moment, looking around suddenly. "I… had forgotten you would need sleeping arrangements as well. I apologize. I will reactivate another capsule bed as soon as I am able to. It should take me no more than a day."

"A needless worry." I waved my hand dismissively. "Beds became a luxury for me years ago. I can sleep on the floor if needed. Should I Draw the same as I did last time?"

"For now." The gray woman nodded. "You have not even advanced to the first stage yet, so it's far too soon to tell which Drawing technique will suit you best. I'll watch you begin all the same, though."

Once again, I knelt on the floor and began reaching out for the different Source energies present in the room. Like before, all three approached me at once, but this time they hesitated, as my own Source energies stirred in response.

That was the problem. The three existed in some amount everywhere under the night sky, but on some level, they interfered with each other. Essence obstructed mana and qi, preventing them from moving freely. Mana disturbed essence and qi with its rapid, ceaseless movement. And qi could subvert both mana and essence by moving both of them in slow, stable, constant patterns. The new incoming Source energies could probably be negotiated in the same way as when I first drew, but now the different energies were demanding that my Soulscape be positioned in a way that would be beneficial to them, and each Source energy wanted something different. Essence wanted my imaginary world to remain in one place long enough for it to stabilize inside of it. Mana wanted to move the planet around quickly and violently, to see what else it could stir out of my soul with rapid movements. Finally, qi wanted my Soulscape to methodically move about in a consistent pattern.

I struggled to find a way to accommodate the opposing demands of three different forces until I cursed myself for missing the obvious and began spinning the Soulscape slowly in place, keeping it stable, active, and consistent. *Just like an actual planet,* I reflected, *or at least how a normal world is supposed to work.*

The three different Sources resisted at first, each wanting a more advantageous position. But when they saw how much room they had to operate in this fashion, without being obstructed by the other two, they relented, incorporating themselves into the world as they had done earlier—essence in the ground, mana in the air, qi within the rivers and seas. As the faintly glowing world spun, its light suddenly pulsed, sending Source energy back into my body. This time, the essence primarily settled within my flesh and bones, the mana into my mind and synapses, the qi into my heart and veins. I felt myself augment further, getting one small step closer to the strength of a normal human being.

"Well done," Vessa said from her bed. "You are balancing your different Source energies beautifully. Your gains from Drawing are minimal, but you have done an excellent job of making sure your different Source energies do not interfere with each other."

"When you say my gains are minimal, do you mean I am not progressing quickly enough?" I asked with concern. "Am I gaining enough power to help Nova?"

"Nova is very new to her power, but her nature as a Beacon will leave her far above you, for now," Vessa answered as she closed her eyes. "But do not worry, Jasper Cloud. You do not need to be stronger than her captors. You only need to be strong enough to help her escape. She and I can take the brunt of the dangers by then. You will no longer need to risk yourself on behalf of either of my bodies then."

"I thought you said that you would probably need my help even after we rescued her," I countered. The ship-woman seemed to be distracted, and contradicting herself, but when she heard my question her eyes blinked back open.

"I did say that," Vessa replied. "Forgive me, Jasper Cloud. I am not very coherent at the moment. I am still far more tired than I would like to believe."

"Then I will let you rest in peace," I answered, sitting down to brace my back against one of the unlit pillar-consoles. "I will try to do the same as well."

"Thank you, Jasper…" the ship-woman began, then hesitated. "Apologies for asking, but… may I be informal with you, and just call you Jasper?"

"Of course," I replied, confused as to why she would even need to ask. "It's still a very common custom for my world to call a person by their first name. I had assumed you were abstaining out of your own customs. Are many worlds more formal than my own?"

"Nearly all are, especially when one party desperately needs the other," Vessa answered, closing her eyes. "Good night, Jasper. Thank you for saving me and feeding me. And thank you for the flower."

I closed my own eyes, puzzled by her inconsistent shyness, and let sleep overtake me.

Chapter 6

I awoke to something soft and pointy brushing my face. I saw Nestor a few inches away, sniffing at me with his whiskered nose. His fur had become dark blue, helping him blend in with the black steel and blue light inside Vessa's ship-body.

Bad-noise, the lifemouse impressed into my mind. *Close-close.*

I listened, hearing a banging noise off in the distance. Judging by the echoes, it was coming from much farther away than the eaterling had when I first heard it, but the beginning echoes were much louder than what I remembered the eaterling making.

A larger, or at least stronger, threat was currently trying to force its way deeper into the Soulship.

I tried to think of what needed to be done. Obviously, I knew I should wake Vessa, but she was still in no condition to fight and had already activated all the defenses she could. There was likely little more she could do to help. Could I handle this threat myself? I had no idea. If I could surprise it like I had the eaterling, possibly. But anything strong enough to make this much noise from this great a distance was probably a threat I couldn't stop with just a loose tile, or a push into a damaged console.

The frustrating thing was that I was currently stronger than I had ever been, more well-fed than I had been even back at the orphanage, thanks to Vessa's miracle food-packets. But I was still weaker than the average Earth adult, and the average Earth adult was still weaker than anything that had Advanced even once with Source energy.

I need to get stronger, I said to myself, clenching my fists together as I rose to my feet.

Yes-yes, Nestor impressed into my mind. *Strength-good. Life-good. Get-strength. Guard-life.*

If we can only live long enough to find that strength, I thought as I walked to Vessa's capsule. I kept my footsteps light just in case whatever monster was raging around in the dark could hear them. I tried to think of anything else I could do if the creature made it into this room. Could Nestor distract him, perhaps? Long enough for me to fire another mana bolt into a weak point?

But there was no real point in planning until I found out what the creature was.

I was about to carefully nudge the Soulship-woman awake when the clanging became louder, and angrier, and two different voices screamed and roared at each other. The invisible assailants thrashed and battled for a few more moments until one of them let out an anguished screech. Then the ship was silent again.

"Not close enough," Vessa murmured sleepily. "Still safe. Go back to bed."

"Does that happen often?" I asked, surprised at how untroubled she was.

"All the time," she murmured without opening her eyes. "Not eaterlings. Too big to get in. Still safe. Wards still holding. Go back to bed."

And with that, she tilted her head and went back to sleep. I wanted to ask her a few more questions, such as the kind of banging I actually would need to listen for to know if our lives were endangered, but she did not wake again. In the end, I had no choice but to assume that she had survived long enough to recognize threats to her life, and probably had some sort of alarm to alert her to something truly dangerous. I leaned back against the dead terminal and re-welcomed sleep.

A disturbingly short amount of time later, Vessa was telling me to wake up.

"I agree, Nestor, you should tickle him again if he does not answer me this time."

"Unnecessary," I groaned, rising slowly and wincing painfully. Apparently I had exaggerated my tolerance for sleeping on uncomfortable surfaces, because my back felt terrible. "I am awake. Again."

"Good," she said, and I turned to look at her. She still looked tired, and still looked like she was slowly recovering, but for the moment, her eyes were bright with purpose. "We have much to do this day. I need to make sure you are ready for it. Did you sleep well enough, though?" she asked suddenly, her eyes glittering with worry. "I had forgotten the noises that the… scavengers sometimes make in my ship-body."

"They were quiet for the rest of the night," I answered her, stretching out my back. "I take it their noises are a common occurrence, though."

"For a very long time," the ship-woman admitted. "I had grown so used to them I had not even thought to warn you. You probably thought another eaterling had found its way into our sanctuary."

"They sounded like they were far larger creatures," I said, looking around the room. Everything looked to be undisturbed, save for the terminal I had used to slay the eaterling on, and even that no longer sparked with dangerous energy. I turned my gaze back to the hallway through which I had originally entered this place, and this time I noticed that the blue lines within it were completely dark.

"They are. And stronger, for that matter. Most of my remaining energy has been spent keeping the more dangerous life forms away from this place. Anything…" She paused to swallow. "Anything that made it in here would be strong enough to kill me. But the more powerful predators would make much greater use of the Source energy they would gain by devouring my flesh-body, and more likely become one of the great terrors in the night sky. So I chose to spend the bulk of my remaining power warding them away from this place, and trusted my ship-body's natural defenses for keeping away the weaker vermin, such as the eaterlings. Had we more time, I would spend more effort in showing you gratitude, Jasper. But until then, I will continue to trust you with my flesh-body's protection." A squeak sounded to my right, and Vessa smiled as she looked down. "And you as well, little friend. I look forward to watching you grow."

"Thank you for the explanation," I said respectfully. Truthfully, I felt insufficient for the task she asked of me, especially after hearing the most recent noises in the dark. "But if you are going to continue sending me to different worlds, how I can I keep you safe? And how should I recognize which noises to ignore and which noises to warn you over?"

"Fair question," the ship-woman conceded. "This vessel you reside in is currently my body as well. Most of it has been depowered, but I can still feel movement in the nearby compartments. If something bypasses my remaining defenses, I will sense its presence, and alert you. If you are currently on another world, I can summon you here myself, and trust you to defend me as you have already done. And next time…" She took a deep breath. "I will trust you to protect me, and not advise you to… do otherwise." She exhaled, and looked back up at me. "Does that address your concerns, Jasper?"

"It does," I answered her. "Thank you."

"Good," she said briskly. "Now back to our plans. The soil you have collected has been immensely helpful. Our next step is to acquire a water source that will benefit us. Now that you have Nestor, you will be able to better navigate through more populated environments. Lifemice are excellent at detecting Source energy, especially energy found in living creatures. He will help you avoid other

Sourcebeasts and practitioners as you navigate to the water sources I need you to harvest samples from."

"That sounds fine, assuming I can convince him that other practitioners should not be trusted."

"He will learn quickly, I am afraid," Vessa said sadly. "And now that you are bonded, he will be able to read your mood much more easily. If you distrust a person or talking Sourcebeast, he will know almost immediately." She turned her head and stared down at the fluffy blue mouse by my ankle. After another moment, Nestor squeaked, and the ship-woman smiled again. "I have spoken with him. He should understand. Now, on to the water samples we will need. As before, we will require three different sources of water. They will all have different trace elements, but the key difference will be their temperatures. One will be a much colder, almost-frozen liquid, and it will be surrounded by snow. It will be very beneficial to your body as well as the inherent essence of all three of us. Including you, little friend," she said to Nestor with another smile, and the little mouse squeaked happily at the attention. "The second will be of lukewarm temperature, from a running source of water. A stream would be ideal, in fact I have one in mind. It will improve mental focus and mana." She shifted, to sit higher in her bed. "You will need to collect a sample from a warm body of liquid, preferably a hot spring. The one I have in mind will greatly refine your body and provide immense benefit to our qi pools. It will also be the most dangerous of the three locations, as the practitioners on this world are primarily qi users, and more likely to frequent the planet's various springs. You should be extremely careful when you collect a sample from here. I am sending you to the most remote of locations, where most practitioners of that world would never bother to search because there are so many more beneficial, and easier to reach, Source treasures to obtain, but that still will not erase the chance of encountering a hostile practitioner. If you or Nestor sense anyone at all, I insist that you hide until the danger has passed. Do you understand?"

"I believe I do." I nodded. "Do you know more of this world than you did the last?"

"Much more," the gray-skinned woman affirmed. "It is a Source-rich world, flush with all three Source energies, but most known for its qi. Its name is Likwon, and I have a Beacon there."

"You do?" I asked, excited. "If I bring her here, can she power you? Can she help us return to Earth and save Nova?"

"She cannot," Vessa said sadly. "I created her in a damaged state, and some of my damage passed to her Soulscape when she was formed. She is much more powerful than my Beacon on Earth, but she cannot handle travel through the night sky. Until her Soulscape is somehow repaired, she will die if she leaves her world. Furthermore," the ship-woman continued, "she has joined a powerful sect, and achieved status within it. Her leaving would be noticed, and possibly draw unwanted attention to my existence. We will not be able to contact her until we are in a much stronger position."

That was unfortunate, but it couldn't be helped. Perhaps, after we brought Nova onboard, Vessa would be strong enough to connect with her other Beacons, although she still had not revealed how many of them she had.

"It would be a freak accident if you actually encountered her," the ship-woman continued. "In fact, the sect she is stationed within is several countries away from where I am sending you. She should have no reason to go there at all, with the resources she has access to at her own sect. But if, for whatever reason, she decides to inexplicably travel hundreds and hundreds of miles to collect Sourcewater already inferior to what her own sect provides her, and encounters you by some accident, she will look like a dark-haired, pale-skinned woman with features your world would consider Asian. Her name will be Lunei, one of the Shining Maidens of the Sparkling Sky Sect, and you should not reveal your connection to me. She will not believe it at any rate, because like Nova, I have not made her aware of her status as a Beacon, for her own safety."

"Can you not simply warn me if she comes close?" I asked, remembering how Vessa had been able to detect Nova's movements back on Earth.

"Not in my damaged state," Vessa admitted. "Right now, both of my bodies are so damaged that it is difficult to even remember how many Beacons I have, much less be able to sense all of their movements. I have a general idea of her health and stage of qi advancement, and I can detect just enough information traffic on her planet to know that she has retained her status in her sect, but I cannot guess her location within the world itself. But Nestor will most likely sense her or any other practitioner of her level long before she arrives. But again, if you do encounter her, do not reveal my existence, either by speaking of me or teleporting in front of her, and excuse yourself from her as soon as you can. None of my Beacons will ever desire to harm you," she said oddly, quickly looking away from me, as if she felt she had been staring too long. "Can you think of any further questions to ask?"

"What should I do if I encounter any other practitioners, and I am unable to hide?" I asked her.

"If that happens, you should return here immediately," she said firmly, turning her gaze back at me. "Do not try to collect any further samples. Return here, and wait for us to try again tomorrow. I mean it. We have time."

"How much time?" I asked, unable to hide my concern. "And how much spare energy do you have available to transport me, if I do not procure the resources you need?"

"Enough," she replied, hesitating just long enough for me to disbelieve her. "And if you die, I have no way of gaining any further resources I need. If you die, Jasper, I have no hope of saving and recovering Nova. I can risk losing time. But I cannot risk losing you."

I wanted to point out that she could simply pull up any random person from any random planet and probably gain a stronger practitioner than myself, but the look on her face told me she would hear none of it. For all I knew, though, she was right. Another practitioner might decide to slay her for her Source energy instead of helping her save the night sky.

"Very well," I said with a defeated sigh. "Do I need to do anything different to prepare this time?"

"Nestor washed the vials while you were sleeping." The ship-woman pointed to the little mouse, who ran up to me with the stoppered vials in his tiny paws. "Just return them to the pack, load it up with more food, and move to where you stood when I teleported you to Techne."

"Very well," I said as I lifted the bag's strap onto my shoulder. It had taken only a moment to pack everything, partly because I had almost nothing to take with me. I did remember to put the Techne ring on my finger and charge it with qi, and found that it could store slightly more Source energy inside it now. Nestor squeaked and climbed his way up to my shoulder. "I believe I am ready."

"I believe so, too," Vessa said calmly. "But be careful all the same… friend Jasper."

With that, the world of steel and dim blue light faded away, and a world of trees and snow took its place.

I looked around to take in the life-flush world, a complete opposite of Techne. Grass, snow, and large rocks covered the ground like patches of paint, while trees of different sizes and colors rose to obstruct my view at eye level. High overhead, large blue clouds sprinkled small batches of snowflakes onto the ground and trees.

At that point, I realized Vessa had dropped me into a lightly snowing environment without so much as a light jacket for protection.

I spent a half-second resenting her for that fact until I remembered her latest lesson and began managing my different Source energies. An inexpensive essence charm made my skin more resistant to the cold, while a simple cantrip sent warm mana cycling through my veins. Finally, I invoked the qi shield technique I had used on the last planet, and found that it blocked most of the cold on its own. The result was that I had become more comfortably warm in light clothing than I ever had been with the thickest of coats, and it had only cost me a negligible amount of Source energy.

I began to feel much more charitable about the woman who was slowly opening up a world of miracles to me.

All-good? Nestor impressed into my mind. I turned to look at the little Sourcebeast on my shoulder, whose dark-blue fur was slowly changing into a light brown, probably to blend in with the dead leaves on the floor. *Go-now?*

Yes, I told the little mouse, turning my attention to the matters at hand. *Lead the way.*

The little mouse hopped down, landing on the grass and snow. Nestor looked up to sniff at the air, and sneezed when an orange leaf landed on his nose.

I chuckled, taking one more moment to look at the beautiful world around me. The forest seemed to be going through a phase where fall and winter jostled each other for their turn, because leaves and snowflakes were falling at the same time. All of the leaves that fell were orange, brown, or bright red, creating one of the most beautiful sights I had ever seen in my entire life. I dropped my guard just long enough to hold out my hands, wanting to bask in all the colors falling from the sky.

I felt the planet inside my soul stir and croon, as enamored as I was by all of the nearby beauty. It pulled on my limbs like a pet scratching at the door, begging me to open the spatial window and let all of the falling snow and leaves inside me.

I decided once again to risk it, remembering what Vessa had told me before. I let the falling snow, leaves, and even the air fall into the world inside my spirit. I found I could now absorb larger objects into my soul, and that I could do so with both hands. Wind and snow and fallen leaves spun into my Soulscape, and I felt my inner planet spin in excitement as it found a place for everything it had gained. In my mind's eye, I saw a tiny bit more detail form into it. The planet began spinning again, and suddenly, without doing anything else, I realized I had begun Drawing. It was not nearly as beneficial as taking up a proper pose, but it allowed me to absorb the three Source energies while still being free to move about.

So as I walked behind Nestor, I continued to let my tiny inner planet absorb whatever it wished, whether it was more leaves and snow, some dirt or pebbles on the forest floor, or just the air itself. As I did so, I continued to transfer the power ring in and out of the Soulscape, emptying it of Source energy, then returning it to my finger and filling it back up, then sending it back into my Soulscape to empty it again.

It was a marvelous feeling. Every movement I made gradually got easier. Breathing felt marvelous, both from the Source energy cycling through me and because this was the freshest air I had been able to breathe in over a decade. The qi in the air was especially rich, and I could feel it surge into my body's organs, pushing out toxins and impurities that had lingered inside of me for all those years spent living on the streets.

Eventually, the rate of Drawing of Source energy slowed to the tiniest of trickles. I put my hands down, but kept cycling my ring in and out of my Soulscape, since the trickle was still more than enough to fill it up in a few minutes. We kept walking through the forest, with Nestor leading me to the first location Vessa had described. No practitioner or Sourcebeast appeared to greet or threaten us, though plenty of small animals skittered about the forest floor, and colorful birds chirped high over our heads. But Nestor and I could not find any danger at all, not even something as mundane as a natural predator. The closest to danger we came was when Nestor detected a small red fox over a stone's throw away, and that animal still hadn't dared to do more than glance curiously in our direction.

The place was so beautiful that it had taken every shred of my willpower to remain vigilant, to remind myself that I was never truly safe, and that safety could never be permanent. Even then, I could not help but smile at everything I had seen: the falling snow, the rioting color of leaves, the lushness of the pine needle trees. I would never have believed that it was even possible to walk through a place with so much natural color, and I wondered if I would ever wish to leave it.

We made it to the first body of water without incident. We followed the growing patches of snow until we reached a large, calm lake, surrounded on all sides by the white powder in the same way that sand would surround a beach. The snow around it looked completely untouched, as if it had fallen yesterday. As I stepped closer, I could tell that the air was thick with invisible flakes of essence.

The lifemouse and I approached cautiously, but as far as we both could tell, no other creature was anywhere near us. I remembered that qi was the richest energy in most areas on this planet, and that we were in a remote area with relatively weak treasures. Even the few essence users and local Sourcebeasts still had better and more convenient options than making use of the essence here, which suggested just how prosperous this world truly was. Even then, Nestor kept watch as I knelt down and withdrew the first vial to dip it into the lake. The water rippled as soon as the glass touched, and I felt a pleasant sensation of cold travel through my shielding and into my fingers.

The Soulscape inside me stirred awake, but I pulled away from the water.

You first, I sent to Nestor. *We go one at a time. I will keep watch while you drink or bathe. Then you will watch for me.*

Nestor squeaked in happy agreement, and scampered through the snow, his fur turning white as his tiny body wiggled its way to the bank. He leaned his whiskered mouth carefully over the water and took a long drink. Through our bond, I felt power flow into him, strengthening his muscles, bones, and organs. Then he waded into the shallow water and dipped his body quickly under the rippling surface, rubbing his paws all over himself. The sight of the fluffy creature cleaning himself was adorable, but I reminded myself to stay on guard and scan the trees for any visitors.

Done-done, my tiny friend said as he crawled next to my ankle and shook himself, sending droplets everywhere. His fur seemed to have gotten even softer, and gained a healthy sheen to it. Beyond that, and a higher concentration of essence, I could see no change in my new friend. *Your-turn.*

I nodded, stepped over the lifemouse, and walked up to the crystalline pool. I knelt over the snow, feeling its cold despite my Source protection, and opened up my Soulscape. My little planetoid happily swallowed up the essence-rich powder, instantly gaining more detail, coloring the small cluster of clouds over its surface. This time, though, I felt the essence and qi inside the snow pass directly into my body from the Soulscape, merging with my own Source energy seamlessly. It felt even more beneficial than the time I had spent Drawing. With that done, I cupped my hands into the water and took a long, careful sip.

My Soulscape absorbed the water directly from my throat without waiting for my permission. It cycled the liquid into itself, whirled it about as if it was testing it, then flushed it back into my body. It felt invigorating, like I had taken the best drink of my life. I could not be sure how I knew, but I felt that my Soulscape had tested and enhanced the water, making it both safer and more potent. I felt flecks of essence settle all over my muscles, organs, and bones, making everything a bit stronger, tougher, and denser.

I stood up, finding that I had once again grown an incremental amount taller. Now, I could almost come up to Mother Anne's chin. I started to undress so that I could bathe, and then decided to see if I could send my clothing directly from my body and into the small world inside my soul. It took almost a minute of concentration, but I was successful. My boots and garments vanished into my special realm of storage and refinement, and I felt my Soulscape immediately go to work on making microscopic improvements to Vessa's gifts.

Having undressed in the most supernatural way possible, I now stepped into the cold pool. Essence particles clung to my skin as I descended, causing a cooling sensation to spread throughout my body. I felt the particles scrub my skin, soak into my pores, then travel directly into my body and continue scrubbing me of impurities that had been brought on by years of combating malnutrition by eating things that only loosely be considered food. It felt as if a lifetime of dirt and grime were cleansed from me, from my skin, and my hair. I could feel my lungs being scrubbed from all of the filthy air I had breathed in. In place of all the dirt and pollutants was a cooling sensation that soothed the damage that a lifetime of contaminants had brought to my body.

I tried to be conscious of the time, but it was hard to pull myself away from the most wonderful bath I had ever taken. Eventually, though, I shook the water from my hair and climbed out of the pool, belatedly realizing I had nothing to dry myself with, then realizing that once again, I could just send all the clinging droplets into my secret spatial world.

A little more than a minute later, I was dry, dressed, and ready. I gave the wonderful pool one last look, thinking I should save more of the essence water, before I realized that my Soulscape had once again acted on its initiative and soaked up several cupfuls of the liquid. It had begun spinning again, letting me Draw while I bathed without realizing it, and even transferred the Source ring to and from my finger without a conscious effort, letting me continue the exercise I had forgotten to maintain during my bath.

It had also grown larger, to where it could store all of this looted material and still have space for more storage. I suspected it could probably hold almost as much weight as I could carry myself. That was far from an impressive amount, but at least it meant that I could continue my own sample collection for the time being.

Go-now? Nestor asked me. *Next-place?*

Yes, I told my tiny friend. *Sorry I got distracted. Let's go.*

He tilted his head, seeming baffled by my apology for a moment. Then his tiny shoulders shrugged and he hopped off to lead the way to the next location Vessa gave us. The forest welcomed us back into its colorful embrace, and I spent most of the time trying not to forget all the lessons life had taught me until now. But it was hard to look for danger in a place more wonderful than any I had seen outside of my parents' illegal works of literature.

Nestor saved me by stopping abruptly in front of me, sniffing the air.

Stop-wait, he warned. *Smell-folk.*

I did exactly as he suggested and froze where I stood, and my Soulscape froze with me, no longer spinning and Drawing on its own. A moment later, I smelled what he had just noticed. A smoky aroma drifted through my nostrils, like that of meat cooked over an open flame.

Go-see? he asked hopefully. *Much-life. Much-food.*

It was hard to tell him no. The smell of cooked meat affected me even after eating one of Vessa's nutrient pouches. But I had remembered the ship-woman's warning about being discovered. Any practitioner that had advanced even once was capable of murdering me easily. At the very least, they could cost us time we would need to save Nova.

We cannot risk being seen, I decided. *But we need to find out who and where they are. Lead me in a way where we can remain hidden but still locate the source of the fire.*

Yes-yes! Nestor sent excitedly, and bounded forward once before crouching low to the ground as he wiggled through the snow and grass. I did what I could to follow him quietly, cursing every time my feet crunched on a twig or thick patch of snow. But nothing reacted to our presence. If a person or animal heard us, they must have chosen not to care. Given how safe the trek had already been for me, I would not have been surprised by that decision, no matter how foolish I thought it was.

After a few minutes, the forest opened up before us, ending just before it reached the edge of a large cliff.

Hiding behind the last few trees still gave us an excellent view of the land down below, where a series of small wooden buildings clustered around the center of a valley. We were high above them, but not far away. I figured we were a few hours of hard walking away from the village, and most of that would simply be the trek downward. Thanks to the essence of Nestor and the eaterling, I was able to make out the details of the people themselves. They were a tall, strong race, with pale skin, black hair, and almond-shaped eyes. They wore thick clothing of fur and hide as they went about their business, the adults cooking, building, or gathering, the children running about laughing and playing. Here and there, I saw what was most likely a practitioner kneeling with eyes closed, probably Drawing the nearby Source energy from their surroundings. I took them to be the protectors of the village.

Somehow, as primitive as their buildings and clothing seemed, the people still seemed much healthier and happier than everyone I knew back at home that didn't directly work for the Glorious State.

Go-see? Nestor asked me hopefully. *Form-pack?*

Definitely not, I replied as I shook my head. *We are on their world without their permission. They may decide we are a threat and attack us.*

But-food, Nestor protested. *Look-safe.*

He had a point. These people looked like happy, peaceful folk, and Nestor and I probably had the most unthreatening of appearances. But I still shook my head.

They may ask us questions, and insist that we answer them. If they do so, they may be forced to answer questions of us themselves by a stronger power on this world. If that happens, Vessa may be discovered, and all our lives will be at risk. Best to wait until we have much more strength and time. For now, we must continue to collect water samples and do what we can to help Vessa recover.

His whiskers twitched, and from our bond, I could tell that he still did not understand the danger another practitioner could pose. But he understood the virtue of hiding from uncertain danger, and he stopped arguing with me. We turned and worked our way back into the forest, Nestor following the signs Vessa had told him to watch for. A short time later we had found the location to take the second sample from: a rapidly moving stream, sparkling with ambient mana.

Nestor sniffed the air and looked about, informing me that he sensed no danger. All the same, we kept our earlier rotation: he kept watch while I collected the sample, I kept watch while he drank and bathed, and then he kept watch again while I tried to benefit from the properties of the stream.

It took him a little longer than the pool had, because Sourcebeasts primarily Advanced through essence energy. They could use other types, and there were even Sourcebeasts proficient in spells and techniques, but usually they had to distill mana and qi into a form that was enough like essence for them to be able to absorb it. I did not fully understand the process, but Vessa assured me that it was a trait exclusive to the creatures themselves, just like Drawing was to practitioners. They could Advance just by growing and consuming any foods with Source energy, whereas practitioners advanced through careful, diligent cultivation and by consuming the exact type of Source energy beneficial to them.

And of course, either group could grow at least somewhat by killing another creature for their Source energy.

But Nestor had finished with his second bath soon enough. This time, when he shook himself dry, his fur crackled slightly.

Close-close, he impressed into my mind. *Grow-soon.*

I took that to mean that he would soon Advance. According to Vessa, that would now provide both of us benefits, as would my own Advancement. At any rate, it was now my turn to partake of the water.

The stream was much smaller than the pool had been. I would not be able to bathe in it. So instead, I once again took a cautious sip while letting my Soulscape clean and enhance the water. Then I dipped my hands back into the running liquid and massaged the water all over my face, scalp, and ears.

A current of energy surged into my brain. I felt old knowledge activate, as if my mind was a house, and there was now enough power to turn on lights for previously darkened rooms. A forgotten memory stirred, one driven into the back of my mind by years of hunger. In it was a hazy memory of my parents, kneeling down in front of me. My father was gripping my shoulders, fiercely whispering something to me. I struggled to remember his words, but to my horror, I couldn't remember a single sentence. The mana was not providing enough power to reveal everything I had never even realized that I had forgotten.

I should have been joyful. I was improving again, and this time it affected the most treasured part of myself, my brain. I felt my awareness expand and my synapses fire faster. But all I could focus on was the newfound fact that in spite of everything that had happened to me in the last ten years, I had lost far, far more than I had ever realized.

I scooped my hands into the water and desperately scrubbed another bowlful all over my skull, and sucked great bowlfuls of the substance inside my personal planet, but I had already gotten all the benefit I would get from this stream. My mind and Soulscape could not process any more of its mana. I was done, much closer to Advancing the stage of my mana, and with a much sharper mind than I had mere minutes ago, but completely unable to fix any of the newly discovered holes still in my brain.

Maybe Vessa can fix me, I thought desperately as I rose to my feet. *Surely she knows how to heal my mind.*

I was still repeating that hope after I had left the stream.

At least, I was repeating it until I caught sight of a great white shape flying high above the trees.

Nestor and I ducked into cover immediately, but the figure flew past us quickly. I was barely able to make out feathery wings on its body, and what I thought were two riders on its back. They turned toward the direction of the nearby village Nestor had found earlier.

Strong-things, the little lifemouse impressed upon my mind. *Sensed-folk. Form-pack?*

I had been unable to sense anything from the flying Sourcebeast's riders, but I suspected that they were not anyone I had the power to deal with if I encountered them.

Definitely not, I impressed into the little mouse. *They may not wish to form a pack with us. Even asking might offend them.*

But-life, Nestor argued with me. *Strong-life. Life-good! Help-much!*

No, I sent to him firmly. *Not all life is good. Remember the spider you saved me from. Remember the giant beast in that tower?*

Not-life, the little rodent insisted stubbornly. *Not-good. These-life! Much-life! Much-good! Help-much!*

It was the Source energy, then, I decided, or at least the Source energy that did not rely on dead things. Even with the bond, Nestor and I had many barriers in our communication. But right now, I could sense his desire to befriend another creature with Source energy, and his inability to realize that other parties might try to harm him filled me with even more dread than discovering the loss of my memories had.

Not all life is good, Nestor, I projected as firmly as I could. *Plenty of life that looks just like I do has chosen to kill, or steal, or destroy.*

But-why? my tiny friend asked me. *Have-life! Life-good! Gain-much! Why-hurt?*

I do not know, I answered the little mouse. *All I know is that some people think they have something to gain from the smallest and pettiest of depravities. We will remain hidden until we are strong enough to defend ourselves. To do otherwise will risk both Vessa and the pack-mate we have back on Earth. Do you want Vessa to be alone? Do you want bad things to find her? Things like the monster you showed me on Techne?*

No-no. My companion shook his furry head. *But-but...*

Trust me, I sent back to the little lifemouse. *Please. Remember our agreement? The promise we made each other?*

Yes-yes, Nestor sent back, as his ears and whiskers drooped. *Hear-hear. Do-do.*

Good, I sent to him. *Now we need to hurry and reach the last place.*

We moved quickly. I suspected that, for whatever reason, the two new practitioners were here for the same bodies of water that we were here for, and probably for similar reasons. They needed remote resources, resources that they needed to use discreetly. So they had come here, because like Vessa, they knew it to be the safest, most remote part of the planet that would still benefit their Advancement. Perhaps that meant that they were close to my own strength, but I refused to be optimistic. Vessa had stressed that most practitioners my age had already Advanced several times, and these people were of enough status to have a Sourcebeast serve as their mount. I would be completely helpless if I encountered them, and they probably would not appreciate my pursuing the same resources they likely intended to use.

Fortunately, they hadn't even arrived in the woods yet, since they were choosing to land in the village. Surely, Nestor and I would have enough time to collect the final sample and leave. We may not have time to use the spring ourselves, but that was alright. I could carry enough in my Soulscape for us to at least drink of the spring's water. And for all I knew Vessa had a host of other resources she would be able to point us toward soon.

Spring-close, the little mouse sent to me. *Stop-soon.*

I heaved a sigh in relief, pausing to rest against a large tree. We had been running for a long time, and my body felt pushed to its limits, in spite of the recent gains it had made today.

Need-food? Nestor asked. The lifemouse had climbed halfway up the tree and was watching me carefully, eyes wide and whiskers twitching. *Food-tree. Help-you.*

I looked up to see large, pink fruits suspended in the branches over my head. They reminded me of peaches, save for the color, and the fact that they were pointed at the bottom.

And, according to my enhanced senses, they gave off faint wisps of qi Source energy.

I could not believe this fortune. After living on the streets of the Global Republic for so long, it was a shock to see fruit-bearing plants at all. But to randomly stumble into fruit that would help me Advance, however slightly? I was overwhelmed. I had no idea how any one place could possibly be so rich in resources, especially when I considered that Vessa had described the rest of this world as far richer than this. The few kilometers I had already traveled through were already rich enough in timber and soil alone for the Glorious State to have stripped this area completely bare, had this location been back on the Global Republic.

I shook my head to clear it of such thoughts. Others were likely coming here. We did not have time to linger, no matter how tired I felt. I needed to eat one of the fruits just so that I would have the energy to keep running.

Wait-here, Nestor told me as he scrambled toward the branches above. *I-get.*

Grateful that the little mouse still had more energy than I did, I walked a few steps over to another tree with a larger, more comfortable-looking trunk, and leaned against it. The branches of this tree poked against the fruit tree, and would probably be easier for my little friend to climb down.

As I briefly rested, the fluffy mouse suddenly turned his head and sniffed.

Life-near, he impressed into my mind. *Make-friends?*

No! I warned, terrified that the little rodent still had not taken my warnings about strangers to heart. *Hide! Hide now!*

I heard a rushing wind, followed by a loud rustle of leaves and branches. I gathered that something large, probably man-sized, had moved quickly through the air before landing in a controlled fashion. I scrambled to get behind the tree as the sound repeated, cursing myself for not finding a better hiding place sooner. But I heard the figure land again before I could find one, too close for me to find any more concealment in time.

I did my best to remain completely still, smothering my Source energy as thoroughly as possible. Through my mental link, I felt Nestor do the same, and closed my eyes in relief.

I heard the unseen figure sniff, as if in judgement over their surroundings. I guessed his gender to be male, though I wouldn't know unless I looked, and I certainly wasn't curious enough to find out at the moment. Aside from that, I could sense that he had been using a qi technique, probably one that let him leap through the air quickly enough to catch up with us. Judging by the power of the technique, I could tell that he had already reached the later stages of the qi Condensation level, meaning he was over halfway through the very first stage of Source Advancement for qi Source energy.

Meaning, according to Vessa, that he could probably kill me with a single slap of his hand.

For a few moments, I heard nothing but the sounds of nearby birds and forest creatures. Then the practitioner spoke.

"Well?" the arrogant, masculine voice asked. "I'm waiting. You can come out now. There's no point in hiding if I can already tell you are here."

I disagreed, and said nothing.

How had he sensed us? I asked myself. Nestor and I had little Source energy to begin with, and we were spending all of our efforts to mask it. For him to arrive at this location so quickly meant he would have detected us at a great distance, which struck me as extremely unlikely.

"You are testing my patience," the figure grated. "I did not come all this way just to encounter a coward. Reveal yourself and attend to me, or I will show no mercy when I discover you."

I suppressed my sigh of relief. If he had truly known where Nestor and I were, he would not have needed us to reveal ourselves. At the very least, he would have made it obvious that he knew which tree I was hiding behind.

Then I realized that I had been understanding the words of a being from another planet.

Mandarin, I realized. He had been speaking in a variant of one of the many outlawed languages my parents had taught me so long ago.

"Are you really so foolish as to think that I won't…" The figure trailed off suddenly. "Ah, a qi plant," he announced. "Of course."

He bounded forward again, landing just inside my peripheral view, then began approaching the Sourceplant. He had a cold, handsome face, with long dark hair, sharp black eyes, skin a good bit paler than my own, and a lightly muscled body covered by white robes cut in a fashion almost identical to what I had seen the undead practitioner on Techne wear. I could see no weapon on his body, not that he would have needed one to deal with me or Nestor.

"Yes, that is exactly what I was sensing," he muttered, eyes appraising the fruit on the tree. "Barely worth harvesting, though. Still, that irritable woman should have let me know the plant was here. Arrogant bitch acts like she doesn't even know who I am…"

He kept muttering, but I was far too shocked to pay further attention to his words. Now that he believed he was alone, the arrogant young man had changed languages again, speaking what I guessed to be his native language. It was one I understood easily, because it was the exact same version of the language everyone on my world had been forced to speak exclusively for the last ten years.

The Sanctioned Speech of the Glorious State.

This man's native tongue was a language supposedly only a decade or so old, and supposedly formed on a planet where people had never even heard of Source energy.

But I had no time to puzzle through the implications, as the stranger had approached the fruit tree. Since my own tree was right next to it, my location was now horribly compromised. One wrong glance would be the only thing needed to reveal my location to an arrogant man whose native language was that of my planet's tyrants.

And even if he did not notice me, little Nestor was hiding in the very branches he was interested in.

"Still nowhere near as productive as the fruit of my own orchard," the young man kept muttering. "But if I eat enough of these, I would be just a little stronger, and this trip would be just a little less humiliating. For that woman to insist that I come all the way out in the middle of nowhere just to perform this rite… breathing," he said, switching back to Mandarin, dark pupils shifting around. "Why do I hear breathing?"

I answered his question with an invisible host of silent expletives. He still had not detected our Source energy, but his hearing had been far sharper than I had thought possible. One of us would now have to reveal ourselves and hope that we would survive.

But before I could move, Nestor had already scampered down the tree, carefully gripping the stem of qi fruit in his mouth. He held the fruit directly in front of the arrogant young man, clearly offering it as a gift and peace offering.

I wanted to scream at him. Because I knew what impressions he was projecting to the unnamed practitioner: *I-help. Make-friend?*

The dark-haired figure regarded my little friend coolly.

"A Sourcebeast as well," he said calmly. "How rare. And a young one at that. Let's see…" he considered as he narrowed his eyes. "If you were of a practitioner race, you'd be just at the very first stage of essence cultivation… the beginning of the Natal stage, if I recall. Congratulations on your very first Advancement," he said in a dispassionate tone. "And since you cannot speak yet, you likely were unable to understand my demand to reveal yourself, or that your essence-speech was useless for announcing yourself to me. Very well," he announced. "I accept your offered fruit, and praise you for having enough intelligence to submit to me."

He raised a pale hand and took the fruit Nestor had offered him. The fluffy mouse squeaked happily.

See-see? he projected to me, full of cheer. *Take-fruit. Be-friend.*

Run, I begged of him. *Run. Please.*

I knew a cruel man when I saw one.

I strengthened my qi shielding, and had already begun to send all of the loose mana and essence into my body to help me leap far enough to reach the little mouse. If I could reach him in time, and was careful enough, I could send the both of us back to the Soulship, where we would be safe. Then I could ask Vessa how someone from another world could know the newest language on my planet, when she had never learned it herself.

"Unfortunately," the practitioner continued in a pitiless voice. "You made the mistake of only bringing me one fruit, so you are a stupid thing after all."

I tensed my legs to leap, but the qi user was far faster than me. His palm flashed through the air and slapped into little Nestor's side with a loud crack. A whimpering squeak tore out of the tiny mouse as he hurtled through the air and landed on the ground, his back twisted in an unnatural position. Time slowed down for me as I leaped forward.

I gritted my teeth as I somehow suppressed my shriek of rage. The arrogant monster of a young man still had not noticed me, distracted by the fact that Nestor was still alive. There was still time to get to my bonded friend. There was still time to take him back to Vessa and find a way to save his life. As these desperate thoughts poured through my mind, the practitioner shrugged and raised his foot over the tiny mouse, not even looking down as he took a bite out of the fruit Nestor had given him.

I dove low and reached my crippled, mewling friend. I had made it. I carefully cupped his body within my palms and reached for the thread of Source energy that would take me back to the Soulship.

Then my new enemy's boot blasted into my back, and the world went white with pain.

His qi-laden stomp blasted through my reinforced qi shielding, slammed into my essence-strengthened back, shredded many of my muscles, fractured my ribs, ripped apart far too many important blood channels, and completely shattered my spine. Numbness warred with pain everywhere below my shoulders, something I had thought impossible, given all the damage to my nervous system.

Worst of all, the pathways maintaining the thread of Source energy that linked me to Vessa were crushed like overstressed metal beams. Except for a small wisp of mana, the rest of my Source energy had scattered uselessly through my body, ignoring any command my mind gave.

"Well this is a surprise," the arrogant practitioner said after swallowing. "There was a trap for me here after all. One from a young fool able to use basic qi and bond with the weakest of Sourcebeasts. I'd be impressed, if you weren't so pathetic. Tell me," he said, and I heard his foot move toward me, but felt nothing. "Who are you? Who sent you? How did you know I would be here?"

I held Nestor tightly and carefully, desperately trying to reconnect with Vessa's ship. It would risk exposing her, but I was now completely empty of wiser plans.

But it was fruitless. My mind was growing hazier. All of my remaining Source energy became even harder to gather. I could not recall how to return to the Soulship, or any of the techniques Vessa had taught me. The only thing I remembered was the spell that would fire a mana bolt.

"Stop acting as if you were dead," the harsh young man snarled impatiently. "I've merely crippled your body and your cultivation, and you should be ashamed at how easy it was for me to do so. I give my frailest maids a greater beating than this every day, and they still attend to their duties. Answer my questions, and I will give you a reasonably clean death, and perform the honor of personally harvesting your remaining Source energy."

Somehow, my arms were still able to answer my commands. I removed one from shielding Nestor, and tried to push myself onto my side. My enemy kicked me impatiently, either to help me turn over or to punish me for not yet answering him. It was enough to roll the top of my body onto my ruined back, though my legs still faced downward.

But I did not let myself focus on that. Instead I raised my finger to perform one final act of defiance, hoping to at least scar my murderer's otherwise-unblemished face as my mind worked out the formula for performing a mana bolt.

His eyes widened as he realized I intended to die fighting back. Then he opened his mouth and began chuckling.

"Go ahead, rat-lover," he laughed, clutching himself. "Go ahead and try to harm me. Pretend I need a reason to break all your fingers before I kill you."

I lowered my finger to aim for his throat, and did my best to comply. It took longer, because my breathing was becoming more and more erratic, and my vision was growing dark. I remembered Vessa saying that mana spells required more mental concentration than essence charms or qi techniques, especially at the earliest stages. But I had almost managed it anyway, before a blast of qi energy sent the practitioner hurtling away from me, straight into the tree I had hid behind earlier.

"Koram!" a young woman's voice screamed. *"What have you done?"*

Long white robes fluttered all around me as a dark-haired, moon-skinned figure landed by my ruined body. I looked up to see onyx eyes sparkle like stars under the night sky, with a faint white light glowing in the center of them.

The glow was different in color and intensity, but somehow it reminded me exactly of both Vessa's and Nova's eyes.

"Hang on," she said quickly to me, speaking in the Mandarin dialect Koram had used earlier. "I will stabilize you, and find a way to tend to your injuries. Can you tell me what happened? Why did my charge attack you?"

I gritted my teeth, not answering her, except to carefully reveal Nestor's pitiful form under my other hand. The little mouse squeaked painfully as he looked up at our savior.

He-hurt, the creature impressed into my mind, and the moon-colored woman's eyes widened in comprehension. *Why-hurt? I-friend... I-help... give-fruit... why-hurt?*

"He tried to attack me, Lunei," Koram gasped painfully from the tree that the powerful woman had slammed him into. "He leaped out at me, like he had been waiting for me all along."

"Shut your lying mouth right now!" the woman bearing the same name that Vessa had warned me to watch for shouted. "Do not speak again until I command it! You are lucky I have not already killed you for attempting murder on my world!"

The once-arrogant young man quickly clamped his mouth shut. Lunei turned her attention back to me, and placed one hand over Nestor and the other over the broken remains of my chest. A cool, soothing white light spread out from her palms and mingled into the broken channels of my body.

I felt qi energy travel soothingly into my veins and arteries, wrapping protectively over them and mending broken blood vessels together, before spreading further into my body and doing the same to my heart, lungs, and other vital organs. The qi did nothing to reset my spine or ribs, however, and my body remained a numb puppet with cut strings, except for my arms and neck. I felt Nestor stir on top of my body, apparently receiving similar treatment.

"Forgive me, stranger," she said softly to me as the light faded from her hands. "I have enough power to keep you alive, but I will have to take you elsewhere to restore the rest of your body, as well as your Source energy. Your bonded companion has explained the incident well enough for me to know my guest was at fault. I assure you, he did not harm you with my permission, and I will see to it that he is punished appropriately. I swear by my name as Lunei, Shining Maiden of the Sparkling Sky Sect, that you will come to no further harm while you are in my care. Might I know your name?"

Her face was soft with concern as she looked at me. But I clenched my teeth together and heaved with visibly painful breaths.

"You see?" Koram said as he finally pulled himself free of the nearby tree. "He will not cooperate—"

"You dare test me again!" Lunei exclaimed as she whirled on my attacker. She stretched out her hand and sent another invisible blast of qi into the vicious man, knocking him once more into the tree he had just crawled out of. "You dare speak again without permission! You dare lie and omit that you attacked another practitioner's bonded Sourcebeast unprovoked, and then did the same to the practitioner himself! If you were not a guest on my world, I would have already executed you myself, and if you were a member of my own sect, your mentor would have been stripped of their position! You bring great shame both to me and to the order you represent, by attacking so junior a practitioner under the night sky!"

The glowing woman turned her attention back to me.

"I apologize again, stranger. I can tell by your appearance that, like Koram, you are not from my world. The fact that you know of this remote location suggests you were directed to come here by someone in authority. I will respect your privacy for now, and will personally provide you with both healing and compensation, but I am honorbound by my sect to ask if you or those you belong to have any ill intentions regarding the Sparkling Sky Sect or the world it resides in. Do you come in peace, stranger from the night sky? Do those you call family mean us harm?"

I nodded, then shook my head. Then, to indicate a possible exception, I pointed to my attacker, then to the damage he had caused both me and Nestor.

"Thank you for answering, stranger from the night sky," Lunei answered softly. "And know that Koram will be punished accordingly, and will never be allowed to harm you again."

I mouthed my thanks to my savior, and Nova gave me a soft, bright smile.

Lunei, the stable portion of my mind corrected. *Her name is Lunei.*

Her smile vanished, and she carefully scooped me up into her long-sleeved robes.

"His damage is more severe than I had originally judged," she said with a frown. "I will take him with us. If I perform the same treatment on him that I was going to perform on you, Koram, I can save his life. Hurry and pull yourself out of the tree, or I will be forced to leave you behind."

"But, Shining Maiden, you were supposed to guide me to the spring yourself!" the young man whined petulantly.

"And you were supposed to stay close by me at all times," Lunei snapped, "and not charge off on your own, and you certainly were not supposed to attack a fellow visitor over a resource so petty as a wisp fruit tree! Now stop talking, and try to keep up, or you will find your own way to the hot spring!"

With that, she bounded into the air, still cradling me and my Sourcebeast in her arms.

My small body proved to be no trouble at all for the average-sized woman. Her arms thrummed with qi as she carried me through the air, cushioning me with every landing. Her destination proved to be the very spring Vessa had directed me to, and her speed put my earlier pace to shame. I felt foolish for underestimating just how easily Nestor and I had been overtaken in these woods, despite the fact that we had a massive head start on the two practitioners that hadn't even bothered to fly here on their winged Sourcebeast.

The air warmed immediately as Lunei carried us out of the trees and into a large clearing. Grass and snow gave way beneath her feet to rock and silt, and I heard a bubbling sound nearby.

"Unnamed stranger, this spring has special properties, many of which I will ask you to keep secret when you leave. We use it sparingly, because it will lose much of its value if those who do not need it ever learn of its existence. Here, those whose bodies had been born with defects, or who have somehow erred drastically on their cultivation of Source energy, can have their damage repaired, giving them another chance at finding their destinies under the night sky. This is not the only such spring on our world, but it is the one we have chosen to keep secret, to protect those with more sensitive histories behind their limitations. Our sect leaders have been asked by Koram's own masters to provide him this boon, and they have chosen me to perform this favor discreetly. That may have been why he was so suspicious when he encountered you, although it certainly did not justify his decision to immediately attack you and your Sourcebeast."

I nodded to show that I understood, although I wondered why this secret spring had a village so close to it, and why they had chosen to land at the village instead of some other, more secret location.

"Please know that I am beyond furious over his actions. The knowledge of this spring's existence is well-guarded. The only way you could have learned of it yourself was to have been told by your master, and your master must have connections with my sect as well. I know that your master must be highly favored, to have learned of the location and sent you here directly, instead of being led here by one of our guides. I do not know why you were sent here on the same day as Koram was, but on behalf of our sect, I must beg forgiveness from your master. The Sparkling Sky Sect has worked hard to preserve the harmony of this world, and does what it can to bring peaceful Advancement to other worlds under the night sky. Know that after you have bathed here, not only will all your injuries be healed, but you will be remade. Any defects brought on by birth or unfortunate events will be corrected, allowing you to reach a higher potential than you might have otherwise. You will be more whole than when Koram found you. This I promise to you under the night sky."

She stared intently at me, evidently wanting to make sure I understood and believed her. I caught myself wishing she would not take so long in getting care for my body. I nodded finally, wincing with the effort. She muttered angry words at herself, then performed her sustaining technique again, erasing the last of my pain and stabilizing me completely, at least for the time being. Through my bond, I could feel Nestor settle into a painless sleep, breathing steadily for the moment.

A loud crash sounded from behind us. Out of the corner of my eye, I saw Koram land into the clearing, panting heavily from trying to keep up with Lunei's pace.

"Shining Maiden," he gasped, "I am here."

"And I must tend to you as well," she said in an aloof tone. "To uphold the vow my sect made to your own charter. But know this, Koram: after today, I will never do so much as look at you. I had no idea the members of your lofty order could behave so shamefully, and put my own sect at such risk by offending this stranger's master."

"He has a master?" the arrogant young man asked incredulously. "How do you know?"

"Because he is at a secret location, can manipulate both essence and qi, and has a type of Sourcebeast that I have never even seen or heard of before as his familiar!" the ivory maiden snapped. "You chose to focus only on his weakness, and did not ask yourself how such a supposedly weak practitioner, clearly from another world, could stumble into this place on his own and survive, without us even realizing he was here before you literally stepped on him! Fool! It is likely that his master brought the boy here himself, and then left him on his own, because he had such a good relationship with my sect that he was both trusted with this spring's location and confident that his disciple could run about unsupervised! Do you have any idea how powerful his master likely is, to have gained such a relationship with my masters, when not even your own group was trusted with the knowledge of this spring, and you yourself were blindfolded for much of the way here?"

The arrogant idiot's eyes widened in surprise.

"I—" he began, but Lunei didn't let him finish.

"No!" she shouted. "You did not think at all, but immediately acted as one of the baser savages so common under our night sky! And in doing so, you risked the safety of my own sect by creating a powerful enemy in this one's master! Is this how the people of your lofty order repay those who help them? By creating more trouble for us? How would your leaders have recompensed us, if you had killed this one, and angered his master? Would they still have enough face after admitting what you have done, and taken the blame on our behalf?"

Koram stammered for a moment, but then he composed himself, wearing the cold, arrogant expression I had seen him wear when we were alone under the fruit tree.

"I mean no disrespect to your sect," he began sarcastically, "but the Glorious Star Charter boasts dozens of worlds under its rule. My master is a powerful expert on the level of many Sect elders, my master's master is an even greater power, and his master rivals the champions of a hundred different sects. I will apologize personally if necessary, but no master worthy of the title would be foolish enough to raise his hand against a son of the Consortium. Forgive me, oh Shining Maiden," he said insincerely, "but your concerns are unwarranted. Now I must ask you to fulfill your sect's obligations, and prepare the spring for my use. But I will not object if you allow my wounded attacker to use it afterwards."

"Your wounded—" Lunei started to say, then sighed deeply, as if she intended to inhale her next words.

"He is stable, is he not?" Koram argued, giving me a dismissive glance. "And he will require more care and time in the spring than I will, correct? Let me go first then, so that you may fulfill your personal obligation first, and then tend to him undistracted. I will use the opportunity to Draw while you take care of him."

"Take care of him," the pale, beautiful woman stated flatly. "You wish me to let you go first, and then leave you unsupervised, while I take care of him. You declare such a wish mere minutes after causing the very delay you are now requesting to avoid."

"As I said, Shining Maiden," the arrogant noble repeated, apparently finding his own spine after remembering the might of his patrons, "he surprised me with his appearance. I am deeply sorry for the misunderstanding. I merely proposed a method to save time for any parties involved."

"Do you now?" Vessa's Beacon asked thoughtfully. She glanced at me, seemed satisfied that I was currently not in pain or danger of death, then rose to her feet. "Do you truly wish me to fulfill my obligation as quickly and thoroughly as possible?"

"Of… course," the young man replied, hesitating at the last moment.

"And you wish to attain the maximum benefit possible from the spa, correct?" the Shining Maiden asked, taking another step forward.

"Absolutely." The affluent practitioner nodded, sounding sure again. "After coming all this way, it would be foolish not to obtain the full benefits of this place."

"I am so glad you agree." The beautiful woman smiled.

She leaped forward, glowing with light, landing next to Koram in the very next breath. Then, without pausing, she drove her palm into his solar plexus. The force of her blow lifted my would-be murderer off the ground, demonstrating once again that she was on a level far above both him and myself.

"If I am to ensure you gain the maximum benefit from the healing spring…" she said as she stepped gracefully to the side, grabbed the front of Koram's robes, and hurled him further into the clearing. "I must make sure to give the spring as much damage to heal as safely possible."

The young noble from another world landed a short walk away from the steaming pool, still wheezing from the force of Lunei's first strike. As he rose to his hands and knees, Lunei landed next to him and stomped on one of his hands. There was a loud crack, and Koram screamed in outrage and pain.

"My hand!" he shrieked. "How dare you break my hand?"

"Quite easily," the Shining Maiden calmly replied, sending another kick into my former tormenter's ribs, making his body crack again. "This will, in fact, give the qi further opportunities to refine your body. The more damage it repairs," she continued as she struck the young master's arm, breaking the forearm of the same limb she had struck moments ago. "The more perfect your refinement will be. Your leaders sent you to us," she continued as she gripped the broken arm in both hands, "for the express purpose of improving you as much as possible, and as discreetly as possible…" She twisted the arm in two different directions, making the elbow bend forward instead of backwards and causing another snapping sound to ring out. Koram screamed again, this time cursing the woman who was torturing him so thoroughly, but she ignored him. "…And this is the most thorough way I know. And I trust this procedure will remain confidential, unless you wish to go bragging about this experience to your peers."

"There is a witness!" Koram screamed, tears streaming down his cheeks from his tightly-closed eyes. "You are torturing me in front of another witness!"

"I suppose that's true," Lunei replied as she yanked the already-shattered arm out of its socket, "but who would believe him? His journey here was supposed to be as confidential, and as *incident-free* as your own, correct? He'd risk exposing his own time here. Besides, he's likely never heard of you. He may not have even heard of your Charter. I don't think he will see you again, or see anyone you will meet. Now, be silent and let me work."

He continued to scream and curse at the white-robed woman, and she continued to strike him and ignore his cries, striking both of his legs and the center of his chest.

"Drat," she said in a monotone voice as Koram rolled his head and went silent. "He passed out. If he had stayed awake for a little longer, he would have gotten more benefit from the pool. Very well, then. I did what I could." She grabbed the non-broken arm and began dragging his body through the rocks and silt. She grimaced in distaste, and began disrobing the young noble, thankfully leaving his loincloth on. Then she unceremoniously dumped Koram's unconscious body into the steaming spring, spending just enough effort to make sure his head stayed above the water.

"I apologize for making you wait, stranger from the night sky," Lunei said in a much softer tone as she looked up at me. "But I had both an obligation to fulfill and a need to ensure this charge of mine would cause no further trouble while he was here. And, I must confess that I desired him to experience a small portion of the pain he had needlessly caused two others. Will you permit me to work on your own wounds now?"

I slowly shook my head and pointed a trembling finger to Nestor's twisted form.

"Of course, stranger," the beautiful woman said as she reached down to gently lift the lifemouse into her own careful hands. "Your companion will receive the best of care. I promise that he will receive just as much benefit as my unworthy charge will. More, in fact," she added darkly, giving Koram a harsh glance. "Since your poor little friend has both suffered more, and remained conscious in the process. It is likely Koram's limitations stem more from his own temperament, than any unfortunate event in his past. But I will speak no more on that."

Lunei walked cautiously over to the steaming pool, whispering soothingly to my damaged little friend all the way.

"Poor, dear, little thing. You will be all better soon. I promise."

She slowly lowered Nestor into the shallowest portion of the spring, carefully positioning him so that he could rest comfortably, even going so far as to wrap a cloth around a small rock so that his head could rest on it. The lifemouse sighed in relief as his broken body settled into the pool.

"I promise that he will make a full recovery, unnamed guest, and emerge healthier than ever. May I please address your own injuries now?" the sect maiden asked respectfully. "It grieves me that you have already waited so long for proper treatment."

Her concern touched me. It reminded me of the way Nova had tried to look out for me, when she had finally gained new opportunities, and noticed that I hadn't kept up with her in both status and health.

That memory hardened my resolve, and I shook my head, forcing words out of my mouth.

"No," I croaked. "Same… me."

She flinched at my initial rejection, then cocked her head at the rest of my words.

"I do not understand your request, stranger," she replied.

I raised my barely working arm and pointed a trembling finger at Koram's unconscious form.

"Same...me...please," I gasped, still finding words difficult. Lunei's qi technique had merely stabilized me. Every bit of damage was still there.

"That should not be necessary, stranger," she replied carefully. "Your body is already badly damaged.

You will reap plenty of benefits just as you are. There is no need to cause you further pain.”

“Need… strength,” I gasped, the qi-induced numbness beginning to fade as I continued to force myself to talk. Apparently Lunei’s technique depended on the patient remaining still. “For...master… please,” I begged. “Will… owe… favor.”

Lunei flinched again at my final words.

“Please do not shame me, wounded stranger,” she said in a grieved tone. “I would lose a great deal of face if I were to demand any kind of debt from you in this moment. I will do as you request, but know that I cannot numb your pain while I am injuring you, due to the nature of my technique. If you would truly do any favor for me, then tell me when you have reached your limits. You will receive less benefit from the spring if you are unconscious.”

I managed to nod, then held up my fingers so that she could see I wanted her to break them.

As Lunei reluctantly walked over to me, I went to that familiar place in my mind, the one I had always gone to back on the streets of the Republic, when the pain of hunger grew too much for me to bear. It was far from enough to distract me completely, but at least I managed to remain silent as the moon-colored woman broke all ten of my fingers.

“Please nod if you wish me to stop, unnamed stranger,” the dark-haired woman asked gently.

I gritted my teeth and shook my head in a firm ‘no.’

“Then I will now move onto your hands themselves, stranger. Forgive me.”

And with that, she continued breaking my body.

I succeeded in remaining silent for the first hand, but the second hand brought out a quick gasp of pain. I worked hard to separate my mind from my body, and motioned with my head for her to persist. The beautiful woman reluctantly continued, moving to my wrists, giving them both a simple crack, then my forearms and biceps, then my shoulders. I had screamed by then, but I had just enough willpower to ask that she keep going. I saw her nod, as if coming to a decision, and then she struck as quickly as possible, hitting dozens of locations on my body as quickly as possible. My shirt, trousers, and shoes shredded under the force of her blows. Beyond that, I could not tell what had happened, because my entire vision had become a red haze of pain. But I knew I was conscious, because I could still feel my body scream silently when she picked me up and quickly carried me into the warm water.

Vapor and liquid rushed into my body, as if they were heroes from the forbidden stories I had read, rushing toward danger to save the lives of others. I felt threads of qi crawl out of the mists and water to probe through my body, examining the damage, trying to find the full extent. It traveled deeper, finding damage to my ability to Draw, both from Koram's attack and from other, more subtle damage that had been caused by a lifetime of neglecting basic needs.

Source energy had already improved my body numerous times in the span of two days. I had unlocked a host of benefits that had gone a long way in changing my appearance of a filthy, sickly child to that of a short, frail young man who at least could pass for an adult. Despite the constant threat of danger and the looming concern over saving my closest friend, I felt profoundly grateful over the improvements to my body, the new certainty of nutritious food, and the discovery of new friends. But the effects of the qi spring were on another level entirely.

Slowly, thread by thread, my body was rebuilt from the ground up. Instead of simply adding enhancements to me, or providing correction to deteriorated muscles and stunted growth, the steaming

Source energy went to the very root of the problem, somehow breaking my body apart in a way that would let it correct problems before they had even formed.

Best and worst of all, the vapors numbed my mind, putting me in a state of half-sleep that made it difficult to feel the pain or fully understand what was happening to my body. All I knew was that my bones, muscles, and organs were repaired in a way that completely reset their potential. Then, the magnificent threads of steaming energy reapplied all the gains I had made in the last two days, adding them wherever they would grant the most benefit. Even the nutrients from Vessa's food packets were reallocated, letting my body gain the benefits from the very beginning, instead of when I was malnourished and almost completely done growing.

Then, after my losses and gains were rebalanced, the qi moved to repairing and fortifying my body. Bones were repaired, then supplemented, making them at once more flexible and more durable, but somehow left with more room to improve, while still merging perfectly with the essence I had gained earlier. I felt my muscles reknit themselves, blasting past the barrier my malnutrition had put over their growth, then expanding further as the benefits gained from absorbing Source energy kicked in. More lights turned on in my brain, and though the memories that had resurfaced earlier still eluded me, other bouts of knowledge came roaring to the front of my brain. More outlawed languages. More purged history.

I wanted to see more, learn more, understand just how I was changing so drastically, but the pleasant numbness of the spring made it difficult for my mind to catch anything more than brief glimpses of reconstruction. After what felt like mere moments, the overwhelming sensations all began to subside. I now felt as if I was relaxing in a normal spa, like the ancients of my world once lounged in. I felt others' eyes on me as I rose out of

the water, but a quick glance showed that my
undergarments had survived.

A second glance showed that my feet were much
farther away than I had remembered, and that my entire
body now had a consistent, visible level of muscle
definition. Even the earlier Source energy hadn't been
enough to completely hide my ribcage, but now my
stomach was covered by abdominal muscles, and my chest
was clearly parted in the middle by pectoral muscles. My
arms and legs likewise now showed years of healthy
nutrition and exercise, in place of the once-obvious signs
of starvation. I looked up and into the eyes of the woman
that had both saved my life and provided me this
opportunity. But before I began to thank her, I realized that
she was now shorter than me. Her forehead only came up
to my nose, now.

And of all things, she seemed impressed.

"Oh. My," she said quietly, her eyes widening as
she looked up at me. "How do you feel, stranger?"

I looked all around me. Koram was still in the
spring, unconscious, with his head lolled against a rock.
Nestor was down by the hem of Lunei's robes, watching
me with his large dark eyes. He had grown slightly, too big
now to be completely hidden by a closed hand, and his fur
rippled with color now, with one side green like the grass
under him and the other white like Lunei's garments. I
wanted to inquire just how he had changed, but I had not
answered my benefactor's question yet.

"Whole," I answered her, stretching to adjust to
my new height and reach. But I realized that was not quite
true. I felt stronger, faster, and greater, but there was an
emptiness inside me now. Not one that made me despair,
but one that made me believe I could reach for more, that I
could even be more, despite now being taller, stronger, and
healthier than I had ever been. "Perhaps not whole," I
corrected, not wanting to lie to this woman who had done

so much for me. "I owe you a great deal of gratitude, Lady Lunei of the Sparkling Sky Sect. Forgive me for not knowing how your culture expresses gratitude, but know I will never forget what you have done for me."

I bowed my head, not knowing what other gestures would be appropriate on this world. But Lunei smiled at me, and suddenly I felt as if something had struck me over the head.

Nova, I managed to think before my mind started swimming. *She has Nova's smile.*

She has Vessa's smile, the next partly coherent thought said.

"Since you feel so grateful," the sect maiden offered, "perhaps you could tell me your name?"

I looked back to make sure Koram was still unconscious, as far as I could tell, and I remembered Vessa's warning about exposing our identities to her Beacon.

But she had saved my life.

"My name is Jasper," I answered her. "Jasper, of a family I wish I could name to you, disciple of one who has expressly forbidden me to reveal their identity. I truly wish that I could tell you more."

"I will respect your privacy, Jasper the Mysterious," Lunei said, still smiling, "but I must ask you to vow that you will keep what you have seen here secret, and to never reveal the location of this spring to anyone. I also ask, despite what occurred, to keep the matter of Koram's presence at this place a secret as well, though I will not ask you to withhold information from your master or your superiors."

"I will do as you ask," I replied, grateful at how accommodating this woman was to me. Her behavior was as much of a contrast to Koram's as Nova's had been to the other officials of the Glorious State.

The similarities of Koram to the Glorious State, including the fact that his charter had a similar name and that he spoke the language fluently, was a much more troubling matter. But I doubted I could ask Lunei about that matter without giving up some of my own secrets, and risking Vessa's discovery.

"Thank you, Jasper the Unnamed," the woman said as she bowed her head. An awkward silence descended, as she waited for me to say something more. "I will await your oath of power, fellow practitioner," she said in a patient, but confused tone.

Because she was waiting for me to perform a vow I had no idea how to make.

"I must ask you to forgive my ignorance," I said, thinking as quickly as I could. "But my master has instructed me to be careful in the making of any vow, no matter how familiar I think I am with the other party's culture. Please explain exactly what I must say, and what actions my body must perform."

"Your master takes your education very seriously, then," Lunei replied graciously. "Very well. I ask you to perform no more than the most basic of Source oaths. Inject either essence or qi into your Soulscape, and swear by your Source and your Strength that you will not reveal the location of this spring, or the incidents occurring after or before the last hour of your visit to anyone but your master or the superiors of your clan, sect, or tribe."

I placed a hand over my chest and did as she asked, injecting a tiny thread of qi into my Soulscape.

"I hereby swear by my Source and Strength that I will not speak of today's events on this planet to anyone except my master and elders, until I have leave by Shining Maiden Lunei or a higher-ranking member of the Sparkling Sky Sect to discuss the matter in detail."

My chest quivered as soon as I finished speaking, but only for a moment. A headache formed in my mind whenever I thought of revealing today's secrets to another, but it became easy to avoid even considering the idea.

As Lunei began speaking to me again, I quietly considered the implications of being able to make supernaturally enforced vows.

"...I must beg one more thing from you, Jasper the Unnamed," she added. "I beg that you ask your master for mercy, despite the attack you suffered. I am prepared to offer compensation on my sect's behalf."

I hesitated, torn between offering my grateful forgiveness and taking any further benefit I could in order to save Nova's life.

"I understand," the woman said, mistaking the nature of my hesitation. "Regardless, I will intercede on my sect's behalf." She twisted a silver ring I had yet to notice on one of her fingers, and the ground in front of us shimmered with pale light. When it faded, I saw a pile of folded garments lying on the ground, with a small leather pouch lying on top of them. "The garments are to replace your own, which I was forced to destroy. They are probably not as good of a quality as your master will likely supply you in the future, but they will serve you well, and when you finally Advance to the qi Condensation stage or Natal essence stage, you will be able to make greater use of them. Judging by your new Source aura, that day is not far," she said with a smile. "The pouch contains pills that will enhance your Source energy. They are predominantly for qi users, but a handful of them will help with Drawing mana or essence energy as well. You may give the mana pills to your master in case he has another disciple that can benefit from them. I understand these items are likely already common for you, but they are all I am currently carrying, and have permission to give. If your master demands further compensation, please ask him to speak with my own elders, and they will discuss the matter."

"That will not be necessary," I said, kneeling down so that I could pick up the bag and the clothing. "These will be sufficient. I will honor your request to keep the spring secret, but my master ordered me to take a small vial of water from this place. May I have your permission to do so?"

"Of course," Lunei replied, blinking her shining dark eyes. "Though I am baffled why your master would need it. This spring's greatest benefit is its privacy. He or she could gain more potent water elsewhere if he truly needed it."

"I am unaware of the reason for the command," I said mildly, which was technically true. I had no idea how Vessa intended to use this water. "All I know is that it is part of my assignment."

"Well, then, take some with my blessing." The kind sect maiden nodded.

I performed the last of my tasks, finding that my Soulscape had already absorbed plenty of the spring water on its own initiative. I struggled to remember if there was anything I needed to do, any favor I needed to ask of Vessa's hidden Beacon. Nothing came to mind, until I glanced down at Koram's unconscious form.

He was a cruel young man, without a doubt the cruelest I had ever met, even when I had struggled for survival all those years before. I would likely never see him again, and Lunei had done much to make him pay for my and Nestor's wounds. I recalled, though, that he had been boasting of other cruelties even as he broke my own body. As soon as he returned home, he would vent his rage on another who, like me, had been under his power.

And if I did not speak up, no one would ever know.

"Shining Maiden Lunei," I began formally. "I stand by my statement to bear you and your sect no ill will, but Koram's actions are another matter. I have found both his actions and his words to me in private utterly abhorrent, and I know my master will bear enmity to both him and the Charter he claims everyone fears. I do not know the extent of your sect's involvement with him, but out of respect for you and your sect, I am willing to further intercede." I injected a loose fleck of essence into my Soulscape, and continued speaking. "I swear by my Source and Strength that if Koram of the Glorious Star Consortium makes a Sourcevow of his own to cease boasting about beating his own maids, and to no longer abuse any servants under his or his family's power, I in turn will drop the matter of violence between us, and urge my master that no further actions are necessary."

My chest quivered again, but I felt nothing beyond that. The remaining conditions of my vow had not been met.

Lunei, for her part, turned her head as if she had been struck.

"He boasted of *what?*" she finally said, her dark eyes blazing with rage. Her body glowed ever so briefly, and it reminded me of the light from a blood-red moon. Then she shook her head, forcing a harsh, frosty expression over her face. "Never mind. If your words were untrue, you would not have risked sealing them with a Sourcevow. But that does not lessen my disappointment. Brutalities toward another practitioner in a secluded wilderness are one thing, but purposefully harming those under one's care is an unconscionable savagery on all the worlds of the night sky. Know that Koram has lost a great deal of face today with my entire sect, both concerning that of his vaunted charter as well as the very last shred of his own standing. Oaths made under duress are much less potent, Jasper the Unnamed, but know that I will do all I can to shame him into doing as you asked."

"Then I must thank you again, honored maiden," I said carefully. "My master detests those who abuse the weak, but is sometimes willing to grant second chances to those who abandon such behavior."

"You are welcome, and in risking yourself to reveal Koram's full character, you have likely saved my sect from future dealings with his charter. But I will have a better chance of convincing him when you are gone, so I must regretfully bid you farewell. Is there anything else I can do for you before you leave, Jasper the Unnamed?"

I tried to think, but there truly was nothing. Lunei's sect apparently only had claim to this spring. Anything else I could possibly want, I could scavenge on my way through the forest. It was time to go. Nestor reluctantly crawled up my shoulder, loath to leave this beautiful place. I could not blame him. I turned to face Vessa's Beacon, knowing I had to extricate myself from her view before I could return to the Soulship, when another question leaped out of my mouth.

"Why have you been so kind to me?" I asked her, unable to stop myself. "My master is clearly not here, and if he had been guarding me, he would have already interfered to protect me from Koram's attack. No one would have known if you had just left me to die. And even if you did not wish to do that, you could have simply required that I make whatever vow you wished, without offering me any compensation at all."

Lunei sighed sadly.

"I have already said that Sourcevows made under duress are not nearly as effective, but you have probably seen less honorable cultivators force others to swear them all the same," the graceful woman answered me. "And after Koram's attack on you, I suppose that such a dark outlook has been reinforced. No doubt you have already met a good number of brutal practitioners, that give our kind a bad name under the night sky. But that does not give me, or my sect, a right to be brutal ourselves and forsake our own goals, our own ideals. I will not bore you with the details of my sect's history, Jasper the Unnamed, but I will answer you with a question of my own: Why did you leap to the defense of a weak and broken Sourcebeast, when you could have better saved yourself by remaining hidden? And why did you burden yourself with a Sourcevow on behalf of those you will likely never meet?"

I wanted to tell her that her question was absurd, until I realized that it wasn't. I bowed my head in both acceptance and apology.

"Thank you for everything, honored Lunei of the Sparkling Sky Sect. I will speak highly of you to my master, for what little my word is worth. Will you permit me to take my leave now?"

"If I must," she said with another blinding smile. "Take care, Jasper the Unnamed. I hope to see you again. You have nice eyes," she said with a wink.

I blinked and stepped backwards, surprised at such carefree compliments.

"You honor me, lady Lunei," I stammered, trying to regain my composure. "I confess I hope to see you again as well." I bowed, and turned to leave her.

Before I passed back into the forest, I turned my head to look back at her.

"You have nice eyes yourself," I dared to say, then kept walking before I could say anything more foolish.

Chapter 7

She made no move to follow me as I walked. I assumed she turned her attention back to Koram, who was still unconscious and therefore necessary for her to keep alive. It surprised me that a cultivator at his level had still not woken up by the time I left, and that he had not been able to handle the same injuries I could, but I would not find my answers here. I passed by the tree of qi Source energy to place a small number of the peach-like fruits into my pack, which Lunei had thoughtfully recovered for me. My Soulscape swallowed the two smallest ones happily and greedily, then pulsed out a desire to absorb a few of the leaves and a single piece of the tree's bark. When it was finally finished, I chose to hike up a densely wooded hill, one that gave me a good view of the hot spring below. I had sworn to keep secret all of the events within an hour of my arrival at the hot spring. I was worried that my Sourcevow would somehow still apply if I returned to the Soulship too soon, so I resolved to spend at least an hour somewhere in seclusion before I returned to Vessa. So until then, I would keep an eye on Koram, and let my Soulscape absorb whatever else it wished.

Koram and Lunei were a great distance away, but my vision had been enhanced several times over since the beginning of the day. I watched Koram finally wake up and remove himself from the steaming outdoor bath and stretch, much like I had. Judging by his movements, he seemed impressed with the changes wrought upon the arm Lunei had so thoroughly broken, and disappointed with the amount of benefits that the rest of his body had gained. Lunei stomped toward him with her hand raised, and he immediately flinched and stopped moving his mouth. The sect maiden lowered her hand and began speaking with a frosted face. He shook his head immediately, and then she spoke again, her mouth moving in a way that suggested clipped, angry sentences. Then she walked right up to him, pointing the finger of one hand directly into his chest while pointing the other far out into the woods, whispering fiercely with bared teeth. Koram's face became even paler, and then he sagged his shoulders and began speaking slowly, as if he was reciting some formal phrase or declaration. Lunei gave him an angry, but satisfied nod and thrust his clothes at him, stomping off out of the clearing. She turned her head to shout what sounded like a threat to leave him behind if he did not keep up as she kept walking. Koram stumbled as he tried to dress and chase after her at the same time.

I was slightly amused, but my mind still played back the name he had called his charter, the power he claimed it wielded, and the fact that his native language was that of the Glorious State's. I would have to get more details from Vessa herself. But I suspected I had found a new enemy, one that I would need to pay careful attention to in the future.

Now, though, Lunei and Koram had walked deep into the woods. This was the ideal time to risk teleporting back to Vessa's Soulship.

We-go? Nestor asked me, twitching his whiskers to confirm no one was nearby.

Yes, I answered, closing my eyes and reaching for the newly-repaired thread of Source energy. *We can go now.*

Wait-wait, the little mouse said, crawling closer to look me in the eye. *Folk… folk-bad?* he asked hesitantly. *All-hurt? Like-him?*

I guessed that he was referring to Koram, and his senseless, brutal reaction to Nestor's offer of friendship.

Folk are bad, I replied sadly. *It's why I tried to keep you hidden from them. Many people will hurt you for any reason at all.*

Wait-wait, he insisted, and I felt that his mind was struggling to articulate something. *You-folk. She-folk?*

He was referring to both me and Lunei. I nodded slowly.

We count as people, too. Yes. But that doesn't change what I said about everyone else.

Ship-folk? Nestor persisted, referring to Vessa. *Friend-folk?* he asked next, and I barely made out that he was meaning Nova, the friend I described to him before.

Well, yes, I answered. *We all count as folk.*

Why-good? the mouse asked. *Why-help? Why-kind? You-folk,* Nestor repeated. *Folk-bad. You-good. Why-good? Why-care?*

I reached into my mind to give him an answer, just before I realized I didn't have one to give.

I... I began helplessly, unable to finish the impression. *I do not know. All I know is that being weak and helpless hurts. And I suspect that it hurts for others just as much as it hurts for myself.*

Yes-yes. Nestor nodded in agreement. *But-but,* he continued, *you-wrong. All-folk. Some-good.*

I had no answer for that childlike declaration. Instead, I spent one last glance to ensure that the two of us were truly alone, and teleported us back to the Soulship.

Vessa's world was much smaller than I had remembered. I still could not see the ceiling of this shadowy place, but all of the nearby devices seemed to have shrunk by over a foot. Several of the inactive ones were now in danger of bruising my shins if I did not watch where I stepped. I navigated my way through the maze, realizing that some devices that had been lit earlier were now dark.

"Jasper?" Vessa's voice called from her capsule bed. "Jasper Cloud? Are you here?"

I froze when I noticed the frightened tone of her voice.

"Yes, Vessa," I answered her. "I have returned. I have the water samples."

"Well done, Jasper," Vessa said, sounding relieved. "But I should tell you to be very quiet right now."

I looked back at the newly unpowered consoles, and realized that many of the other lights on the floor had been turned off as well. Before I could ask what was going on, more banging noises sounded out in the distance.

"Those are not the same things as last night, are they?" I asked the ship-woman in a cautious whisper.

"No, friend Jasper, they are not," Vessa answered me quietly and tensely. "These are creatures I cannot keep out. I am sorry to say that we are in danger again."

"This is not your fault," I whispered to the bedridden woman as I reached the capsule and leaned over the edge to check on her. She looked paler than she had before I left, as if she had already spent all of the energy she had just gained yesterday.

I worried for her.

"Tell me how I can help," I said quietly as two more bangs sounded out. "And when this is over, tell me why you did not summon me earlier."

"I tried," she whispered, looking at me with wet eyes. "You did not return. Something had broken your connection here. I thought you had died." Her gray eyes grew wider, and brighter, as she took in my form. "You... look different. Your body now fits your face."

"Thank you," I replied, choosing to take her words as a compliment. "Now please tell me what I should do."

"I do not know," she whispered back. "There were not supposed to be this many small things on my ship-body." She looked at me again, then awkwardly looked away. "You are much stronger now. Close to Advancing, even, to the first stage of every Source. Perhaps..." She trailed off, considering.

"Perhaps I could fight for you again," I finished for her. "You said a single grown man with a lit match could have protected you from the last eaterling. I would say I now qualify."

"You do," Vessa said, still not turning to look at me. "And I apologize for many of the words I said back then. It had been too long since I had seen a living being. I was tired, and hungry… and my mind was not well," she added awkwardly.

"You are apologizing again for things you should never have been judged for in the first place," I said as gently as I could, worried about her current loss of composure. Was this dark world getting to her? Was she going to relapse to the broken state I had first found her in?

"How long until it gets in?" I asked her, still watching her carefully. Her breathing looked fine, at least. Assuming she breathed like a human, instead of an alien woman who was also a starship. But as far as I could tell, she was unhurt. Merely very tired, and scared.

And possibly hungry, I reminded myself, reaching into my pack as she answered.

"There is more than one," she answered quietly. "And I do not know how long they will take. They have been trying to break their way in for the last hour. The eaterling took just a little longer than that, but I have reinforced several doorways since then. I thought it would be enough, and then devoted the rest of my power to further repairs. I had not realized so many small and wretched things had found their way onto my vessel, or I would have been more cautious." She frowned for a moment, eyes narrowing in thought. "We will have at least a few more minutes until they break in. Just when I was hoping to… what are you doing?" she asked as she finally looked up at me.

"You sound tired, frustrated, and hungry," I answered her as I held out the pouch of liquid food and the qi plum. "If your body is like mine, you will have an easier time thinking if you have something to eat. Would you like a food packet, or one of the qi plums I found?"

Vessa stared at me for a moment without answering.

"I just told you," she began, her voice becoming just a bit more heated, "that my sanctum is about to be breached again, unless the intruders decide to give up and go away. This is not the time for a meal."

"If I am distracting you, I apologize," I persisted, still holding out the food, "but if there is nothing left for you to do right now, and the enemy is still at least minutes away, then perhaps now is the best time to get back some energy. And while you eat, I can deposit the samples into your capsule. Would you like me to get you anything else?"

The banging continued. Vessa's stare turned into a glare.

"You are neither my ship-parent, nor my ship's butler, to speak to me in such a fashion," she said in her iciest tone yet. Then she snatched both food items out of my hands. "But thank you. You are right. The qi plums are an excellent find. If you have more, you and Nestor should both consume one immediately. They are perhaps the weakest of Sourcefruits, but every little bit will help right now. Processing the water samples will take too much time and energy at the moment, so we will wait to see if we survive these next few minutes."

With that, she tore open the food pouch with her teeth, took a big bite out of the qi plum, and then washed it down with the green liquid from the food packet. She shot me another glare, as if she was daring me to say anything about her current eating habits, so I backed away and focused on procuring my own food, tossing one of the plums to Nestor so he could eat as well. The little mouse managed to catch the fruit in the air and began nibbling away.

I did my best to follow my own advice, closing my eyes to help me ignore all the violent background noises as I bit into the Sourcefruit.

Like everything else I had encountered in that last planet—excluding Koram— the fruit provided a soothing sensation as it entered my mouth. As bites traveled down my throat, my Soulscape opened up to purify and enhance them while I finished swallowing.

To my surprise, the fruit re-entered my body with wisps of mana and flecks of essence attached. As it circulated, I felt all of my Source energy levels increase, both in current amount and in total capacity.

"Go ahead and eat another fruit," Vessa said around another large bite of her own. "You too, Nes. Eat all you can. I'll take the leftovers."

The banging intensified until I heard a loud screech, as if something metal was finally forced open. It continued after a moment of silence, sounding a bit closer.

"Two more doors left," the ship-woman said before she took a long drink from the food pouch. "Hurry up and eat all you can."

I took her at her word, tossed Nestor another plum, and began eating the next as rapidly as possible. A decade of hard living kicked in, and the next thing I knew, both my lifemouse friend and I had finished off three more plums each. I washed down the remnants of my messy meal with the sweet liquid from the food pouch and tossed a second one to Nestor so that he could do the same, then walked over and handed the last two plums to Vessa.

"Thank you," she said absently as she stuffed them into her mouth. "Now get me a napkin for my face. Please," she added at the last minute, still glaring at me. I walked over to the same closet where I had found my first new set of clothes and fetched her a small cloth.

"Is there any chance one of these containers also holds some kind of weapon?" I asked, but she shook her head and swallowed another large bite of Sourcefruit.

"Would have given it to you the first time if there was," she mumbled with a full mouth, hurriedly swallowing another bite of plum. Then she closed her eyes and sighed, glowing faintly from the fruit's influx of qi. "The weapons were all lost with the last of my crew, when they fought to hide and seal me here. But you are here, and I have taught you to be a weapon yourself. You have a chance now, Jasper Cloud."

I privately disagreed with Vessa's assessment that my body could easily replace a firearm or large blade, but there was no point in voicing my concerns or openly questioning her new confidence in me at this particular time. I would have to see for myself just what my new body was capable of.

Since I was done eating, I opened the bag that Lunei had given me and began to go through the medicinal pellets. Vessa's eyes snapped back over to me, widening at the sight of my palm full of Source pharmaceuticals.

"Where did you get those?" she asked me, finally taking in my new clothing as well. "And where did you get those new garments? Why did you change out of your old ones?"

The pounding from down the hall intensified. More screeching began, as if another door was about to break.

"I had an unavoidable encounter with another practitioner, who reacted favorably to my discovery. These new clothes and pills were a gift. She said I was to ask you which pills I should take."

"She?" Vessa narrowed her eyes at me. "I can perhaps understand her being extremely generous with the cultivation resources, but why would she think you needed clothing? Your old clothes were fine," she finished with an offended edge. I wondered what I had done to insult her.

"In her defense," I began carefully, determined to show that there was a perfectly valid reason for all of this. "These garments were a necessary and practical gift. My old garments were destroyed when she tore them off of me."

The ship-woman's eyes widened, prompting me to rethink what I had just said.

"You mean while I was up here worrying whether or not you were dead—never mind," she said quickly, as the second door began screeching again. "We will discuss this issue at great length much later. For now, take the orange pill, the green pill, and the blue pill, then give the small white one to Nestor. After that, give me the large purple one in the center of your palm. Then, and *only then*, I want you to take the biggest pill, the black one with the flame motif. Do not take that one before you have finished all of your other instructions, and as soon as you take that one, you should put the rest of the pills away and begin to Draw. And in the future, I want you to be more cautious about accepting random gifts of clothing and drugs from women you do not know."

I accepted her admonishment, realizing just in time that saying more would only upset her right now.

The pills proved to be chewable, so I did not worry about taking water with them. As everyone finished taking their medicine, we heard the second door screech and give way.

"Don't pay them any attention right now," Vessa commanded sharply. "Put all of your focus on Drawing. I will alert you when you should stop."

Nestor and I complied immediately, the little mouse unable to Draw, but able to concentrate on digesting what he had just consumed. I sat down in a meditating position to cultivate all the power available to me.

My inner planet began spinning in a faster, more stable rotation than it had before.

More loose flecks of essence began settling. Mana gathered together as it floated through my body, thickening from a single wisp into a strand of vapor. Qi rotated rapidly through my body in a faster, but somehow more viscous, stream.

Muscles I couldn't identify started to ache, as if I were straining to push through an invisible barrier with all three of my Source energies. essence thickened and spread until it covered almost all of my insides, but the last few flecks failed to collect, and fell off. The tiny cloud of mana gathered more and more vapor, but the final few trails still floated just out of reach. My qi kept circulating faster and faster through my body, in a more exact pattern each time, straining to create some unknown form…

As the last door began to screech, the scant amount of qi in my body *condensed,* forming a single drop. It landed in the center of my soul, and my Soulscape moved to superimpose over it.

The next moment, power blasted out of me.

I exhaled with a gasp as my eyes snapped open. I pitched forward, arresting my fall with both hands, but too full of energy to stop moving, so I swept my legs out from under me and twisted them upward. I lifted my entire body up into a handstand, then used my arms to launch myself into the air, twisting to land in a crouch behind one of the taller terminals.

My senses had finally caught up, letting me scan the environment. The room was still dark, but Vessa had raised many of the terminals, to the point where they were much higher than they had been the first time I had entered here. Scraping footsteps told me that creatures similar to the last eaterling were running down the halls, probably no more than two, if I had to guess. They were hiding their Source energy, but imperfectly, leaving large patches on their body open for me to detect and roughly estimate their amount of essence.

I realized that I could also gauge their potential strength, and that I was not impressed with what I found.

Don't talk, the words in front of my eyes said. *They will be close enough to hear very soon.*

I remained still. I could hear hungry rasps accompanying the scraping footsteps. I concentrated on sealing the Source energy emanating from my body, and activated the technique that let me form a thin, invisible shield of qi over my own body. I noted that it had become much thicker than it was before, three times thicker than my fingernail.

They know my entire crew is dead, Vessa wrote, *so they will not expect anyone but me to be here. But they will still be wary of me, so I will not be able to help you as much as I wish.*

That was not a problem, but I chose not to interrupt her.

They are here, she wrote quickly. *Do not move. I will tell you when they are close enough to strike.*

With that said, I closed my eyes and listened to the noises in the room.

The two creatures must have stopped running when they reached our room, because I no longer heard footsteps. Instead, I heard them sniff at the air.

"Human?" one of the things rasped in a language I somehow understood, but did not know. "A human was here. Careful."

I heard more sniffing, and then the second creature hissed.

"Gone, now," the second one said. "I cannot taste it in the air. The scent of the dead crew, maybe. Perhaps one lingered here before it died."

Eaterlings, I finally decided. They sounded and acted just like the last creature I had slain.

"Why did it linger?" the first one asked, before it began making wet, chuckling noises. "Never mind. I know. Maybe it was her lover. Am I right, little ship-girl?" the creature called out in a gloating voice. "Did you have a little lover that died? Is that why you are quiet now?"

Vessa did not answer it. I felt my hand clench, but I forced myself to remain silent as well.

"Do not be foolish," the second creature snarled. "This ship was one of the newest models. She would have been too young to have a lover."

"A foster parent, then," the first eaterling continued to gloat. "This little ship-girl had a false father, or mother, that lingered. How long did they stay, little ship? Did they leave in the end, or were you able to watch them die?"

Bad-thing! Nestor sent to my mind, and I realized the little mouse was creating actual words instead of impressions now. *Speak-hurt! We-kill?*

Can you understand them? I asked my friend, reaching out to sense him.

To my surprise, I found that he had surpassed his gains at the pool, and already Advanced to the next substage of the Natal stage.

Yes-yes! the lifemouse snarled in my mind. *Speak-hurt! Speak-hate! Mock-friend! We-kill!*

The creatures were still arguing as their clawed feet scraped against the floor. For whatever reason, they had completely abandoned stealth, choosing to believe that they were safe now that they were in the same room as their prey.

Yes, I thought back to my little mouse, surprised to find his fury, but approving nonetheless. *We-kill.*

Don't let them anger you, Vessa wrote to me, as the monsters continued to advanced and demean my friend in the capsule-bed. *They are always this cruel and stupid. It's one of the reasons their kind stays so weak. If they bred any less quickly, my people would have been able to wipe them out long ago.*

Very well, I wrote back to her, and kept listening for the monsters to get closer, speaking all the way.

"How much power do you think we will gain from her?"

"In her weakened state?" the second one replied. "Still more than enough for us both to Advance several times over. Perhaps by then, you will be smarter, when we are made new."

"I can't wait," the first one breathed, missing the insult of its packmate. "They always acted like they were better than us. Do you think she will beg before she dies? Do you think she will cry?"

"We have time to make her," the second hissed back vehemently. "Nothing else is down here."

"Good," the first one rasped eagerly. "Gooood…"

Nestor sent a spike of anger through our bond. I answered it with my own rage.

Keep ignoring them, Vessa pleaded. *This is not new. Others have said worse in the past.*

That knowledge angers me even more, I wrote back in my mind. *But I will do my best to be patient, and wait for your command to act.*

So I waited, and tried not to concentrate on how proud the two oversized vermin were of their cannibalistic hunger.

Eventually though, the second one sniffed again.

"We may not be alone," it warned, and to my surprise, I heard chittering in its voice. "The human's smell is stronger."

Both of them stopped moving forward. I heard shifting, sniffing, and hissing. They were looking for me.

"Can you smell Source?" the first one asked, hesitating. "Could he be strong?"

"No Source," the second one replied after a moment. "Not that I can smell or taste."

"Then why care?" the first one demanded. "If it was strong enough to hide from us, the human should have struck us by now! Perhaps she found a stray from Earth!"

"A stray from Earth would not smell like this," the other corrected. "If a human is still here, it is not one from Earth."

"Does it matter?" the first one argued, before it suddenly raised its voice. "Ship-girl! Tell us where the human is, and we will kill you before we eat you!"

"She will not tell you, idiot!" the other monster hissed. "Her kind protected humans! Watching them die broke them!"

"Then we should find it, so that we can break it in front of her! Human!" the first hissed excitedly. "If you show yourself, we promise not to hurt your ship-girl! We will leave and go home!"

"I did not say I was sure one was here!" the second snapped.

Just then, Nestor made a scraping noise from across the room.

"Human!" the first one shouted in an excited tone. "I found the human! I found the human!"

I heard the monster's feet scrape rapidly across the tiles as it took off toward the direction of the sound.

Which happened to take it right past me.

Now! Vessa typed quickly, but I was already moving. My enhanced senses help me predict the stupid thing's route. I rose quickly from behind the tall terminal and drove my elbow out to intercept it.

We saw each other a moment before impact. It looked much like I had expected, a bipedal mixture of rat and lizard, like the last eaterling had been. Now that I could see it, I corrected my stance to better aim for the monster's center mass, linking my hands together to better brace my attack.

My enemy had just enough time to widen its yellow eyes in surprise before my elbow lifted it off the floor and knocked it backwards into an awkward pile of limbs and tail. I rushed forward to stomp on its head, but it pushed itself out of the way at the last moment. It skittered to an upright position just in time for me to step forward and drive my fist into its jaw.

The thing reeled backwards, staggering from the force of my blow, as if I had hit it with one of Vessa's loose tiles. *No wonder she said I was a weapon now,* I thought as I kept advancing forward, trying to keep the pressure up on the giant rat-lizard. A clawed limb swiped at my face, but I intercepted its wrist with my forearm. I felt my qi shield take most of the blow, and the sleeve of Lunei's robe inexplicably stopped the rest of the attack's force.

I kept moving quickly, before the rest of the eaterling's limbs could come into play. I slammed my fist repeatedly into the creature's face and body as fast as I could. I could feel the qi shielding on my fists reinforce my blows, turning my defense into a weapon that broke scales and bruised fur all over the giant vermin's mismatched body.

Then I had to jump backwards to deal with the second eaterling was racing toward me through the shadows. It dashed between two dark terminals and swiped a long, brown claw at my retreating figure. The jagged appendage scraped painfully along my thigh but failed to penetrate my qi and robes.

"Spread out," the larger eaterling hissed as it skittered into view. "Approach him from his side."

Its appearance surprised me. It was at least a head taller than its more foolish companion, which brought it to roughly my eye level. What caught my attention the most, though, was the brown carapace on its back, leg, and arm. It was as if, as these creatures grew in power, they gained more features of different pests. I clamped down on my revulsion to keep my head in the fight, stepping backwards to keep the other monster from encircling me.

"A young male," the rat-lizard hissed as it glared at me. "Did the ship-girl find a mate after all, little human? Did she woo you?"

"Step forward for your answer," I replied as calmly as I could, keeping both of them in front of me.

"What?" The eaterling stopped and tilted its head. "Why—"

I burned a tiny amount of mana and rushed forward immediately, pummeling the monster in a short series of blows that knocked it backfirst into the edge of one of Vessa's inactive devices. Its cry of pain told me that it had landed hard enough for whatever Source-based protection it used to be completely overpowered, but I had no time to finish it off, because the larger eaterling struck out with its roach-claw. The blow narrowly missed my face, and I had to catch the next blows on my robed forearms, losing part of my qi shield in the process.

My return kick made the monster leap backward and skitter away, and the two of us watched each other, panting.

"A qi user," the thing rasped between breaths. "You've Advanced to the Condensation stage. You might even be at the second drop. Close to my level of essence advancement."

I kept my fists raised protectively and said nothing.

"You can't stay here," the monster rasped, keeping its own guard up as it watched me. "Not for very long. This is a broken ship stranded between stars, and your people have too many complicated needs. You will starve, or get sick, or get lonely, and then you will die."

I kept my guard up and said nothing.

But my inner planet started spinning again. I felt the energy from the black pill run through it, and my loose essence and mana started agitating.

"You could leave," the monster offered, taking a tiny step closer. "There is a way out. If you run down the tunnel we came through, the larger creatures will not be able to catch you. Just stick to the small tunnels until you find one of the smaller pod-ships. Use that to escape this place. Go. Take whatever food you need. We will not chase. We just want the ship-girl."

"That's it?" I asked skeptically, not dropping my guard. "You'd let me go, as long as I leave you two alone?"

"We do not need you," the eaterling insisted, stepping closer to the shadows. "Just the ship-girl. Her body will give us all the food and power we will ever need. Just go and leave her with us. She cannot help you anyway. She is already broken."

"Why don't you leave yourself?" I asked, keeping my expression neutral, and forbidding my arms to punch the creature every time it referred to Vessa. "This place is full of danger, and you have a safe way out."

"I am eaterling," the rat-roach said in a raspy laugh. "Every place is dangerous for us. The other races judge us for our hungers. Places like this are our best homes. Go. All I want is to eat whatever I want, and in the way I want, without interference. Just leave us alone with the little ship-girl, and you can go save yourself. Find a female of your own race, a better one, one that isn't broken."

A growl crawled out of my mouth in response to the insult, and the giant vermin chuckled.

"Have it your way then, idiot."

The other eaterling leaped outward at the same time I pointed my finger at it.

While its friend had been talking, it had pulled itself back to its feet and quietly been creeping toward me. We had finished talking just as it lunged toward me, mouth stretched wide open.

Had I been born yesterday, or recently received a sharp blow to the head, it would have been an effective tactic.

As it was, though, I recognized the roach eaterling's stalling tactic for what it was right at the start, and bided my time for its weaker, damaged friend to finally move.

The mana bolt had gotten simpler for me to perform since my time on Lunei's world. I had completed the spell in time to direct the finger-sized energy arrow right into my enemy's open mouth.

Vessa had taught me that the mana bolt spell was one of the easiest attacks to counter by any practitioner or Sourcebeast. All it took was for the target to activate any sort of protective charm, technique, or spell, and the magical arrow would be thwarted. The spell was still useful to a junior practitioner though, partly because it cost very little mana, was easy to cast, easiest to learn, and served as a good foundation for other spells.

Finally, to targets that lacked or had exhausted their source protection, it struck with the same force as a bullet shot from a modern firearm.

The eaterling's essence protection charm had been completely depleted by the earlier beatings I had given it. Its body had been improved by passive essence, but that protection was minimal at this stage, and concentrated on its skin, bone, and muscles.

So my bolt shot into its mouth, discharged its magical payload through the inside of the monster's skull, and then still had enough force to blast out of the back of the creature's head.

The remaining eaterling stumbled at the sight of its partner's death. I pivoted and launched into it.

That's it, my mother's voice said in my mind. *Keep moving. Hesitation will get you killed.*

Another light turned on in my mind. Muscle memory I should not have had guided my next punch around the monster's hastily raised talon to slam into its shoulder. It dodged the next blow, and the next blow after that. Then the roach-rat-lizard's scaled fist struck me and pushed me back. It disengaged from me, and we began circling each other, watching for an opening to close in again.

More lights were turning on. More lessons I should not have kept over the years returned to me. How to better throw a punch. The best place to take a blow on the arm. How to look for tells to predict an enemy's next action. None of these lessons made me anything close to a martial expert, but they were enough to keep my courage from crumbling, at least in the face of this weak, ugly thing.

The roach eaterling leaped forward, and I pounced with it, while angry pieces of my insides burned brighter and brighter.

The sensations had begun after I had eaten the black pill. At first, they had only been an uncomfortable feeling in my belly. When I began this battle, they climbed out and warmed my torso. When I slew the first eaterling, they began to burn out to my limbs.

Now, as I hurtled toward my remaining opponent, it surged through my Source energies, slamming my essence and mana against the barriers preventing them from Advancing as my qi had, and piercing right through. The cloud of mana hovering inside of me had completely gathered all stray vapors, and hovered directly over my

Soulscape. The last flecks of essence finished covering my body, and began to rumble directly under my inner planet.

The essence under my Soulscape cracked just enough to create a crude mosaic, the shape suggesting some kind of four-legged, undefined small animal. The rumbling cloud above my spiritual world shifted to reveal an ore-like vein of some shiny gray substance inside of it. My inner planet began spinning again, circulating the single droplet of qi throughout my body, and the cloud and mosaic glowed in response.

Awareness flooded my mind and nerves. Power flooded my muscles. I adjusted my charge to collide into the side of the roach eaterling, dig my hands into the edges of its back-carapace, heave it over my head, and hurl it through the air.

It bounced off another unlit terminal, its carapace cracking, but otherwise taking the fall much better than the last eaterling had. It rolled to its feet and began scampering away from me with wide eyes.

"Tri-practitioner!" the monster shouted. "You are a tri-practitioner, that has Advanced in all three Sources!"

It was right. Vessa had called this the tin stage of mana and the natal stage of essence. Neither they nor the first drop of the qi condensation stage provided a large amount of power by themselves. All together, though, they made me faster, stronger, and tougher than my opponent could hope to handle, and it knew it.

"Who are you?" the monster screeched as it continued to skitter away from me. "Where did she find you? How is she building you up so evenly, and so quickly? You were nothing mere moments ago!"

"Do you remember when I advised you to leave a few minutes ago?" I asked as I stepped forward. "Back before I killed your companion? Back when you were still taunting the woman I chose to protect?"

"English," the monster said, eyes bulging ever wider. "You are from that planet! The world of different tongues and tribes!"

"If I were not already planning to kill you, I would ask you what you mean by that," I told the thing, taking another step forward.

There was no longer any need to hurry. We both knew this fight was over. I only delayed now to give my body time to adjust to the now-mightier soul inside it.

"I can help you," the monster said, tripping over its own tail and hastily landing backwards on its hands. It kept pleading as it scooted backwards. "I can guide you around the rest of the ship!"

"What a kind offer," I said quietly, stepping forward again. "Do you remember when you said you would make the woman I chose to protect beg and cry before you killed her? Before you ate her, rather? What exactly did you mean by that?"

"Nothing," the creature said, still scooting backwards. "I meant nothing! I can help you protect her! I can find things that will help her recover! Help her re-power pieces of this ship! Do you not want that? Do you not want to see her healthy? Do you not want her to be able to leave that capsule and walk around?"

"Those are all generous concessions," I acknowledged as I continued advancing. "Would you mind holding still for a few moments?"

Something about my tone must have disturbed it, because the creature finally pushed off the floor with its scaly tail and darted towards Vessa's capsule.

I growled and chased after it. My thrice-augmented legs helped me close the distance between us quickly, but it was going to be a near thing. The monster began leaping on top of deactivated pedestals to maneuver better.

But after it landed from its third leap, a small furry form intercepted it with a leap of its own. Nestor's blue and black body darted onto the eaterling's snout and leaped off immediately, leaving the creature to scream and clutch its face in his wake.

I raced toward my wounded enemy. The monster had a clear path to Vessa's bed now. I had to end this quickly. But just before I caught up with the creature, a thin gray hand lifted out of Vessa's capsule and fired a burning ray into the monster's skull.

The eaterling's scream lasted for a half-moment, then cut off immediately. The monster's actual head did the exact same thing, falling to the ground in a tumbling cloud of ash. The ship-woman sighed from her bed.

"Ugh," she groaned, withdrawing her hand back into the capsule. "My mentors were all so very wrong. Exercise is overrated."

Nestor squeaked as he leaped onto my shoulder. He latched on to my new robe as I raced to Vessa's side, worried for my friend.

"I had the thing," I admonished as I reached her bed. "There was no reason to risk yourself in combat."

"That was *why* I did it," Vessa replied tiredly. "It was a safe opportunity to spend leftover Source energy that has been collecting in my flesh-body, and to recycle it with the energy gained from killing the thing."

"I thought practitioners weren't supposed to kill creatures for their Source energy?" I said back as I looked over her, checking her body for wounds or other trauma. Her eyes were focused and her breathing looked fine, though she panted heavily.

"They're not supposed to make a *habit* of killing things for their Source energy," the ship-woman corrected me. "Not without Drawing heavily between kills to avoid imbalance. That's especially true just after Advancing, so you will need to begin immediately, since you have just

Advanced three times. And, it's also a problem because it's murder. But occasionally killing a Sourcebeast, fellow practitioner, or hybrid such as an eaterling in self-defense is safe, beneficial, and frequently necessary, given how violent the night sky has become. Now," she panted, still clearly exhausted. "You should take a moment to rest, but after that I want you to begin Drawing as soon as possible. The pills I had you take before the fight will help with that. I'm sorry there wasn't time to tell you what they did," the prone woman added uncomfortably. "But they were all designed to either help you survive the fight or gain as much power as you could safely keep. Especially the black one."

"No offense taken," I replied, taking two empty food pouches and walking over to one of the pillars I recognized. "I am getting a drink of water. Would you like one as well?"

She sent me yet another inexplicably annoyed look.

"You do not need to keep anticipating my needs before I voice them," she finally said. "But, yes. I am thirsty as well. Thank you. And thank you for saving my life again. I appreciate the risks you are constantly taking on my behalf."

I handed her a small pouch full of water.

"You are welcome, Nova," I said easily, then froze. "Vessa," I corrected, "you are welcome, Vessa."

She gave me a wide smile as she took my offered drink, all of her previous irritation gone. I hurried away to follow her instructions.

Chapter 8

"Already?" Vessa asked as I rose to my feet. "You are already finished?"

"You instructed me to stop when I became very drowsy and no more energy drifted into my body," I replied hesitantly, worried that I had done something horribly wrong.

"Yes, that's all correct," she said as she propped herself up to examine me. "But you had just Advanced three times, each in a different type of Source energy. You should take at least another hour to… do what you have already done perfectly." She trailed off, sighing. "Okay. I think I see what happened. This is a good thing. Technically."

"Did something go wrong?" I asked her. "I thought I followed your instructions exactly."

"You did." she acknowledged. "They were good instructions. They should have worked flawlessly. These circumstances are inconvenient and unfair for the both of us. But especially me."

"Do go on," I said dryly, not sure what to make of Vessa's complaint.

"Your Soulscape," she answered. "It refined the energy for you. Helped your qi move everything around in a healthy pattern. It made the process work safer and more quickly than any other post-combat Draw I have ever seen."

"Alright," I said with a nod. "That explains everything, except why you are upset."

"I am upset because it did all of that without providing further benefits. And yes, I was thrilled to discover that you could also store and refine items inside your Soulscape. I wasn't lying about that being rare or beneficial. The problem, Jasper, is that you gained far, far more power from combat than you should have, and are technically gaining much less than other practitioners do from Drawing itself. If I had only seen you Draw so far, and had not known what planet you had come from, I would have guessed that you were of inferior talent for being a Source practitioner. Even though you have access to all three Source energies, I would have been surprised if you ever advanced to the second stage of any of them. I would have judged your limits to be around the fifth drop of the condensation stage, or the fourth crack of the natal stage, or the third wisp of the tin stage, and none of those together."

"Those ranks still mean nothing to me, by the way," I interjected.

"We've been over this," Vessa sighed. "Every first stage is divided into ten substages. The majority of both people and beasts everywhere under the night sky never make it to the tenth substage no matter what Source they practice. Because many strong beings form their own nations and communities, the concentration of power is far from uniform. But since practitioners of each Source energy have their own established traditions, they all have their different names, at least for the first stage. Qi condensation is divided into drops, the tin mana stage is divided into wisps, and the natal essence stage is divided into cracks. Get ten of the same substage, and you can advance to the next stage, which will be qi Pool, Copper mana, or Wailing essence."

"Since I need ten of any to keep Advancing, can I simply refer to them all as substages?"

"Not without offending any number of passionate practitioners, who all insist that their particular branch of Source energy is unique or better than the other two," Vessa sighed again. "Just memorize the names, Jasper. You will have fewer duels to the death that way."

"Noted." I nodded.

"But that isn't even the point," Vessa persisted. "Because while most normal people never Advance twice, practitioners often make it to at *least* the second stage. So do Sourcebeasts and monsters. As a layperson, you would have been fine Drawing. You might live fifty years longer than people from your world normally do. But you're trying to be a practitioner, and that's a different matter entirely."

"Considering what has just happened in the past two days, I feel very happy with my progress," I said defensively, hoping she was wrong about my future. I rather enjoyed the gains to my body and would prefer for them to continue.

"Yes," Vessa admitted, "because of what just happened. You gained an abnormal amount of power both from killing the eaterlings and from the resources you used. Your Soulscape seems designed to help you acquire and store treasure, and to process Source resources. But that's it," she announced. "No benefits to Drawing normally. No unique combat skills."

"Combat skills," I noted, focusing on those two words. She may have mentioned that fact before, but I was having trouble remembering all of this new information. "You mean Soulscapes can help other practitioners fight? As in improving their strength, reflexes, or instincts?"

"No," Vessa replied. "I mean your Soulscape could have been a giant flaming sword that would have appeared in combat to help you battle. Or, for that matter, a pair of wings that appeared on your back to help you fly quickly through the air. Or a spiritual hammer that helped you break or build things, letting you make constructs in the middle of a battle. Or even a set of gills that allowed you to breathe in hostile environments, such as underwater or even in space. But the true combat style Soulscapes usually grant benefits that directly help in a fight," she emphasized. "Had you a combat-oriented Soulscape, you would have torn those two eaterlings apart even faster, even though Soulscape combat is one of the most intense arts to use. It's usually the trump card in a fight. So when you go up against other practitioners, who either want to kill *you* for your Source energy, or just want the same resource you just found, you will be at a huge disadvantage if they have a combat-style Soulscape. At the same time, your Soulscape depends on you fighting and acquiring resources, without really making it easier to do so."

"That has not been a problem so far," I argued, wanting her to focus on the fact that I had Advanced three times in less than two full days.

"Only because you have not had to compete with anyone for resources," Vessa countered. "Eaterlings do not count as a challenge, not for a real practitioner. And so far," she added with an edge to her voice, "the only practitioner you *have* encountered was a woman that, by your own words, chose to tear your clothes off and then gift you treasure."

"When you put it that way, I realized I described the event badly," I replied awkwardly.

"Perhaps you have," she allowed primly. "So now that we are safe, maybe you could explain further? Especially since you were supposed to teleport here immediately if you encountered anyone? And since I tried to teleport you myself when the eaterlings arrived, and I couldn't reach you at all?"

"Very well," I began. "Nestor and I were still working to acquire the last sample you wanted when we saw two practitioners flying high over our heads on a winged beast—"

"And one of them leaped off of it to pounce upon you and tear your clothes off?" Vessa interrupted acidly.

"No, and that really isn't the most important part of the story," I argued, confused as to why she thought otherwise. "May I please continue?"

"By all means," Vessa replied, still glaring.

"Thank you," I said, sensing that we were probably fighting. "The couple was some distance away, and had not seen us. We did not immediately return to the Soulship because we felt we had time to grab the last sample you needed without being discovered."

"Even though I told you to teleport as soon as you saw another practitioner, no matter what?" Vessa interrupted again. "Even though I told you that we could always try again tomorrow? Or the day after that?"

"Correct," I replied evenly, giving her a glare of my own now. "Your pardon, Nova, but I did not believe you when you said you would be alright if we waited that long. Vessa," I corrected, shaking my head. "Your name is Vessa. Apologies. I think I need more sleep."

"No," Vessa said in a soft, stricken voice. "You're fine, Jasper. Don't worry about it. I'm sorry I snapped at you. Please continue."

"Thank you," I said back, relieved that we were no longer fighting. "Nestor and I hurried as quickly as we could to reach the qi spring in order to get the last sample. On the way there, we stopped briefly to rest at what turned out to be a tree of qi plums. Nestor offered to collect some fruit for us, and I let him do so while resting at a more comfortable tree. Separating was the mistake that kept us from teleporting."

"If that was when you encountered the woman practitioner, I disagree," Vessa rebutted, but without any heat in her voice. "Since she proved to be friendly, you could have simply teleported as soon as Nestor came back down. It would not have mattered if she had seen you, because she would likely never see you again."

"Even if she was Lunei?" I asked quietly.

"Lunei?" Vessa asked me with a start, sitting up in her partially raised bed, then wincing from the effort. "You met Lunei in the middle of nowhere? At one of the most secluded spots of the planet?"

"It was precisely her and one other, who kept me from departing immediately," I said confidently. "She looked exactly as you described her, and she named herself Shining Maiden Lunei of the Sparkling Sky Sect."

"And she was the one to tear your clothes off?" Vessa asked, her acid tone returning.

"I *really* should have phrased that better, but yes," I provided reluctantly.

"Jasper Cloud," the ship-woman began angrily. "I don't appreciate you insinuating that I lack the amount of self-control needed to avoid just tearing your clothes off as soon I get you alone in the middle of the woods!"

"That's not what—" I began, then finished processing her words. "Wait. Why did you just say 'I'? We were talking about your Beacon."

"A slip of the tongue," Vessa said quickly. "Completely unimportant. What's important is the slanderous allegation you are leveling at one of my Beacons, about how she lost control over the first green-eyed man I saw—she! She saw!"

"Ancient American gods!" I shouted. "She did it to save my life, all right? And you are the first person to ever care about my green eyes! May I please explain what happened?"

My outburst shocked Vessa into silence, and I felt ashamed. I reminded myself that the poor woman had been starving, bedridden, and terrified for a length of time I could not even fathom.

"I'm sorry, Jasper," the ship-woman finally replied. "Please continue. I won't interrupt again."

"Thank you," I said to her. "And I should not have yelled at you." I took a breath to ensure that I was calm again. When she gave me a small smile, I continued. "While Nestor and I were separated, we encountered the male practitioner traveling with Lunei. We both hid, and tried to wait for him to leave. But Nestor was forced to hide in the fruit tree that the practitioner was interested in."

Not-true, Nestor said sadly in our minds. *My-fault. Gave-fruit.*

Vessa tilted her head in confusion.

"That was dangerous, since you have Source energy, but most practitioners are likely to react favorably to a Sourcebeast willing to share resources with them."

"This one chose to punish our friend for not offering a greater gift, and struck the little mouse with a fistful of qi energy."

Vessa gasped in horror.

"That would have crippled him!"

Yes-yes, Nestor said sadly. *Hurt-much.*

The ship-woman crooned pitifully and held out her hands to the little mouse.

Go, I told my friend. *Let her look at you, so that she knows you are better.*

The small lifemouse squeaked and crawled down my shoulder and into Vessa's palms.

"You poor thing," she whispered to him, bringing him to her cheek and nuzzling the furry creature. "I'm so sorry that happened."

My-fault, my bonded friend squeaked softly. *Bad-folk. Hurt-him.*

He pointed his fur-plumed tail in my direction. Vessa gave me a concerned look.

"I tried to catch Nestor and teleport us away. That was when our attacker struck me, and somehow damaged my ability to teleport."

"Then he crippled your cultivation," Vessa breathed. "And probably broke your body as well. Blast it all, Jasper. That wasn't supposed to happen."

"I believe you," I replied, nodding once in agreement. "Lunei arrived then, and saved us from him."

"What was she even doing traveling with such a vicious brute?" the ship-woman demanded. "I'm surprised she even associated with him at all!"

"His attack on the two of us both shocked and infuriated her," I answered. "He was not part of her sect, but a visitor from another world, like I was, and she was his guide to the qi spring. Since I obviously knew of the spring, she assumed I had permission to be there as well, making her charge's attack on me all the more serious."

Vessa held up a finger for permission to interject, and I nodded.

"Did he say the name of his planet, sect, or clan?"

"He did not exactly," I replied. "But his name was Koram, and he was at the later part of the qi Condensation stage. He boasted about belonging to a charter that supposedly numbered over a dozen worlds, and that he claimed had a number of powerful masters. I will ask you more questions about that in a moment, but for now, know that Lunei beat him severely for his attack on us."

"Good," the ship-woman said firmly as she petted Nestor's fur. "Please continue."

"Lunei personally carried me to the spring herself. She explained that in addition to providing benefits to my qi, it would also repair any damage done to my body or cultivation, and exponentially enhance whatever it healed. After she provided evidence by further damaging Koram, I begged her to injure my body completely to receive a greater benefit from the spring. That act was what destroyed my old garments."

"Oh," Vessa said simply, looking pained. "Jasper… the qi spring would have fixed you without doing that. I didn't tell you about its specific ability because I was confident it would change nothing, and I did not wish to shame you by drawing attention to a condition you were never responsible for.”

“I understand,” I said with another nod. “But right now, I am responsible for the care of a currently bedridden woman, and am the only person able to aid Nova when we return to Earth. It was not a question of whether I needed to change or not, it was a question of just how much I was needed.”

Vessa opened her mouth to say more, closed it, and then looked away. Nestor gave a concerned squeak as he sniffed at her cheek. I chose to continue speaking.

“Afterwards, she moved us into the spring, and our bodies recovered to the state they are now. She gave me these clothing and pills as a final apology for Koram’s attack.”

“Did you extract compensation from him as well?” the ship-woman asked as she continued to pet Nestor, still looking away from me. “You would have been entitled to it under these conditions.”

“Koram was still unconscious. He did not have the same tolerance for pain,” I said, sounding smug and not caring. “I asked Lunei to extract a Sourcevow of better behavior from him, and made one in turn, stating that I would not speak of the day’s events with anyone but my master, unless Lunei’s sect gives me permission to speak more freely.”

“That… was well done,” the gray-eyed woman confessed. “I owe you an apology for lashing out at you, Jasper Cloud. I became afraid when I could not contact you, and I did not handle my fear well. I am… unused to companionship now. And it will take time for me to relearn proper behavior. I ask for your patience.”

“Nov—Vessa,” I corrected. “Please look at me.”

She slowly turned her head back towards my direction.

"Do I still look frail?" I asked, showing off arms that bulged with well-sculpted muscle definition. "Do I still look starved? Do I have a roof over my head, instead of being exposed to the rain and snow?" I pointed to the ceiling. "And, most of all, I am no longer completely defenseless against anyone who wishes to cause me harm. Do you see why I bear you no ill will at all?"

"I…" she began, and looked away again. "Thank you, Jasper Cloud. I am grateful for your protection and your care. And I will continue to do all I can for you. I hope you soar far one day, farther and higher than any other practitioner under the night sky."

"I appreciate that," I told her. "Would you like me to add the water samples to your capsule?"

"Yes, please," she said, touching a button on the inside of her tube. "While you do that, did you have any questions for me?"

"I did," I remembered, pouring one of the vials down the new curved holes that opened up on the side of her chamber. "I wish to know why Koram knew the language of my world. And why I can understand everyone I've ever encountered out here, despite the fact that they all come from other worlds."

"That's no trouble to answer," Vessa replied as she shifted in her bed. "I spoke before on how your planet was a library for my race. At one time, the memories of over a thousand different worlds resided in your great library. All of the languages your people speak today—or spoke until recent events on your world, at least—were languages from other worlds that your elders decided to preserve by teaching to their own people."

"That does not sound possible," I said, carefully pouring another one of the vials into Vessa's personal device. "Even if there had been some record of my people gaining a language from another world, it still does not explain how our languages had remained similar enough for me to understand the Mandarin-like speech on Lunei's world. English alone has changed so much over a thousand years that its last speakers would not be able to understand the first."

"I have no answer for you." Vessa shrugged from her bed as I emptied the last vial. "All I know is that the languages of different worlds have changed with much the same rapidity as your own, and in similar fashions. Maybe someone has ensured that these languages have remained consistent, even when they were spoken on different worlds. And time passes far more slowly on your own planet, remember? That is why we still have a chance to save Nova. Barely any time at all has passed on your world right now."

"That is another thing I have a hard time understanding," I said, as Nestor hopped up and held out his paw. I gave him one of the empty vials and he ran to the water dispenser and began cleaning it. "How could time pass so differently on these different worlds?"

"I… don't remember," Vessa said suddenly, sounding surprised. "Wait," she said, staring upward quietly for a moment. "No… I don't remember." She grimaced in frustration. "Damage. My ship-body has sustained too much damage. I have forgotten that I am still a long way from recovery. We need to find a way to bring more of this place online."

"Should that be our next task?" I asked, finally realizing that I felt tired. I had gone to another planet, been broken, put back together, battled two human-sized monsters in a duel to the death, then finished communicating with the energies of the universe while under the effects of unknown medical supplements. It had been a long day.

"We will see," Vessa replied. "After seeing you and Nestor battle those eaterlings, I am starting to feel much more confident about showing you the rest of the Ship.”

“Just to clarify,” I began, “because I know you have already explained this, but you are the ship itself, yes? And a young woman? At the same time?”

She had already explained this at least once, but I felt as if I had lost many details in between scavenging food and dirt from foreign worlds, fighting rat-lizard-roach-men, and letting mysterious energy supposedly from the universe itself unlock hidden potential within my body.

Vessa sighed as she brushed a strand of black hair out of her face.

“I had forgotten how difficult my people’s nature is to understand,” she muttered, looking down for a moment. “I am among the youngest of my race, but our creation is shrouded in secret, even by the oldest Soulships. Either none of us ever learned how we were made, or the oldest of us took some silent vow with them to their graves. I can tell you this much: As far as I learned, I was born at the same time that I was made, into the arms of a family I do not remember, and who did not keep me. I know only that I came to be in some shipyard far away, perhaps at the very edge of the night sky. Half of my mind is in this body of flesh, and half of my mind is in this massive ship. I cannot even remember how the two are joined, but my flesh-body cannot leave this ship easily, and not for a long amount of time. But I can create another body and send it to grow up on another world and stay there indefinitely.”

“That is another thing I am unclear on,” I spoke up, as Nestor brought me a freshly-cleaned vial and held out his paws to take another. “When I first spoke to you, you said your Beacons were also yourself. That Nova was also you. What does that mean? Do you divide your consciousness further? Did I grow up with a part of you, those years in the orphanage and on the streets?”

And did a part of yourself fall in love with me? I did not add.

"I…" The ship-woman looked away in embarrassment. "I said many things when we first met, things that were mere gibberish. Forgive me. I was not well. But did you say you had more questions about that rival practitioner?"

"Very well," I said, not because I fully believed her, but because I knew I could not force her to talk against her will, and I did have more questions about my newest enemy. "Tell me what the Glorious Star Charter is, and why its practitioner spoke the same tongue as the official language of the Glorious State."

Vessa blinked, and this time I knew it was genuine surprise.

"I have never heard of that language until very recently. By the time I had retreated into the trap around your planet, I had been repelled by assailants who spoke languages I had never heard before, but I had no time to really study them. If more of my data storage could be powered, I might be able to examine the files and see if they are similar to what your people speak."

"The monster on my world," I mused, "that dragon thing, told Nova and I that they had been waiting for you. That they had left a trap for you to entice you to recover your Beacon. If that is true, and they are part of this new Charter, then Lunei and your other Beacons are in danger."

"They may well be." Vessa nodded. "Though not as much as Nova is. The other Beacons have Drawn Source energy and Advanced several times at least, and most have the backing of a powerful sect, country, or tribe. More than that, these new enemies may not even be aware of their presence, since I have worked so hard to keep them secret."

"How did they find Nova, then?" I asked, watching as Nestor ran back to the water dispenser. He crawled into the largest cubby on it, hit the nearby button with his tail, and began showering himself.

"I do not know," Vessa admitted, propping herself up to see what I was looking at. She smiled at the sight of the tiny mouse enjoying the running water, even though our conversation had turned serious. "But I had been rushed when I created Nova. I was desperately trying to create a Beacon that could link directly with me and help me repair further. I had to risk omitting a half-dozen failsafes that normally prevent my Beacons from being discovered, and just trusted that she would be fine because of her remote location. I was wrong. But after we save her, we will have time to find out more about our enemies. And by then, we can plan how to combat them."

"But first, we need to finish acquiring a way to return to my world, and to ensure I am strong enough to help Nova escape," I finished for her. "What do I need to do next?"

"Rest and train," Vessa replied firmly. "Now that you have Advanced, I can teach you more powerful arts. You've still got a long way to go, but at least you can't just be slapped to death by any random practitioner. Furthermore, thanks to your decision to take a dangerous and unnecessary risk by not leaving at the first sign of danger, and somehow surviving, we still have time that we can spend to guarantee Nova's escape. However, I encourage you not to learn the wrong lessons from your actions and to stop taking needless risks regarding your own safety."

I started to shrug, then stopped myself, realizing just in time that Vessa would not appreciate the gesture.

But hopefully we raised you right anyway, my father spoke from my memories. *Because she'll need you to throw everything on the line for her, when the time comes.*

I blinked and shook my head. Another light in my mind had turned on, for a room I had never remembered until this moment.

"Sorry," I said, as Vessa continued to stare at me. "I will try to be more careful. Losing me would endanger us all."

"I'm glad you realize that," the ship-woman said firmly. "Speaking of unnecessary risks, now would be a good time for you to realize that you need to rest for a bit. I was able to reactivate one of the bed-capsules for you. It has not been used in ages, but it should be better than sleeping on the floor."

A section of tiles on the floor opened up, and a capsule similar to Vessa's rose from the floor. It opened from the top, revealing some sort of synthetic padding inside, much like Vessa's had.

I started to say that I wasn't tired, that I had just gotten a long rest on the floor and at least two relaxing baths today. I could begin training, I almost said, until I realized just how comfortable all that padding looked, and remembered how sore the floor had made me yesterday.

"I'll take a quick nap," I conceded, removing my boots and climbing into the capsule. "Only a quick one. After that, I would like to immediately resume… how is this so soft and firm at the same time?" I asked.

Vessa chuckled, and my eyes closed before I heard her answer.

"He's beautiful, isn't he?" my mother said as I pretended to sleep. I had found they would talk more when they thought I wasn't listening.

"He is," my father answered. "Tall for his age, and he's not even six. He'll grow up to be strong."

"I hope he doesn't need to be," my mother answered, as she talked to my father outside my bedroom door.

"I hope he doesn't either," my father admitted. "But if she comes soon enough, he won't have to be. It will be our jobs instead."

"What if she doesn't come at all?" my mother asked hopefully.

"Then he'll have a nice and safe life, and pass the duty down to his children, in case she comes during their lifetime."

"What if she never comes?" my mother asked, this time sounding worried.

"She will, honey," my father said soothingly. "She'll have to, so that our world does not go dark."

"She may not even know about us," my mother kept arguing, as was her habit. Father said it made her a better fighter than him, because she never gave up until her conscience let her.

"It's not her job to know about us," my father corrected patiently, a habit he had developed to balance with hers. Mother said it made him a better guardian than her, because he never forgot what was important. "It's her job to keep all the lights in the night sky shining. Our role is to protect her long enough for her to be able to do so."

"It should be more than us," my mother countered. "It should not be just our family. I don't want it to be his burden."

"I don't either," my father answered. "But you know what happened to the other Knights. The fewer our number, the safer we all are. For now, at least," my father added. I heard him step forward, and I guessed he moved to hold my mother.

"I want that to change, then," my mother growled, apparently leaning into his embrace. "I want justice for all that they've done."

"So do I," my father said quietly, but firmly. "And if she returns in either his time or ours, we will ensure that the others are avenged. But for now, we keep him safe, and we train him, as your parents trained us."

"I hope we have time to get him as ready as he needs to be," my mother whispered. "I hope he can go as far as she can take anyone, if that day comes. And then I hope he not only lives, but makes every one of those monsters pay for what they've done."

I wanted to hear more, but my mind had chosen that moment to wake up.

My eyes opened to reveal that I was back in the world of shadows, steel, and blue light. As I rose to my feet, I saw that Vessa had elevated her inner bed enough to where she could look out at me from her capsule.

"Sleep well?" she asked me, with a smug expression on her face.

"Yes, surprisingly," I answered her, not wanting to admit that I could spend a little longer in that wonderful bed. But my back and other muscles felt incredible. "I hadn't known a short nap could do this much for me."

"I wouldn't know either," Vessa replied in a cocky tone, "because you slept for eight hours."

"I…" I began, unable to really finish. "What?"

"The beds are well-designed," Vessa answered, still smiling. "They are supposed to help me care for my crew under the worst of circumstances, for an inordinate amount of time. Because of that, they take a great deal of power to activate, or it would have been the first thing I had done for you," she added uncomfortably. "As things are, though, it will continue to help condition my body. But enough of that. I suspect you are eager to continue training."

"I would like to learn just how many new miracles I can perform now, yes," I replied with a grin. "Something tells me that you should probably teach me some sort of art that involves fire, given how quickly everything up here burns."

"About that," Vessa interjected. "You're right, but I also want you to remember that fire burns oxygen, and that you are in space."

"Oh," I said sheepishly. "Right. Are we in danger of running out?"

"No, but producing enough for us to live indefinitely is one of the many reasons I remain confined to this bed. Which is no longer as comfortable as it first was," she admitted grumpily. "Speaking of which, that trick you did yesterday with my damaged devices saved my life, and I will never stop being grateful. But know that every part of my ship-body that breaks is something I must spend a great deal of energy to fix, or learn to do without. So I am going to teach you a few more arts that will help you with a broader range of situations, without risking more power than you know how to handle. So listen very carefully…"

She taught me a skill for each of my three Source energies. The first was a simple essence charm that let me increase my speed. Practitioners could inherently spend spare energy from any of the three Sources to augment themselves, but it was far more efficient to use an actual art instead. Essence had the least amount of spare Source energy, but its charms were among the most efficient for enhancing the body's normal functions. The charm's benefit wouldn't last forever, but it might help me dodge a fatal blow or escape an enemy I could not hope to defeat.

The second was a mana spell, similar to the mana bolt spell I had learned earlier. This one allowed me to create a tiny coin of flame no bigger than my thumb and send it at an enemy. It actually did less damage than the mana bolt, at least to a foe without Source protection, but it was just as cheap, could exhaust an opponent's force protection faster, and provided a controllable amount of flame that I could use to light a campfire or some other purpose.

The final art was the most complicated, and the hardest for me to maintain. It was a qi technique that intensified rejuvenating energy into the drop I received when I Advanced to the Condensation stage. If I practiced concentrating, I could maintain a passive technique that would slowly rejuvenate me if I grew tired, or was lightly injured, closing small cuts instantly, or I could expend the technique to immediately fix a broken limb or a life-threatening wound. Doing the latter wouldn't remove the injury completely, but it would stabilize me enough so that I could get further care later. If I had both the time and the need, I could perform the technique multiple times.

"And that's it," Vessa said as she took a deep breath. "Now I need to send you beyond the safety of this room, to a more dangerous location of the ship. I need you to bring the crew emergency drive back online."

"Very well." I nodded. "But I expect you to tell me what and where it is."

"The crew emergency drive is the last backup for my ship outside this current room. Its purpose is to help the crew briefly take over control of my ship-body's engines in the event that both of my minds become incapacitated or otherwise overwhelmed. It allows them just enough power to maintain life support and have my ship make long-distance jumps to a hopefully safe location, although it needs time to charge after every use. It's the closest nearby room, and at peak function, had a small stockpile of weapons, rations, and other emergency goods. I expect the room to have been largely picked clean by now, but if you can reach it, I'll have enough power to return to your world, reactivate my stealth drives, recover Nova, and hopefully escape from Earth once more before my pursuers realize we've returned."

"How exactly are you even being pursued?" I asked.

"By rivals who have their own various methods of traveling through the night sky," the ship-woman answered me. "The only reason they have been so cautious is because they know my ship-body has already been… infested," she said with a grimace, "by powerful Sourcebeasts and other creatures. I have kept those things confined to the outer areas of myself just as much to discourage boarders as to preserve my sanity."

"I am sorry you have to do that," I said quietly, and probably uselessly. This woman had already suffered far more than I could have ever imagined. "I will do what I can to help you recover more of yourself."

"I know," she said, looking away from me. "I know you are willing to help me in any way you can. I do not know *why* you are so willing to help me, Jasper, but I've finally realized that you had already made up your mind to protect and care for me long before you had a chance to get something in return."

"You are my only link to Nova," I answered quietly, because that much was true.

"That's not enough to check on me like you do, Jasper," she replied in a frustrated tone. "I've been confined to this bed for ages. I'm clearly able to survive inside without anything else, but you still bother to ask if I would like some real food. Or if I am warm enough, or if I would like any water from the container you made to carry it." She pointed to the food pouch I had turned into a makeshift waterskin. "You even bothered to make two of them, so that there would always be one available for me. And yes I know they're not hard to make, Jasper. The point is that you thought to make one at all for me. And then you share Sourcefruits, a treasure literally capable of extending your own lifespan, with me."

"What is your point?" I asked in consternation.

"My point is you didn't need to make sure I had a potted plant to keep me company!" Vessa suddenly shouted, pointing at the half-wilted flower I had brought back from Techne. "You care about me, Jasper, and I don't know why! And don't say it's about Nova, because you could hold me hostage right now and make me do whatever you wanted! You could have been the one issuing commands and setting terms and making me prove that you can trust me, but instead you're doing everything you can to make my life easier, even though you're not one of my old crew or from a world that remembers any sort of debt to my race!"

"Is that true?" I asked in a serious tone, wondering just how much of that dream was a real memory. "Was there anyone at all on my world who knew about Soulships? And if they didn't, how did the tyrants there know how to trap Nova?"

Vessa blinked, opened her mouth, and then closed it again.

"I don't know," she admitted softly. "As far as I am aware, your planet didn't have any recent contact with a Soulship, despite it being a center for learning back in ancient times. Before I put a Beacon down there, the last recorded contact your people had with a Soulship was roughly five thousand years ago. But I don't even have access to most of my memories right now," the ship-woman sighed as she put a hand to her face. "So I could have been totally wrong, and given myself away all those years ago when I snuck down and planted Nova into that world. And now I'm yelling at the only person willing to help me fix that mistake, because I can't handle him being so nice to me."

I could think of nothing to say, and she did not want me to touch her, so I remained silent. But Nestor scampered into view and crawled inside her capsule, nuzzling at the hand covering her face.

"And you're also nice to me for no real reason, little friend," the gray-skinned woman said, smiling as she moved her hand to scratch his tiny head. "I guess I just forgot how to handle that. I've spent too much time alone in the dark. Sorry about that, Jasper. Shall I continue explaining what I need you to do?"

"Please do," I answered the woman. She took another breath and began speaking again.

"Now back to your questions. I have only the dimmest of senses beyond the walls of my ship-body, so I cannot even be sure as to what is pursuing me. All I know is that large objects that generate Source energy have been following me in the distance, for the last dozen or so jumps. The only exception to that was the last jump I made, back when you killed the first eaterling and gave me just enough power to escape from Earth. But unless we get the emergency drive back online, it's only a matter of time before they discover me again. So now I must risk you traveling down those same halls that so many eaterlings have already crawled through. As I said, I have kept the more dangerous predators away from my inner areas, but you have seen and heard for yourself the creatures that still lurk in the halls just beyond here. I don't know what exactly you'll find further down, but you should be as quiet as possible. Anything that gets past you will almost certainly get to me, and I won't be able to fight it off unless I get *very* lucky."

"Then the smart thing to do is to have Nestor scout before I go in," I offered. I was not thrilled with the idea of risking my newest friend, but he had already proven more capable than I was, both in noticing danger and hiding from it.

As long as he never mistook that danger for a potential new friend, I thought uncomfortably. But after meeting Koram, there was probably little chance of that happening. I hoped.

But Nestor only squeaked happily over the idea.

Yes-yes! he sent to both our minds. *I-help!*

"Thank you, and be careful," Vessa said to the fluffy creature. "But yes, Jasper, that was exactly what I was going to suggest. Nestor can scout ahead, and communicate what he sees, and then we can go from there. Once you have cleared the room of danger, we can reactivate it. To do that..." The gray-skinned woman took a deep breath. "My flesh-body will need to enter the room, and stay there for a small portion of time. Which means I will need to be carried there."

"Alright." I nodded. "I will come back and get you when it's safe."

"There it is again," the woman muttered under her breath. "Promise me one thing, Jasper," she said as she raised her voice. "When you actually feel like complaining, please do so. Just so I know."

"I complained quite a bit back on Earth, when you were speaking to me through dangerous text."

"Yes, I remember that," Vessa replied. "And now that I have had more sleep, food, and Source energy, I realize that sending any kind of global broadcast at all was an extremely foolish risk. I was counting on the fact that I was already being pursued by the unknown enemies I mentioned earlier. But you have not complained since, no matter how dangerous the tasks have been, and that has made me uncomfortable."

"I assure you that I am not secretly planning to drop you," I said dryly.

"Yes, I know," Vessa muttered irritably. "I just expected you to complain about carrying an unkempt, half-starved woman who hasn't changed her clothing in ages down a long hallway. But that's a stupid thing for me to obsess on to begin with, so I'll get back to the point. You will have to secure the room, carry me to the room, and then make sure I can concentrate on reconnecting to the room. All without even knowing what you will find down there, and whether or not you will be strong enough to beat it.”

“Is that likely?” I countered. “Because if I can’t find a way to clear the area of your monstrous squatters, then it seems like we will be stuck here forever. Unless you can keep sending me to other nearby worlds and finding things that will help you somehow.”

“No.” Vessa shook her head. “We’ve exhausted most of the helpful resources in the worlds within my reach. I could keep finding small resources that would benefit you, but it wouldn’t make up for the power spent teleporting you to the planet in the first place. But yes, I’m confident that you could probably handle anything weak enough to get this close. Assuming you don’t make a foolish mistake and die in battle, because you’re so inexperienced.”

“I suppose I should watch out for that then,” I said wryly.

“Yes,” the ship-woman sighed. “You should. But once that’s done, you come get me, guard me while I bring the room back online, and then carry me back here, since this capsule still serves as my command station. With that room online, we will be able to return to Earth with enough power to remain under stealth, free Nova, and leave safely. Hopefully before our enemies even notice we ever arrived in the first place.”

I suspected that was overly optimistic, but I remained silent. I had no better ideas.

“Then Nestor and I should be going,” I said as I turned around. “If he gets too far ahead of me, I might not be able to help if something goes wrong.”

“Jasper,” Vessa said suddenly, “please be careful. Okay?”

I looked back at her, and saw that her eyes were shining brightly with gray light.

"I will be," I promised her, leaning down to pick up the broken tile I had used to kill the first eaterling. There hadn't been enough time to grab it before the second group attacked, not while Drawing the Source energy and getting ready to Advance. "And just so you know, Vessa… my real friends call me Jas."

With that, I hefted my improvised weapon and headed toward the dark hallway.

Chapter 9

The light from the tiles dimmed significantly when I entered the hallway. I recognized it as the same corridor I had walked down after I was first teleported. I hadn't had a chance to get my bearings then, but now I saw that if I had gone in the opposite direction Vessa had told me to, I would have reached the room with the crew emergency drive. Which meant that I would have either encountered one of the barriers Vessa had put up to keep her infesters out, or I would have walked straight into a nest of hostile lifeforms and died immediately.

That sobering reminder prompted me to stop walking forward, and to check the shadows more cautiously. I began to wonder just how loud my footsteps had sounded to anything else that might have been looking down the hallway.

Wait-wait, Nestor advised, reminding me of the plan. *I-go. You-stay. I-hide. I-seek.*

Right, I agreed, telling myself to calm down. *Don't go too far ahead. And be careful.*

Yes-yes, the little rodent replied dismissively to me. *I-know.*

And don't try to make any friends, I insisted. *Come get me first.*

The lifemouse turned his head to give me a dirty look and an indignant squeak, and then his fur became a mottled brown and black, and he scampered down by the wall and vanished.

I worked on keeping my own energy as masked as possible, and waited for a report from him.

Safe-safe, he sent to me. *Clear-clear.*

I walked forward quietly and carefully, drawing on all of my experience honed over years of walking down alleyways without being noticed by those who would do me harm. After a few minutes, I heard a soft squeak to my right, and realized I had caught up with Nestor again.

Go-now? the little mouse asked me, still invisible in the corner between the floor and the wall. I nodded at him, having trouble finding him even with my enhanced vision. I caught sight of a patch of black and dark blue shifting for one moment, but that was it. I didn't hear so much as a single scrape from his tiny claws. It took reaching through my link with him to know that he had finally left.

I waited as patiently as I could, keeping a tiny portion of my mind focused on that link as I absently fingered the tile in my hands. It had deformed significantly in my first fight on this vessel, with one edge rusted brown from slicing the eaterling's throat. I wondered if it was still more useful than my bare fists and feet, and when I would find a better weapon.

There is no such thing as a better weapon, my mother's voice trickled into my mind. *There are only good and bad circumstances for each weapon. That is why, when you get older, we are going to teach you how to use as many weapons and tools as possible, and hope it will help you stay alive.*

I froze as I recognized the memory. She had said that to me a year before their arrest, back when it was still legal for citizens to possess knowledge of self-defense. Years of starvation and stress had driven the memory from my mind until now, but in this moment, my now-healthier mind had recalled two things: that my parents had possessed extensive knowledge of various martial arts, and that the Glorious State had made no mention of such subjects, instead openly objecting to their possession of 'slanderous historical records,' and 'hateful, blasphemous ideologies.' They had been convicted as 'educational terrorists,' and unlike many violent offenders, that penalty had brought an automatic death sentence.

Clear-clear, Nestor said to my mind, shaking me from my memories. *Come-now. See-thing.*

I gripped my improvised weapon tightly, and slowly began walking down the hall. This time, I used my link to spot Nestor. He was waiting for me at a corner, where the hallway took a perpendicular turn to the right. I pressed close against the wall, even though he had assured me that nothing was nearby.

More-turns, he explained to my mind. *Then-door.*

Is the door still broken? I asked, remembering that Vessa had repaired it, only for more eaterlings to batter it down once again.

Yes-yes. Wait-here. I-check.

I nodded, and he snuck off once again, with only a ripple through our bonded link as a clue that he had left.

This time, I fully concentrated on sensing Nestor through our link. We were much closer to our goal, which meant Nestor could run into trouble at any moment. And if that same trouble got past him, there were no more barriers to stop it from reaching Vessa's capsule. I felt frustrated that she had left the door unrepaired the whole time I had been sleeping, but it probably would have cost her too much energy to repair, and had already failed to protect us two times in as many days.

Through my link, I could feel Nestor slowing down as he reached an unfamiliar area. He had probably gone just beyond the first broken door, and was carefully watching the shadows beyond it. Then I felt him carefully creep forward, sniffing and searching, until he was finally satisfied with what he didn't see.

Clear-clear. Come-close. Stay-quiet.

That last warning was new, and I crept all the more carefully because of it.

After traveling past two more corners, I reached the first door Vessa had described. It was a giant piece of metal that had somehow been beaten open. That baffled me, because the eaterlings did not seem nearly strong enough to batter their way through metal that was several inches thick. But when I looked more closely, I saw literally thousands of dents on the other side of the broken barrier, far too many to have come from just the three eaterlings that had forced their way through.

They must have been trying for ages, I realized, looking at the different claw marks, and realizing they came in different shapes and different sizes. *All of them. Everything small enough to have made it this far. And they must have kept at it, coming again and again, sometimes working together...* That thought trailed off as I saw the periodic brown stain here and there among the floor and walls, the same color of stain that my own improvised weapon sported. And sometimes fighting among themselves, I decided, remembering the sounds of combat I had heard last night, as one invisible creature had slaughtered a smaller one. From the echoes, I guessed that the sounds had come from much deeper within the Soulship, but there was no reason not to believe that other fights had happened at this very spot. *All for the opportunity to devour the half-starved woman in the room behind me...*

No wonder she could recognize the different sounds of things bumping and snarling within the shadows of her ship. She had been forced to listen to them thrash and pant against her bedroom door for decades, or perhaps even longer, all while unable to do so much as stand on her own power. To suffer through such an experience while still retaining even an ounce of sanity afterwards must have taken willpower far beyond my ability to comprehend.

I stepped carefully through the ruins of the door, focusing on the hallway before me. I could see the destroyed remains of the next barrier a dozen feet or so ahead of me, and the one beyond that, just a little further away. This must have been a final opportunity to prevent forced entry into Vessa's remaining sanctum, and judging by the damage and recent events, each door had failed at least twice.

No wonder she hadn't bothered putting them down again. Not only were they in no condition to even stop eaterlings, they were probably too badly damaged to repair with whatever power and resources she had left.

Nestor stopped me just before I stepped through the second barrier.

Heard-noise. Wait-here. I-check.

I took what cover I could behind the bent, battered barrier and nodded at him.

Be careful, I begged, just as I felt him scamper off through our link.

I took comfort in the fact that I could barely sense him myself, hefted my unwieldy tile, and listened for whatever I could.

And as I did, I concentrated on his own senses through our bonded link.

I could tell that he was moving even more cautiously now that he had sensed actual danger. He crept forward slowly, sniffing and scanning his surroundings every three steps. But the noise he had just heard was getting farther away, and that had puzzled him. He knew by now that anything creeping along these halls was something hunting for Vessa. There was no reason to draw back now that the barriers had been destroyed.

Unless, of course, the creature had either sensed us and was trying to draw us into a trap, or was a scout that had gone to report back. So we either needed to halt our advance immediately, or follow closely behind and catch it before it could alert its pack that the way forward was clear.

See-thing, Nestor sent to me, and through our link, I could tell that he had detected a creature that he was familiar with. *Like-rest.*

More eaterlings then, I thought. *Good.*

But why was that the only creature able to make it down here? Was it because they were so weak? Or did it have to do with something else?

Smell-more, he sent to me. *Smell-new. Just-came.* After a moment, the little mouse spoke again. *Smell-death. Just-fought. Just-killed.*

They had either fought among themselves or taken down a rival group, I decided. The frequent infighting among the parasites in this ship must have gone a long way to providing Vessa as much time as she had between attacks. But now all barriers were down for good, and more and more attackers were likely to notice and press forward.

I had to kill them, and then secure the room, so that the three of us could have a new chokepoint. Hopefully, Vessa would have more tools to protect us when she brought this room back online.

It also meant that I couldn't wait forever. Every second I delayed risked giving more attackers the time they needed to find this location, and I couldn't count on them fighting among themselves every time.

Thing-left, Nestor spoke again. *Hear-talk. I-wait? I-watch?*

Hang on, I sent to the little mouse. *I'm coming closer.*

I crept up to the last barrier and tucked myself behind the largest piece of remaining metal, listening carefully. I thought I could hear whispering off in the distance, but I couldn't make out anything more.

Will they hear me if I come closer? I asked my forward scout. I got an impression of him shaking his fluffy head.

Talk-much. Not-look. Not-care. May-fight.

That would have to do. Every second I delayed just gave more parasites time to discover this location. I pressed forward, careful to avoid stepping near the dimly lit tiles.

It became much harder to see, even with my enhanced senses, but eventually I began to hear the echoes of an argument. Once again, it was in an Earth language my parents had made sure to teach me—French, of all things.

"I told you the way is clear!" an eaterling's voice hissed down the halls. "Why are we not going now?"

"Because you just said the way is clear, idiot!" a deeper voice hissed, sounding somewhat like the larger eaterling I had killed before. "That means someone has already gone down!"

"All the more reason to hurry!" a third voice, high-pitched like the first, spoke up. "They could be running toward her flesh-body even as we speak!"

"Or they could have already devoured her, and left the way open as bait for more prey!" the second voice argued back.

"If something had devoured the Soulship's core, it would not have needed to hide," the fourth, and deepest voice, spoke up. "It would have Advanced several stages, and been able to hunt and devour whoever it wished, at whatever pace it wished."

"Maybe a large group brought the barriers down, and are currently fighting over her right now," the first spoke up. "Or maybe they already fought, and she was able to kill the survivors."

"Which means she would be stronger now," the second voice butted in, "maybe even able to kill the four of us!"

Good, I thought as I crept closer. *There are only four of them.*

That was not excellent news, but I had already proven able to handle two of the creatures in a fistfight, and I was now armed. *Perhaps I could drop one or more of them by surprise at the very start...*

"Unlikely," the fourth creature rumbled in the shadows beyond me. "Anything weak enough to bypass the wards of this place will be too weak to help her recover enough to fend off a serious attack. At best, she would be a match for one of us right now."

"All the more important for us to rush her before she can recover more!" the third, high-pitched voice said. "She could be completely helpless right now, trying to Draw Source power!"

"Or she could have gained a protector, who has been defending her all this time," the second spoke up. But the first voice scoffed at it.

"Protector? Why would anything bother to protect her, when she has so much power ripe for the taking?"

"You all felt the surge of energy when we were in the vents," the second voice answered. "A few of her systems are still active. She might have summoned a creature from a nearby planet to help her."

"For free?" the third voice scoffed. "When they can just take her power instead?"

"Not for free," the fourth voice spoke up. "She has knowledge of many different arts, and her form is said to be very beautiful, even in its current, damaged shape. She could be guaranteeing protection by training or seducing her new visitor."

"Ha!" the first creature laughed with a rasping voice. "It would take a weak and foolish male to be willing to submit to such a crippled creature as her! We would overpower him easily, and then take his own energy! I'd like to see her face then!"

You-mad, Nestor noted, sensing my anger through our bond. *You-kill?*

Yes, I thought back as my jaw clenched, struggling to remain calm. *That was already a foregone conclusion, though.*

I had realized long ago that the universe was cruel to helpless things, and readily embraced that knowledge as truth. But it was a fact that I had never been able to find peace with, no matter how hard I tried.

"Regardless of what we will find," the fourth voice spoke up again, in a tone that said it would brook no argument, "the fact remains that we cannot stay here. This room has already been picked clean, but we still had to fight a rival group to move in. Someone else will come after us, through the same vent we crawled through. We will go see what lies ahead, and make our decision then."

"I hope she is alone," the first voice hissed wickedly. "I want to see her cry. I want to see her beg for her life."

You will die long before you enter her room, I silently promised the wretched thing, coming close enough to where I could finally see their location.

They were in a room at the very end of the darkened hallway, one with another door that had been warped and battered out of its frame. Oddly enough, there was more light in the room beyond the door than in my current hallway, despite its supposed loss of power. Gray-blue light leaked from beyond the deformed barrier, disrupted by the constantly moving shadows of the beings inside the room.

I reached the entrance just as the four disgusting creatures came to a reluctant agreement, ducking behind the remains of the barrier. I sensed Nestor hiding next to the wall opposite from my own.

Now that we were closer, he tried to project his senses through our bond more clearly. I couldn't see from his own eyes or hear from his own ears, but he was able to share his understanding of what he had seen.

Four man-sized figures similar to the ones he had helped us fight earlier were about to walk through the doorway. Two of them were almost identical to the first eaterling Nestor had seen me kill, while a third looked much like the roach-rat he had struck across the face before Vessa had finished it off. The final, largest one had facial features that the little mouse couldn't recognize, other than the fact that it had a more even mix of fur, scale, and chitin over its body. Nestor suspected that it was better balanced than the other three monsters, and was probably the leader of the pack.

More importantly, all of them were holding some kind of weapon. The two weaker eaterlings carried short, dagger-like pieces of metal, the roach-rat carried a long, sharpened pole, and the unidentified eaterling carried something Nestor had trouble identifying, a short, blunt rod with strange carvings on it. It worried him because he could tell that the rod was not sharpened scrap, like the other items.

We would have to be careful of that one, but the best way to do so was to maintain the element of surprise. Which, fortunately, we could do. Nestor had seen three other bodies in the room. They were quickly dissolving, but the patches of fur and scale suggested that they were a rival pack of eaterlings. Their deaths would provide their slayers with Source energy, but as far as Nestor could tell, all but the largest of the eaterlings had been wounded in the fight, meaning their Source protection was likely close to empty. Furthermore, the blood in the air would help mask my scent.

Nestor saw them move to the opening. I made my plan quickly, relying on the shared senses of our bond to time things just right.

I let the first one pass through the door without incident, one of the two weaker eaterlings. The second was the spear-wielding roach monster, and behind him was another rat-lizard.

As the roach cleared the broken doorway, I stepped out from the warped metal sheet I had been hiding behind, activated my speed charm, and drove the sharp end of the tile straight into the abomination's neck.

The first blow made the creature shriek loud enough to make the two rat-lizards jump in surprise. The next blow made something crunch in the monster's body, and the third rapid blow following made the blasted thing's head loll as it fell to the floor. As it fell, I pointed my finger at the eaterling in the hallway and discharged my new fire spell into its chest. The wretched thing caught flame immediately and began shrieking as my lifemouse companion pounced on its face.

My speed charm was fading quickly. The other knife-wielding eaterling stabbed at me, but it was in a panic, and the blow went wide. I ducked anyway to pick up the roach-man's spear, jamming it into my attacker's body just as my charm deactivated. As it tried to pull my weapon out of its body, I slammed the tile I was still holding in my other hand awkwardly into the monster's head. The tile's corner caught the already-wounded creature on its temple and my third foe slumped down to join the first.

I stomped quickly on both of their heads to make sure they were dead. But the mistake almost killed me, because the final eaterling had pointed the rod at me and sent a blast of red energy radiating out of it.

I noticed the monster's actions just in time to get the large tile up in defense. The improvised barrier blunted the attack somewhat, until the center of the tile melted. The blast traveled right through to impact the qi shield covering my chest and pierced through it before finally being stopped by the protection of Lumei's robes, though much of the heat still blasted its way across my body. By then, the tile had grown hot enough to burn my hand, and I fell to the floor, smoking from two locations. My healing qi technique activated immediately, halting the cooking process that was already occurring on my epidermis and dulling the pain just enough for me to think and see past it.

The last eaterling was walking cautiously toward me, and I finally had time to get a good look at it. Its carapace was evenly distributed, forming a breastplate and also coating its hands and feet in a way that gave it clawed gauntlets and sabatons. Its legs and arms were covered with reptilian scales, and every joint of its body had thick brown fur, especially around its hips. Finally, it had the head of a spotted, furry hyena.

"Tri-practitioner?" the monster snarled in a deep voice, keeping its rod pointed at me. "So she had a protector after all. But why do you bother?" it asked, sounding curious. "You cannot save her. Far too many others are hungry for her."

"Who said I was the only protector?" I said with a chuckle, thinking quickly. "And if you had known just what she had to offer, you would have kept her alive as well."

"Tell me then," the revolting thing intoned, its metal rod still trained on me. "If the reward is great enough, I may spare you both."

But I knew the creature wasn't planning to spare me, even if I could convince it to spare Vessa. It hadn't shown so much as a shred of anger when I killed its three compatriots, meaning it would have no loyalty to me, either. Even if it decided Vessa really had something to offer in exchange for her life, it would have no desire to share the reward with me. I couldn't blame it for that line of thinking. Because if I had the same motives, I probably would have done the same thing.

"Fine!" I spat, raising my hands in front of me and sounding as defeated as possible. "I will speak! Just lower the weapon, and I will speak!"

"No," the hyena-roach growled back. "Talk, or I shoot you again."

That confirmed my opinion that it was the smartest of the group, something I should have already figured out when it made sure it was the last to exit the other room.

"Do you know of the planet Techne?" I asked, keeping the monster's attention focused on me.

"No," the hyena-roach repeated. "You have five seconds to make me interested enough to let you finish."

"We just jumped near that planet yesterday," I explained quickly. "She made me go down there. I gather resources for her. I found something there. A lost civilization. Full of treasure."

"You shouldn't have come back here, then," my enemy replied, sounding dangerously bored.

"She used them to fix me!" I said hastily. "I come from Earth. My people are not able to Draw Source energy at all! But you can tell I've just Advanced!"

"How?" the creature asked, sounding interested.

"There is a whole network of qi springs down there. Too many for its guardian to keep watch over. She used the water from one to refine my body. Correct its deformities. Then she put me on a special regimen that has allowed me to Advance already, even though I never Drew Source energy before yesterday. And she wants me to gather other treasure she knows about as well. And..." I trailed off, gasping for breath.

"And what?" the monster demanded, just as Nestor leaped out of the shadows in front of its face.

The eaterling instinctively brought its weapon hand up. I activated my speed charm and jumped to the side, snatching the spear off the floor as I did so. My enemy aimed its weapon back at me, then snarled in pain as Nestor climbed down and bit the thing in its furry hips.

Yuck-yuck! my mouse projected in strong disgust. *Male-beast!*

I would have found that amusing if I had time, but instead I used my new speed to deflect the monster's weapon, making its next beam fire off into the wall, hopefully not causing any further damage to Vessa. Then I shifted my spear to stab into the furry joint of its elbow as deeply as I could, let go of the weapon when it was wrenched out of my grip, and lunged forward to strike the thing in the jaw.

My enhanced speed let me duck its return swing and land another blow on its side. The carapace cracked but held. I stepped to the side to dodge a horizontal swipe, punched the ugly thing in the face again, and finally took a vicious blow to the chest just my speed charm expired.

My own protection held, but the blow still knocked me breathless onto the floor. As I rolled to my feet, the eaterling swiped Nestor off its body and wrenched the spear out of its elbow joint.

It flipped the weapon around to attack me with it, and I burned the last of my essence to activate my speed charm a final time and snatch up the rod it had dropped.

I had no idea how to activate its beam. I wasn't even sure I would be able to, or if it would take some of my Source energy to operate, energy I couldn't spare because I had already used so much in this fight. But I could still use it as a sturdy, metal club, and that was all I needed from it right now.

The rod was as long as my forearm and thick enough to be a police baton. I lunged toward my enemy, taking a grazing stab on my hip from its spear, and slammed the metal rod onto its unarmored head with as much force as I could. Then, before my speed charm could fade for the third time, I struck it again, and again, and again. The fourth blow brought the creature to its knees, and as it struggled to bring its spear back up, I dodged to the side and sent a blast of burning mana into its damaged face.

The eaterling leader fell onto its back screaming and batting at its burning snout with its good arm. As my body burned with fatigue, I snatched up the spear it dropped and stabbed into its prone form, piercing its carapace and twisting the weapon as much as I could, until my last enemy finally stopped moving. Power flooded into my body, the largest amount I had yet received, and reinforced three more times as trails from the other dead eaterlings finally drifted into me.

I panted in relief, looked at the other three bodies to make sure they were still on the floor, and then stabbed the burning eaterling in the throat to make sure it was dead.

Nestor? I asked in my mind, but I detected him through the link. The little mouse was fine except for a bruise from the eaterling's blow.

Here-here, he replied anyway, *foes-dead. Room-clear. Go-see?*

I nodded tiredly, reactivating my rejuvenation technique, and wincing as I realized just how little qi energy I had left. My essence and mana were both completely spent already, and it terrified me how quickly they had run out. Had I paid slightly less attention, or had just one more foe I had been unable to take by surprise, the fight would have gone completely differently. In fact, the last eaterling had me dead to rights until Nestor had distracted it. I had been grossly overconfident due to how powerful I felt after Advancing. The near-death experience was humbling.

But I would have to contemplate the matter later. Right now, I needed to step through the wrecked doorway and see how I could secure the room beyond.

I gave myself one more moment to catch my breath and recover from my wounds. Then I followed Nestor around the damaged doorway and into the room containing the crew emergency drive.

It was a large, triangular room, roughly twice the size of the living room back at my old orphanage. The floor was lit by some kind of glowing white tube that curved around the bottom of the wall. The opposite wall featured two metal doors, several times thicker than the ones the eaterlings had broken down, which glowed with purple-blue energy. A few feet away from that door was a waist-high barricade, several inches thick. Beyond that was another barricade that rose to a point well over my head and formed a small square, with an entrance near my current position. Inside that barricade were three waist-high terminals similar to the ones Vessa had in her sanctuary.

I had no clue whatsoever regarding how to turn them on, but they had to be the system for the crew emergency drive that Vessa had told me about.

Directly on the other side of the barricade lay the forms of the rat-like eaterlings the crew in the hallway had apparently battled. As I looked at the corpses, it struck me that I had spent at least one day in the presence of one dead body and at least eight hours in the presence of two more, but hadn't noticed them since then. By all accounts, Vessa's sanctuary should reek of death, but I hadn't even thought of the corpses, and Vessa had made no mention of them whatsoever. I would have to ask her about that later.

For now, though, I needed to identify how Vessa's pests had been entering this room. The main door showed no signs of damage and probably never would, though I had to wonder what was maintaining the field of violet energy over it. Then I remembered the monsters mentioning something about a vent, and I began checking the nearby walls. There were a few ventilation shafts no bigger than my fist, but then I noticed that one small section on the wall to my right was oddly discolored. When I ran my hand over it, the wall slid open, revealing a dark corridor traveling upward, which I couldn't see the end of. It was so narrow that even my old emaciated body would have been uncomfortable while traveling through it, but the eaterlings must have been determined enough to stuff their wiry bodies down the chute and somehow manage it. The air smelled foul, and as I listened, I thought I heard something chitter far off in the distance, followed by an unmistakable clanging noise. I stepped back hurriedly, and the wall closed up again.

A secret passageway. Probably intended for the crew to launch surprise attacks from this location. But it was a horrible vulnerability in an otherwise-secure location. At the very least, there should have been a way to seal the door from this side of the corridor. And I couldn't imagine Vessa not knowing about it, either.

This was her body. If there was even a possibility for her invaders to be able to use this entrance, she should have stressed that I check it. Maybe her ship-body's damage was affecting her more than she let on, but I didn't believe that she would forget about such an important location this close to her sanctuary.

I'd have to ask her about it when I went back to her, but in the meantime, I had to find a way to seal it or we'd keep getting unwanted guests. I closed my eyes and concentrated, trying to sense the patterns of Source energy moving all around me. It took over a minute of intense scrutiny for me to realize it, but the Source energy naturally present in the environment purposefully avoided a hand-shaped indentation next to the secret door, as if the indentation had been designed to avoid accidental contact.

I shrugged, injected one of my last remaining threads of qi into my palm, and then risked placing it into the invisible depression on the wall. A moment later, I felt the different Source energies shift, and the invisible door settled audibly into the wall. I stepped back a few feet and repeated the process of searching for an opening, and this time, nothing moved.

So it locks and unlocks with Source energy, I realized, *but that doesn't explain why the crew left it unlocked. Or why Vessa didn't know it was unlocked to begin with, although it's clear she could no longer sense this room.*

Nestor and I did one last check to make sure we weren't missing any other hidden openings, and then we slowly walked back down the corridor. By then, my qi technique had repaired most of the burn on my torso as well as the scrape on my thigh, mending both wounds to a degree that left nothing more than a dull ache.

On the way out, I stopped to loot the weapons on the dead eaterlings, particularly the crude knives and makeshift spear. The shivs were small enough to catch my Soulscape's interest, so I allowed it to suck them right up. But as I rose to my feet, I noticed that the corpses still didn't smell, and that parts of their bodies were missing, as if they had crumbled away. I specifically didn't remember doing damage like that, especially to the ones I had just bashed to death with a tile, and hurried back all the faster, worried that some flesh-eating virus had been released into the air.

A deep sigh of relief breathed out from Vessa's capsule upon my return.

"You're both in one piece," she said as she raised her head to look at me. "I could tell you survived the battle because you were in the hallway, but I didn't know how badly you had gotten hurt. Wait," she said suddenly, looking at me worriedly. "How badly *did* you get hurt?"

"Aside from a random blow or two, I took a spear to the thigh and some kind of heat-blast to the chest," I said casually. "Both of which have already healed. The skills you taught me wound up saving my life."

"A heat blast?" Vessa asked in a baffled tone. "They were more eaterlings, right?" I nodded. "How did they—wait, did one of them have a short metal rod when they fought you?"

I held up the club-like wand so that she could see it.

"Ah," she said. "That's how. One of the crew's old weapons. Blaster and close combat rolled into one item, since not every practitioner can do both on their own. Its main weakness is that the blaster function depends on your own Source energy, so it won't be much stronger than the same blasts a mana user can create on their own. Remember that if you continue to use it."

"I will," I answered, "because at the very least, it's a wonderful replacement to the old tile. Speaking of the crew, why didn't you bring up the secret door in the emergency drive room?"

"Because it was a secret," Vessa answered, as if the answer were already obvious. "Not even most of the old crew knew about it, and the ones that did always made sure it stayed locked. How did you even find out about it?"

"Well, for starters, it was discolored and unlocked, and it opened as soon as I waved my hand over it," I answered dryly. "I was able to lock it again with Source energy, but I don't know how effective that will be, because I already heard noises in the corridor beyond it, and I have no idea if there is a way to unlock it from the other side."

"There isn't," Vessa sighed again, covering her face with her hands. "It was supposed to be a hidden passageway for the crew to use for dire emergencies, if portions of the ship were overrun and they needed to reach key areas in secret, or to help me do maintenance on hard-to-reach areas. But only the command crew even knew of it, and protocol was for the passageways to stay locked unless the captain or I commanded otherwise. And even then, I should have been able to feel someone unlock them.”

“Is there any way they can unlock on their own?” I asked quietly. “Could the lock have lost power over the years—or decades, or however long you have been in this condition?”

“None,” the ship-woman answered me, still covering her face. “All my doors have self-contained power systems until they’re breached. And that specific door is no easier to breach than the wall itself. Someone must have unlocked it, and then chose not to tell anyone. Which probably means I had a traitor aboard my old crew,” she added bitterly, her voice thick with grief.

“But if that is the case, wouldn’t a traitor have done more than just unlock a single door?” I pointed out. “And why would they let someone else in, rather than taking your power for themselves instead?”

“I don’t know,” she replied. “But that’s a good point. I need to get more of myself online, so that I can remember exactly what happened. Which means I need to quit wasting time, and get to that room as soon as possible.”

“Alright,” I said, putting the spear down, and tucking the rod into a loop on my belt. “Let’s figure out how I can best carry you.”

“About that,” she said, looking away from me. “I think it would be better if I tried to walk on my own power.”

“You can do that now?” I asked, surprised.

“I… think so,” she answered awkwardly, then grew more confident. “I mean, yes. Yes, I can. If you can just help me out of this bed, I should be fine. Really.”

I didn't believe her for a minute. Vessa was an exotic, captivating woman, but her frame looked even more painfully thin than my own used to. With enough rest, food, and care, she might one day recover, but for now, she needed me, Nestor, and anyone else who was around to be patient with the fact that she had a lot of needs right now.

I had plenty of incentive to be patient with her, but I also remembered just how horrible it felt to be so weak. She was going to fight me on this, and not letting her try at all would do far more damage in the long run.

"Fine," I said as I walked toward her capsule, stopping by the clothing container to grab a spare blanket and drape it over one shoulder. "I won't argue with you, on the condition that you let me help you if you wind up needing it."

The ship-woman frowned at me as she tilted her head enough to glance at me.

"I'm trying to do you a favor, Jas," she told me in an annoyed tone. "I've been cooped up in that steel cage of a bed for probably hundreds of years. It takes care of most of my hygiene needs, but it can't fix the fact that I haven't bathed or showered in centuries. Just trust me on this one, will you?"

"As you wish," I said as I held out my hand. "Tell me when you want me to pull you out."

"Don't worry about it," she answered me as she grabbed my palm and heaved.

I felt absolutely no force whatsoever, but chose not to say so out loud. Vessa grunted once, and then compromised. She wrapped her other hand around my wrist and tightened her grip.

"Okay, go ahead and pull," she told me. "But slowly."

I nodded, and then carefully drew my hand back.

The stubborn woman's arms shook as I slowly lifted her out of the open tube with one hand. Even with my increased strength, it scared me that she was so light. I could have lifted her easily with both hands back before I Advanced even once, and I might have even been able to carry her in my old body.

But pointing out how frail she was would only make her resent me, so I kept my mouth shut and tried to help her figure out what her limits were. She surprised me by lifting one leg, and then the second, over the edge of the tube while maintaining her death grip on my arm. She managed to catch her balance on the capsule's edge and steady herself, giving a short, fierce cry over her victory.

"Okay, Jas," she said confidently, "if you'll slowly walk me to the floor, I should be fine. Just stay close by in case I need to lean on your arm or something."

"As you wish," I repeated, suddenly reminded at just how stubborn Nova could be when she wanted to prove a point. I pulled just enough for her to slowly gain her balance and begin moving off the edge to the floor. I kept my other hand ready to catch her if she couldn't stand on her own. Once again, she surprised us both by standing on her own power. She gave me a triumphant, dazzling smile, lifted a shaking leg forward to take a single step, and promptly began to fall.

I caught her with both hands. She gritted her teeth, and pulled on my arm to try again, but this time, she couldn't even support her weight with both legs, and she sagged against my arms.

"Blast it," she said, turning her face from me. "Blast it, blast it, blast it. My first time taking a step in forever, and I almost fall flat on my face."

I nodded, knowing she probably did not wish me to say anything. She looked up at me then with a glare.

"Fine, Jas," she mumbled. "You win. You get to carry an unwashed, unkempt, half-starved, crippled waif of a girl wherever you want. And there's not a thing she can do to stop you. Any questions?"

"Yes," I answered her. "Are you cold?"

"What?" she asked, still annoyed.

"You said before that your capsule kept you warm. Are you cold right now?"

"No," she said, shivering slightly. I glanced at her arm and saw goosebumps form on her pale-gray skin.

"Alright," I answered, shifting the blanket off my shoulder, and briefly wondering why there were blankets at all when her crew already had miracle beds. "I'm going to carry you in front of my chest with both arms. Tell me if I hurt you or jostle you too much, or if you get too warm or cold."

"Jas, you don't have to—" she complained as I wrapped the blanket around her. "Really, this is unnecessary—" I very gently lifted her up by the shoulders and knees. "I mean it, this is embarrassing—" I cradled her against my chest, and she suddenly sighed, and leaned her head against me. "Fine. Thank you. This is nice. Just pretend I was able to clean up a bit before you had to do this."

"Same here," I offered. "Since I just finished killing eaterlings."

"Ugh," she said, covering her face. "Don't remind me. Those things are bad enough when they're alive."

"Speaking of which," I said as I began walking back toward the corridor, Nestor squeaking as he ran past my feet. "Are their bodies supposed to crumble apart on their own?"

"Yes," the feather-light woman answered. "It's one of my sanitation features. If a foreign contaminant dies and loses its Source energy, the energy in my ship-body begins to break it down and scrub it clean of viruses or bacteria. That way, my entire crew doesn't risk getting sick if they kill something carrying a plague, or any life form with corrosive blood. But that only works for areas that I have regained power in, so be careful if you ever explore deeper into my ship-body. Your qi shield will protect you from most contaminants, but fending off enough pathogens will still tax it over time. I should get you some kind of portable filtration device, but I need more power to do that. It wasn't a priority because this deep, an oxygen loss meant we would all be doomed anyway, because my ship-body was going to break apart."

"Thank you, and watch out," I said as I stepped carefully through the first of the ruined doorways, making sure not to bang or cut Vessa's body on the broken metal.

"Ugh," she sighed at the damage. "And I had to spend so much power just to reactivate them. Now, they've broken so badly that we can't even open or close them without extensive repairs. Hopefully, the rest of the doors will keep holding, like they have until now."

"I saw no damage on the doors in the drive room," I offered as I carefully stepped through the next broken doorway. "If what I did to the hidden passageway closed it off enough, we should finally be safe."

"I wouldn't say that," Vessa warned as we ducked under the final wrecked barrier. "It tends to guarantee that something else will go wrong. But at the very least, we'll both sleep a little better."

"And when Nova comes on board, we might be able to help you reclaim more rooms," I pointed out as I turned another corner.

She was still very light, and she seemed as if she was getting drowsy as she rested her head against my chest.

"Yes, that is the idea," Vessa admitted with her eyes closed. "A lot of things should be easier when I bring my Beacon on board. Thank you again, Jas," she murmured. "Thank you again for everything you have been willing to do for me."

"You are very welcome," I said back as I cautiously turned a corner. Nestor had gone ahead just to make sure the room was still safe, but a happy squeak confirmed that no new trouble had shown up. "And I wouldn't give up any of this, Vessa. Not the food. Not the clean clothes. Not the bed. Not the whole, healthy new body, or the magic that came with it."

"You'll get more," she promised sleepily, starting to doze in my grip. "I will give all the help I can, to help someone like you go far."

Her words sounded curious to me, but we had passed the last corner and arrived at the hallway where I had battled the eaterlings earlier. A question occurred to me as I stepped around the dissolving bodies.

"Vessa," I began, "why do the eaterlings change so much as they Advance? And how many different stages are there?"

"Mmmm?" she mumbled from my chest, before blinking her eyes open. "Oh. That. Everyone's form changes a bit when they Advance, Jas," the ship-woman yawned. "Especially full-fledged Sourcebeasts. You will see Nestor's body change when he gets more powerful, though I don't know exactly how, since his growth will be modified by his bond with you. Mana-using practitioners change the least, although some will take on traits of a specific element of mana."

"So are eaterlings practitioners or Sourcebeasts?" I asked as I stepped between two more dead bodies, subconsciously holding the lighter woman more carefully all because of it. "Because I keep hearing you refer to them as monsters."

"That's a much better description, frankly," Vessa muttered darkly as she tilted her head to glare at the final corpse. "The line between practitioner and Sourcebeast blurs a good bit, except with races like your own. Eaterlings are actually an offshoot of several different races. Their history is complicated and frankly gross, but the short of it is that they took on practices like cannibalism to more thoroughly absorb Source energy, and it led to uneven advancements, where their minds lagged far behind the progress of their bodies and grew warped over handling the difference. When they were cast out of their communities on account of their depravities, a small group of them gathered together to form packs of their own. They somehow managed to interbreed, and what you see at your feet is the result."

"And they're this common?" I asked giving the last foe, the hyena-roach that had nearly killed me, a glare of my own as I walked past him. "And should I be worried about killing this many in only two days?"

"At the lawless edges of the night sky, yes, they are this common," Vessa confided sadly. "They are extremely easy to kill, even in large numbers, but they breed rapidly unless you make an active effort to stamp them out, which most worlds do now as a matter of habit. But no, Jasper. You will be fine as long as you take time to Draw later, and your Soulscape seems to be helping you absorb and purify energy by itself. That said, I am impressed you killed this many on your own. You have a good instinct for battle, Jasper Cloud."

I recalled my near death and felt very differently about that, but by then, I had carried her into the room containing the emergency drive. At this, she shifted around in my arms to get a better look around.

"Good, good…" she said quietly, scanning the doors and the walls. "This should all hold…"

Then she sighed, and looked back down.

"They're all gone, though," she murmured. "I already knew they were dead… but I hadn't known it would hit me so hard. I..." She swallowed. "I need a minute. Is that okay?"

I nodded, shifting her slightly so that we could both be more comfortable. Vessa pressed her face against my chest and heaved into my clothes for a few moments. I felt Nestor crawl up my pant leg and burrow against her neck, squeaking softly at her. Eventually, she stopped quivering, and composed herself, giving the fluffy mouse a smile and a gentle pat on the head.

"Are you alright?" I asked, worried. "Do you need more time?"

It ached, to hold someone so frail, and then see them grieve so deeply, and so quickly. I felt inadequate to the task of supporting her, but I was all she had. But Vessa shook her head as she removed it from my chest.

"I need a lot more time, just to get better from all the thoughts that have been in my head until two days ago. But you cannot give me that time, or Nova and many others will die. So I will bury myself into tasks that must be completed until we are all safe enough for me to risk finding out how I am feeling. But thank you, Jas… again," she added as she looked away from me.

"You're welcome," I said awkwardly. "Do I need to keep carrying you, or should I set you down next to the terminals behind the barricade?"

"Set me down right in front of them," the ship-woman commanded. I picked what looked to be the most comfortable, cleanest spot, and lowered her carefully onto the floor, blanket and all. She gave me a look that I had learned to recognize as grateful and annoyed at the same time, and then she pulled the blanket around her shoulders, touched the terminal with her other hand, and closed her eyes. "I'm beginning now," she told me. "You don't need to do anything but make sure nothing disturbs me for a bit. Which means you probably shouldn't try to talk to me either, unless something catches on fire or tries to kill us," she added as an afterthought.

"Noted," I replied with a grin. "I will shut up and let you work."

She gave me a wry smile with her eyes still closed. Then she frowned in concentration, and a blue glow flowed from her and into the device she was touching.

All of the lights flickered for a moment, despite having their own sustainable power source. Then they inexplicably dimmed, leaving the room dark except for the faint blue glow coming from behind the barricade.

Nestor and I stood watch while I wondered what we would even do if something larger than an eaterling suddenly forced its way in.

A loud bang from beyond the metal doors answered my thoughts.

It wasn't coming from directly behind the door. I had no idea how far away the actual source of the sound was. But another loud clang rang out moments later from somewhere beyond the hidden door, as if in response.

Nestor hunched down, fur raising and tail thrashing worriedly.

Not-near, the fluffy rodent assured me. *Can't-smell. Still-safe.*

Good, I answered, but the lifemouse still did not relax. In fact, Nestor hadn't seemed this worried even when he was showing me the giant winged monster that consumed the dead back on his world. *Why are you still afraid then?* I asked my friend.

Don't-know, he said to my mind as his whiskers twitched. *Don't-know.*

I wanted to try and comfort him, but then something whispered from the walls.

I drew the battle-rod and whirled to face the direction of the sound, but saw nothing. I thought my sight to be a lie. No whisper loud enough to be noticed could have come from beyond my field of vision.

But the next whisper from beyond the farthest metal door disproved that very thought.

"Heerrrrrre…"

Somehow, the voice was able to crawl through over a foot of Source-imbued metal, travel across the room, passing several barricades, and shudder its way up and down every pore of my body before it twisted its way into my ears.

More banging sounded. This noise came from much closer.

"Heerrrrrre…"

This time, the whisper slithered through the now-seamless secret door before it crawled up my spine.

I suppressed my shuddering long enough to realize that this whisper had both a different pitch and tone from the first, meaning that it came from a different voice. Then I began shuddering again.

"Sheeeeeee's…" the wall whispered again, "heeeeeeerrrrrre."

Chittering came next. The sound I had only thought I had heard when I poked my head down the shaft before.

"Doooowwwwwwn…" the voice somewhere behind the farthest door said. "Heeeerrrrrre."

Behind the barricade, Vessa continued to glow, and the new shadows continued to dance. I pointed my weapon at every one of them, ignoring my own demands to calm down.

"Yesssssssss…" A third voice crawled out from behind the other door. "Fooounnd… herrrrr…dowwwwnnnn...here!"

More banging, this time coming from the final door.

"Giiiivvvvve…" the first voice hissed, as the banging from its door grew louder.

"Giivvvvve…" the third voice said, over its own crashing, slamming sounds.

"Giiiiivvvvvvvvve," the second voice hissed from the wall, and I swore the chittering sounded no farther than a short hallway down.

"Her!" the voices all shouted as one, bringing a cacophony of angry sounds.

Scared-scared, Nestor spoke up, reminding me that I was not alone. Sanity forced its way through a loose window back into my mind.

Go next to Vessa, and make sure she is still alright, I commanded, taking a deep breath and tightening my grip on the battle-rod. The shadows continued to dance, and something beyond my view continued to beg and hiss and batter about, but nothing else loomed out from the dark.

"Giiiiivvve…" the three voices demanded in unison, growing louder, more menacing. "Givvve her!"

And then, they went silent.

But the banging and chittering did not.

The shadows continued to dance as the terminals nearby lit up briefly, flickering as if they were ancient light bulbs. *She's doing it,* I thought. She was bringing the room back online. I had no idea whether that would help with the voices, but at least it meant that something would change soon.

Providing I could stay sane that long.

"Givvve," the voice in the wall said, its hiss less pronounced. "Give… me… her..."

The clearer the voice became, the closer it sounded. It now sounded directly behind the sealed wall.

"No!" the voice behind the first door boomed, making metal everywhere rattle. "Give… *me*… her!"

"NO!" the voice behind the final door screeched in a warbled voice. Something started slamming against the barrier, making the purple screen over it shimmer and come to light. "MINE! MINE! SHE! MINE!"

"MINE!" the other two voices shouted. "MINE!"

"MINE!" another voice answered, and by now they were too loud for me to keep track of where they were coming from.

"MINE!"

"MINE!"

"OPEN!" they began shouting next, each voice trying to drown the other two out. Scratching noises sounded from every closed exit. "OPEN! OPEN! OPEN NOW!"

My skull ached as panic and pain tried to pound their way out. I dropped the baton so that I could clutch my skull with both hands, to push back against the forces trying to blast it apart. *What was I thinking*? I asked myself. I couldn't stand against forces like this. These were not lizards and cockroaches. These were things that could reach straight into my skull and force me to see things, hear things that could not be there.

That was it, I decided. Something was attacking my sanity. After all, there was no way these giant monsters could ever be this close to Vessa's sanctuary.

Except that Nestor had clearly heard the voices too, and even now, he was shivering next to the Soulship's flesh-body.

"Give!"

"Me!"

"Her!" the voices all shouted in competition.

"Open!"

My hand flinched, and with a dawning horror, I realized I actually knew how to open one of the doors in the room, and just might be driven insane enough to do it.

I don't want to, I said in my soul. I didn't want to give this woman to the mad things, lurking within these walls.

But would I do it anyway, to save my own skin?

Was that not what I deeply believed? Was that not what I warned others to believe, because no one would look after them?

"Give!" the doors shook.

"Me!" the walls shook.

"HER!" the floor shook.

Nestor shuddered where he hid. Vessa remained quiet on the ground, lost in whatever world she went to repair her metal second-body.

Two days, an evil part of my mind pointed out. I had known her for less than two full days. Did I really care about her enough to oppose the lost, hungry gods howling and bumping about in the dark? Did I really owe her this sanity-wrecking battle? Why was this my job again?

It doesn't have to be, a deep, calm voice that I had not heard in over a decade spoke within my mind. *You don't have to take up our mantle, son. No one's going to make you care for her.*

The memory of my father's words came clear as day, though I still could not recall the time and place he had said them at.

It's not your job, and it may never be. And even if you do meet her, you don't owe her anything. She won't know who you are. She doesn't even know who we are. She'll probably depend on you, but she's depended on many before, and they've all left her. Even though they owed her more than you probably ever will.

All I can tell you, son, my father continued, *is that she is worth protecting, and that you won't regret doing so, not ever. And you can protect her, son. It may not be a job they ever gave us, but it's a role our line knows by blood, and by training that we've passed down as carefully as we could. Make your own choice about her, but don't let anyone tell you that you shouldn't, or can't.*

As his memory finished speaking, my Soulscape began to spin.

My fingers found the baton. My feet began moving step by step toward Nestor and Vessa. My Soulscape pulled in their direction.

"GIVE! ME! HER!" the mad beasts in the dark all screamed, banging and chittering and scratching at every door. But the words of my long-dead father had quieted all my fear.

I knelt down next to her, the only other person living in this dark, gibbering world, still touching the glowing terminal with her eyes closed, breathing as if she was asleep, Nestor huddled fearfully but protectively against her. She still looked frail, still looked brave, still looked beautiful. The planet inside my soul tugged for her, tugged for Nestor, though it was not nearly large enough yet to contain either of them. But I reached for them anyway, and this time I felt my planet *push.*

It wasn't trying to pull them inside of itself. It was trying to get outward, to cover them.

And in my madness and fear and quiet confidence, I let it.

Pain burst out of my palm as a tiny, steady trickle of Source energy poured out of me. It felt as though my soul had been punctured and was now leaking all over the floor. But the planet inside me stretched its way out, widening and venting atmosphere until it could cover my last two friends in this darkened, steel world.

"GIVE! ME! HER—"

The voices trailed off immediately, as if someone had smothered them on the spot. After a moment, they spoke up again, but this time not nearly so loud and intense.

"Where… her?" they asked each other, puzzled, before turning angry again.

"You… took!" one of them accused, only to be rebutted by the other two.

"No! You! Took! Give!" they all shouted at once, fading away as they continued to argue with each other.

The lights flickered once more, then fully came back on, chasing the shifting shadows away. The terminals all let out a quiet, steady hum as blue power lit their surfaces.

Best of all, my gray-skinned friend opened her eyes and smiled.

The invisible power from my Soulscape retracted back inside of me. When no voices returned, I sighed in relief.

"It worked," she said, too distracted to notice me pulling back my invisible shield. "I can feel this place again. I can feel the walls and floor and doors."

"Anything on the other side of them?" I asked carefully, trying not to sound too worried.

Her lids closed halfway as she considered my question.

"No… not at this time," she said firmly. "Actually, they all seem as if they've been untouched for a while. Same thing with the secret door, except I can tell when you opened, closed, and locked it recently."

"Oh," I sighed in relief. "Good."

"Why?" she asked suspiciously. "Did something happen? I couldn't hear anything while I was working."

Much-noise, Nestor projected into both of our minds. *Much-fear. Bad-bad.*

"Oh, you poor thing," the women said sympathetically as she reached for the little mouse, caressing his fluffy head. "That sounds like it was terrifying."

"Something beyond the doors reacted when you brought the room online," I said to her. "Something that wanted you specifically. There were more than one, and they didn't want to share you with each other."

The ship-woman took a deep breath as she answered me.

"I think I know what those things are. My mind is still very hazy, but the short of it is that ages ago, the other Soulships and I gathered to battle something that came from beyond the night sky. I can't remember exactly what it was because of my damage, but I remember that it was hard for our sensors to detect their forms, or even their numbers. Every one of us had to abandon our planets to meet them in one great battle, because they were already darkening the worlds beyond our reach. I can't remember everything that happened, not even whether we were victorious or defeated, but I could hear brothers and sisters and mothers and fathers of mine all die in great plumes of fire and pain. In the end, we either drove the nightmare back or were forced to retreat, but something else was waiting for us on the way back to our worlds, something different, that I still can't remember. We did an immediate emergency jump to another grouping of worlds, and again, a different enemy was waiting for us, forcing us to jump again, and then again, and then again, each time with the strongest Soulship sacrificing him or herself so that the rest of us could escape. In the end, only I was left, damaged and confused and unable to stop running, because something else would decide to come after me if I ever did. Eventually, I calmed down enough to think, and realize that no one was chasing after me. So I hid for a few centuries with what was left of my crew, until one day, we were able to figure out that most worlds couldn't even remember the existence of my race. So I started to try and do my job again, because it was all I knew how to do, and because I wanted to keep the night from burning apart in case the things beyond it returned again."

She closed her eyes as she spoke, and I thought she was seeing the past under her pale eyelids.

"It was a mistake. I became hunted again, and new hunters mixed with the old. Packs of Sourcebeasts and schools of practitioners saw my ship-body as a treasure, one they were willing to fight, kill, and conquer for. And old foes, ones I could remember only with great difficulty, picked up my scent and began chasing me again. So I resumed running, still trying to hold the night sky together wherever I could, hiding Beacons on worlds to give what little help they were able. But I kept getting damaged, and losing crew, and then one night, I realized that boarders had snuck in somehow without my systems noticing. Some of them had been dormant for a long time, waiting for me to get weakened even further. And then they all struck—no, they struck one by one—no, that's not right either." She covered her face again. "I can't remember exactly what happened. All I can remember was my crew frantically fighting and falling back, pulling me away from the fight myself and dying as they worked to get me to safety. In the end, the last of them carried me to these rooms, strapped me into this capsule, then fought their way back out to clear and seal as many rooms as they could. None of them ever came back."

She pressed her face into her hands, as if she was trying to bury it.

"Then I began to run out of power. I can survive indefinitely in near hibernation, but the truth is that both my ship and flesh-body have too many needs, and I can't perform many functions without meeting at least a third of them. That's why I've risked sending you planet to planet and had you gather silly things like water and dirt, just so that I could process the trace elements in them. Making you scavenge the most common of resources, and right after you saved my life, of all things."

"If you are really sorry," I said gently to the brave, broken woman, "then tell me what else you need from me, so that I can help you further. If you can, do so without feeling any shame, because right now, my life depends on the health and safety of your own."

I scooted closer to her, in case she wanted to be touched or held, but she just shook her head.

"I won't need much more from you, Jasper," she said confidently. "I discovered a trick when I made Nova. I can't explain how it all works, but she and I will be able to repower each other. She'll Advance quickly, and be able to take on the dangerous tasks I've forced you to keep doing. You can work on your own Advancement in relative peace, and when the time comes, we will see what we can do to save your world. Or at least, what's left of it," she added uncomfortably. We both knew why.

"But for now, though," she continued, changing the subject. "I've done everything I need in here. Activating this room has already given me more power. I'll be able to jump us to new locations, and more frequently—including your own world, so that we can go back and get Nova. And I'll be able to do all of that from our sanctuary." She suddenly grimaced. "I just won't be able to do all of that while getting up and walking on my own. So I'm going to need you to carry me again, Jasper. If you don't mind."

No one's going to make you care for her, son, my father's voice echoed in my brain.

I extended my hand for Vessa, making a decision she might never know I had just made.

Chapter 10

We jumped again. Vessa re-seized control of her ship-body's engines, activated the power of her backup drive, and sent us hurtling through the night sky, guiding the ship to the location of Nova, her newest Beacon. Unlike the last jump, this one was slower, and more controlled. Where the last jump had been a desperate attempt to use speed and surprise to travel in a location her pursuers could not determine or easily reach, this jump would be a careful, controlled path, arriving much slower, and harder to detect now that Vessa could activate her emergency stealth systems. They would not last a very long time, but I only had a limited window to get Nova away from the cage drake anyway.

What I had a much harder time understanding, however, was the fact that we would spend so many days traveling through space while Nova was still in danger. When I brought that concern up once again, Vessa patiently reminded me that only moments had passed back on Earth, because time inside the Soulship advances at a much faster pace. I did not understand the workings behind it, but right now, every day inside the Soulship was only a moment back on Earth. It was not always a consistent difference, Vessa had said, but at the very least time would always pass a little more quickly inside Vessa's ship-body than it would in the worlds under the night sky. Vessa's race had depended on this difference to help them manage and protect the many worlds under their care.

So we spent days traveling back to Earth.

And in that time, I rested, and Drew, and trained, as my inner planet spun frantically inside of me.

It was not that beneficial. Most practitioners spent years just to Advance to the very first stage, which was why they tried to begin the practice of Drawing in their early childhoods. My Advancing to the first stage of every Source art so soon was a massive stroke of fortune, but it still put me far behind other practitioners my age, such as Koram. Vessa refused to answer me when I asked just how many small children there were that were far beyond my level.

But that would not matter, she assured me. I did not need to slay Nova's captors. I only needed to divert their focus enough for Nova to break free of them. Vessa would recover us both afterwards. Every ounce of power or skill I gained made that task just a little more possible.

But the time for training soon passed, and we arrived once more outside of Earth's orbit. I watched as Vessa closed her eyes and concentrated on what exterior senses she could still control with her ship-body.

"They're still here," she said as she stared at her eyelids. "Same number, and as far as I can tell, they're the same ships that had been chasing me all this time. I wish I could get a visual on them," she said with a frown, opening her eyes. "But all I have right now are the crudest of my scans."

"What about my world?" I asked anxiously. "What about Nova?"

"Still in the exact same location, Jasper," the ship-woman said calmly. "Neither her nor the cage drake have moved yet. Other people and creatures are approaching the location, however. So work fast. And don't die," she added worriedly. "I mean it. I'm pretty sure it would break Nova's heart. And… you're the first creature I've met down here in ages that didn't want to hurt or eat me. I've really come to appreciate that," she said as she looked away. "So be careful, okay? Both you and Nestor."

"I'll do my best," I promised as Nestor squeaked in agreement. I picked up the crude spear and examined it. It had come a long way from being a random piece of scrap metal. I had sharpened its edge to the best of my limited ability, and Vessa had used a bit of her mana to enchant it. It was still far inferior to that of a practitioner's Sourceweapon or the warbatons Vessa's crew had been using, but she assured me that I could count on it to injure the cage drake and pierce most protection arts around my level of Advancement.

The baton had received no further modifications and was currently tucked into my belt. I had a plan for the weapon.

"Ready," I announced as I walked next to the proper device. Nestor crawled into the front pocket of my robe.

"Alright," Vessa said as she gave me one last look from her capsule bed. "I'm teleporting you to the position we talked about before. It should give you your best chance. But remember, all you need to do is help Nova escape. Once that's done, come back here immediately, if I don't beam you aboard myself. Now go, and good luck."

That was the last thing she said to me, before my body traded a world of metal and darkness for a world of tall buildings and a blue familiar, sky.

The change was disorienting, but I forced myself to remember that Vessa had teleported me far above the ground below. I spun my body around and watched the earth approach. It would meet me in moments, for I was less than thirty feet in the air. But I saw my target in time and plummeted down spear-first into the cage drake's body.

The Sourcebeast, or monster—I had no clue as to which it truly classified as—had been concentrating on expelling its shadowy breath all over Nova. I caught a glimpse of her glowing blue body as she tried to break free of the dark encirclement, but it was a losing battle for her.

I remembered Vessa's warning, that the cage drake had been bred for hunting and trapping, not fighting as I drove my spear toward the creature's serpentine neck.

The monster noticed me just in time to whip its neck out of the way and try to knock me away with its shadowy wing. To the surprise of us both, my improved polearm shredded through the smoggy membrane and stabbed into the monster's flank. That prompted a startled shriek of rage from the beast as it twisted its body and struck out with one of its clawed limbs.

But I was already moving. I pulled my spear out of the wound and leaped backward, holding it up in a parry to catch the incoming talons. The blow overpowered my guard and slammed into me, as I figured it would, but it blunted the attack just enough to keep the drake-thing's claws from penetrating my Source-augmented robe.

I rolled backwards and landed back on my feet, feeling my chest for injuries and noting that Nestor had already leaped off of me. That was a good thing, but I did my best to forget about the little mouse and turn my full attention to the opponent in front of me.

Glowing purple eyes glared at me from an alligator-like snout. The cage drake had abandoned its breath attack in order to turn and deal with me, this new figure in strange robes that had literally fallen from the sky to do battle with it. Far behind it, I saw Nova glow even brighter as she tried to drive off the cage-like smoke still circling around her. She would need more help to get free of the last of it, but that was not my duty.

My duty was dealing with the large, dark thing resembling the classic monster from my parents' illegal fairy tales.

Wings flapped more smoke into the air, at an irregular pattern since one had been shredded.

"Who are you?" the monster hissed. "And how did you break the laws of this world by wielding a Source?"

"I have no idea what you are talking about," I told the creature, happy to trade words with it since it would distract the dragon-thing further. As it visibly grew angrier, I spoke up once more. "But I have a question for you that may answer your own: why did they spare me all those years ago, instead of killing me with the rest?"

The monster had begun rearing up to attack me, but then it suddenly cocked its snout.

"What? Wait." Its purple eyes narrowed. "You are him. The scrawny one that the little boat threw her life away to save. What happened to you?"

"Food, clothing, and shelter, mostly," I answered with a shrug. "Apparently it was enough to make a difference."

"Ridiculous," the monster scoffed. "You were past the age most Earth bodies stopped growing. The only way you could have possibly changed this much was through essence or qi, and no Earthling can manipulate such forces."

"Why?" I asked. "Why are my people the only ones denied the ability to enhance ourselves?"

"Who knows?" The creature shrugged, making its wings flap once more. "The legends say that long ago, your race traded the right to Draw and harness Source energy in exchange for a supposedly greater power, one that you foolishly squandered some few ages ago. But that does not matter. Tell me which of the energies you gained, how you possibly gained it, and why she threw you back down before she left."

Before she left…

I caught myself from reacting to the creature's words as I realized none of Vessa's foes knew that she had returned. But of course they hadn't. It had been mere moments on Earth since we had left. And she had returned under stealth, somehow invisible to their eyes and detection arts. They may not even be aware of how quickly time can pass inside of a Soulship. Her being here would be a total impossibility in their eyes.

"She threw me back down because I wasn't the one she wanted, I became like this by touching the glowing power inside of her. I have never even heard of Source power before today, and have no idea what the differences between them are," I lied easily to each of the drake's questions. "Now tell me why I was spared when my own parents were not."

"Ask your leaders," the monster snarled, as it raised a massive paw and stepped forward. "They make the decision regarding which of you live and which of you die. But you have injured me, angered me, and probably lied to me, all while having climbed only the first rung of a thousand-mile-long ladder to power and immortality. So I will break your body and teach you humility, and then give you over to the lapdogs of this world. Then you may ask them for as many lies as you wish to hear."

"Fair enough," I said as I crouched low. "But for the record, I know why you had them ban the old stories of my people."

"They were full of stories of my race," the drake rumbled, suddenly seeming much larger as it continued to grow closer. Another massive paw pulled it closer still. "They did not need to know of our existence."

"Then your kind are all fools," I answered bluntly. "The fairy tales never taught us that dragons, or monsters, or bogey men were real. We did not need them for that." I shifted my footing and raised my spear. "We needed them to teach us that monsters can be killed."

With that, I burned my speed charm and charged the creature.

The cage drake hissed in surprise, rearing backward and blasting out with its breath weapon, but I was already dodging to the side. I reared my spear back and threw it forward, hoping again to hit the creature's neck, but once again it parried with a wing and diverted the missile into its other flank, giving both wings and sides of its torso matching wounds. Once again it shrieked in pain and lashed out at me with one of its claws.

Had I more time, I would have been surprised at how easy this fight was going, because the monster was clearly two full stages of Advancement beyond me at the very least, and an essence user at that. As it was, however, I chose to focus on using my superior speed to tumble below the next blow and barrel into the monster.

I bounced right off, of course. The thing was several times my size and at the Blooded stage of essence Advancement. But my attack still earned a pained hiss from the thing, because I had drawn my two makeshift daggers back from my Soulscape just before impacting fist-first.

The monster writhed backwards and struck me with its massive tail. I felt my qi shield give way, my robes do what little they could to absorb the blow, and then I was flying through the air. But before I could crash back into the ground, I somersaulted to land on my side while keeping my arm straight as it slapped the ground, discharging just enough of the kinetic energy to keep my bones intact.

As I rose painfully from the floor, clutching the new bruises the dragon-thing's tail had given me, I found that my enemy had not pressed the attack. Instead, it hung back cautiously, watching me with new interest.

"Training," it hissed, circling me slowly. "They gave you training after all. Your breeders taught you battle, as well as all the other forbidden knowledge."

"That bothers you?" I demanded. "The fact that I retained knowledge of how to take a fall all those years ago?"

"Of course it does," the dragon-thing snarled. "The fact that they were able to teach you that knowledge at such a young age, and still have you retain it after years and years of neglect, means that you are one of *them*. A legend your rulers should never have forgotten to fear! It means your breeders were slain for the wrong reasons, and that you very well should have been slain with them!"

I bared my teeth and brandished the single dagger I had managed to retain from my earlier fall.

"You're welcome to correct the mistake yourself," I taunted, pacing toward the monster's injured side in a slow, careful circle. "That's assuming that dragons are not afraid of legends themselves."

"Insolent wretch!" the shadowy drake roared. "You are a hundred years too young to taunt one of my kind and live! The rest of you stay back!" the beast suddenly roared, as if it was speaking to someone far behind me. "He is mine to kill! You are not permitted to interfere!"

I could not believe my good fortune when I heard its words. But its next act made me question my gratitude, as the massive creature tensed its limbs and vaulted straight at me.

I burned my speed charm again, but it was not enough. A claw twice the size of my head caught my torso and slammed me painfully against the alleyway wall, too quickly for me to do anything about the impact.

"Natal stage," the monster sneered as I stabbed at its paw with my remaining dagger, this time not bothered by the pain. "You grasp the weakest of the mysteries, and think yourself special enough to challenge those who are gods!"

"You are no god," I gasped, raising a finger, as if I wanted to admonish the onyx-colored creature. "I have seen far mightier things than you."

With that, and since my speed charm was still active, I quickly traced out a mana spell and sent a fiery bolt straight at the monster's face.

The burning missile took my enemy completely by surprise as it scorched the monster's face. It screamed as it clutched its face and tried to crush me in its grip, found that it had been thwarted by my qi shield, and finally slammed me against the wall two more times before throwing me back onto the pavement.

I rolled and slapped the ground, but still heard at least one bone crack audibly. Something in my side made me scream in pain as I rose back to my feet, rushing to Nova now that the monster was no longer between us. On the way over, I burned the active portion of my recovery technique to hold my body together long enough to win this fight.

"Tri-practitioner!" the monster screamed in surprise. "A tri-practitioner has been hiding all this time on a sealed world! How did you all let this happen?"

I ignored him as I rushed toward my goal. The darkness was starting to fade around Nova. If I could just get to it before my charm ran out…

"ENOUGH!" the draconic voice behind me boomed, and shadowy chains blasted all around me. "I will make an example of you here and now, and orders be damned!"

Shadows tightened around my limbs and neck, choking me and painfully bending my joints backwards. I managed one single step forward, gave one last look at the shroud of smoke covering my childhood friend, saw how her figure thrashed inside of it.

Then I smiled, twisted with the chains so that I could move downward, and ducked.

The last of the chain-like smoke vanished as it was slashed apart. A tall, beautiful, blonde woman stepped out from it as she pointed the war-baton that the tiny yet surprisingly strong mouse on her shoulder had given to her after it crawled through a crack in the darkness that had suppressed her.

"Let go of him," the woman commanded in a powerful tone, as she pressed down on the weapon's glowing rune.

A burning red beam as thick as my head blasted out from the baton and toward the cage drake's head. The monster's eyes widened at the sight of its prey breaking free, but it had been too busy containing me for it to dodge in time. The blast incinerated its way clear through the monster's skull, and the drake's body slumped to the floor in a cloud of ash and Source energy, the latter drifting toward us in translucent streams.

Shouting began all around us. I heard footsteps rush toward our direction. Beyond all of that, something bellowed powerfully, with enough force to harm my ears and shatter windows.

"We need to go," I said, pulling my way free of the dissolving chains. I looked back to see Vessa standing before me in all of her glory, blue eyes shining with a faint glow, blonde hair whipping about as Source energy trailed into her…

No, Nova. Her name was Nova.

I told myself her name again and again. But I could not shake the fact that I now saw the faces of two different women whenever I looked at my childhood friend.

The shock of Source energy trailing into my own body shook me back into action. It surged into me on a level that put my brain and body into overdrive, making me *need* to act, *need* to think.

"Nova—no, Vessa—no, Nova," I said as I moved in front of her. My friend was watching me with a bewildered expression, as if she could not believe what she saw. "We need to go. Right now. Can you take my hands?"

"Jasper?" the beautiful woman asked, sounding dazed. "I… it's really you. You came back… and you've changed."

I chose not to press her. She had just helped me escape moments ago into the sky above, only for me to come hurtling right back down and battle her captor in a new body, along with a tiny mouse both small enough to climb through the cracks of her shadowy prison while still being strong enough to drag an advanced alien weapon that she somehow recognized up to where she could grip it. I was lucky she had managed to go along with my outrageous plan at all.

So I carefully put my arms around her as the Soulship's power enveloped both of us. The next second, Earth's broken world vanished from our eyes.

Chapter 11

Nova stumbled into my arms as we reappeared inside Vessa's ship-body. It hurt, because she was still holding the war-baton, and she poked my chest with it.

"What?" she said as her light-blue eyes looked all around. "Where are we—no, why do I know where we are?" she asked, her expression sharpening. "And what happened to you, Jas?" she demanded, eyes narrowing. "Why do you look different? And are you really Jas? Prove it!"

She pulled herself out of my grip and pointed the baton at me.

Vessa hadn't pulled us back next to her capsule, for some reason. We were in the hallway, at the entrance to her sanctuary.

Nova blinked, and then suddenly swiped in front of her face, as if she was knocking away something only she could see.

"Don't interrupt!" she shouted at no one in particular. "I'm not going along with any of this, until I know he's really Jas, and that he's really okay!" Her eyes locked back onto my own. "Prove it," she demanded, sounding angry, and frightened, of all things. "Prove to me that you're really Jas, and that you really remember me, and that this isn't some trap designed to mess with my hopes and dreams!"

I carefully stepped backwards, slowly raising my hands.

"How do you want me to prove it, Nova?" I asked, trusting that Nova still had enough power to jump us to safety without my help.

Vessa, I reminded myself. *Nova is the Beacon, Vessa is the Soulship. Ancient American gods, this is hard.*

"Tell me how we first met!" she demanded, jabbing the baton forward. "Tell me where, and what happened!"

"We met on the streets, and you know I know that," I said firmly. "And I never told you everything that was happening. I'm not sure you ever figured it out."

"I *did* figure it out!" she snapped. "Tell me anyway!"

Banging sounded out in the distance again. It was farther away, and possibly not even able to enter here, but one of the many things lurking in this ship had grown agitated again. I sighed as I began to recount the story.

"It was about eight years ago," I said to the suspicious, trembling woman. "I had already been homeless for two years. You had apparently only been on the streets for a couple days at most. You may have only been on your first day. I wouldn't know, because I never asked."

"Tell me what happened," Nova repeated, not lowering the weapon. "Tell me all of it."

"One second," I asked as I turned my head toward the sanctuary. "Vessa, get us out of here if you need to! Don't wait for us to work this out!"

"Got it," the woman shouted back from her capsule.

"No more talking to her," the blonde woman said with an angry, and... possessive, edge. "Tell me how we met!"

"You were clearly lost and scared. You had just lost your foster parents, and you had nowhere to go. You looked at everyone nearby with pleading eyes, like you wanted them to stop and help you, but you didn't know how to ask them for help. You just wanted someone that was an adult to notice you and make everything better."

"How many?" she asked next. "How many of them stopped to try and help me?"

"Of the adults in the street? None of them," I said, annoyed. "Of course no one stopped to help you. They had their own problems. You were so ignorant of that, I felt bad for you, but then a man in front of a building called out to you, and asked you to come over and talk to him."

"And what did he say?" my oldest friend demanded. "What did he do?"

"Nova…" I pleaded, because I had always hated this part of the story.

"Tell me, if you're really Jas!" the beautiful, angry woman demanded. "Tell me what he tried to do, and what you did afterwards!"

"He tried to get you to go into the building with him!" I snapped, angry I had to recall this memory. "He said he had a bed, and warm clothes, and food and candy, and if you just agreed to do whatever he asked, you could live there as long as you wanted, and that you would both make a lot of money! He was a brothel owner, Nova, and he thought he could make money by preying on an innocent and pretty little girl!"

The words spat out of my mouth, but not fast enough. I still felt like I wanted to throw up.

"Now can you please stop pointing that weapon at me?" I asked, feeling disgusted and guilty for still having the memory.

Liquid lines streamed down from Nova's eyes. She lowered the weapon slightly, pointing it to where it would barely graze my body, but then she shook her head.

"Tell me what you did," she insisted, with still-streaming eyes.

"Ancient American gods, Nova, I barely did anything at all! I didn't try to stop or expose him, and it wouldn't have mattered if I did, because I was too weak and no one else would've cared if they knew what he did! I just threw myself at his feet and begged for him to take me, too!"

"You told him I was your sister," Nova stammered, eyes shining with more water. "You said no one else would take us because our parents were terrorists, and that everyone thought they'd get in trouble if they helped us!

"...And then you told him that you'd work twice as hard as I would, and then you grabbed his leg and kept begging and mentioning how our parents were terrorists. So he panicked, and kicked you away, and said he didn't want either of us. Then he ran inside his house and locked the door."

"And then I yelled at you," I said bitterly. "I shouted that you can't trust anyone anymore, now that you're on the street. That the next time you believe someone who wants you to come with them, you'll wind up dead or wishing you were dead. That if you wanted to live to see tomorrow, you needed to get smarter, and to do it right now, or else you'd wind up like one of the bodies I kept finding when I woke up the next day."

"And then when I started to cry," Nova said in a trembling voice. "You said you were sorry, and that you shouldn't have yelled. You took my hand and told me that you didn't know what to do either on your first day, but that you figured it out, so I probably would, too. Then you asked if I had eaten anything today or had any warmer clothes, and when I shook my head, you told me you had hidden some food, and a spare blanket, and a safe place to sleep for the night. You said that you would show me how to survive 'just for today,' so that I could get the hang of it, and not wind up like those bodies you had just talked about." She sniffed for a moment, still trembling. "And then the next day when I woke up and cried because I knew I would be on my own, you told me you could help me 'one more day.' And then it was 'one more day,' for the next eight years, Jas," she said as her voice cracked and she finally began to cry. "It was 'one more day' even when

I didn't help us find food and just screwed everything up, even when I started to get bigger than you, because you always shared *too much* of your own food with me, Jas. And when I got citizenship and was allowed to learn in school, you always tried to help me with my homework, because you somehow knew more than what they taught me, and then you got swarmed by the other kids who wanted help from you too, and you spent all your spare time helping other kids study for a school you were never allowed to attend!" The blonde woman let out a sobbing heave.

"So I need to ask you, Jas, even though I'm scared to find out the answer and I'm scared to ask you something you never noticed yourself! Did anything else change, when you got this new body, the one I always felt like you deserved, even though it didn't matter to me, because I can't see you as anything other than a hero mounted on a horse? Are you still the same Jas that knew the world was rotten, but kept building his own tiny better one, that he tried to make room for us all to live in? Is that you, Jas? Are you still my Jas?"

By now, she had lowered the baton completely, though I saw that she had kept her finger off the activation rune the whole time. I sighed, threw my hesitation to the wind, and pulled her into an embrace, not knowing what to tell her.

Nestor crawled back up her shoulder and squeaked, nuzzling his fluffy face against her cheek.

This-friend? he asked, and Nova's eyes widened, letting me know he had spoken to her as well.

"Yeah, Nestor," I said out loud, since the lifemouse could apparently understand people when they spoke verbally now. "This is the friend I was telling you about. Nova, meet Nestor."

Jas-friend? the little mouse asked, apparently able to say my name, now that he recognized the one-syllable version of it. *Jas-good,* the fluffy creature told Nova firmly. *Jas-help. Jas-save. Cares-you,* the little rodent affirmed. *Loves-you,* he added, taking me by surprise.

But Nova smiled at me, and just now I realized that she had to look upward to do so.

That would have to do for now, I realized, and the banging started up again.

"We'd better get you to Vessa," I said, wondering how I was going to handle this next meeting.

I gently led my friend by the hand into Vessa's sanctuary. Nova looked all around at the blue lights and dark metal tiles, eyes widening at the sight of the different terminals and other devices, either in surprise or uncanny recognition.

"Hurry," Vessa said from her capsule, raising a pale-gray hand. She looked tired again, a fact that frustrated me.

She also looked like Nova, which confused me. I had sworn both of these women had looked different a day ago.

"I thought I told you to already jump," I said irritably as I brought my oldest friend over to my newest—not counting Nestor.

"Trying to," Vessa answered. "But it's better if I have enough power to do it under stealth. Is your friend finally ready?"

"I'm here," Nova said confidently, stepping forward. "Now tell me why I was…" Her voice trailed off as she made eye contact with Vessa, and the shining orbs of both women widened in recognition.

"You," Nova said to her, stepping forward.

"You," the gray ship-woman answered, reaching for her Beacon with a trembling hand.

"You're…" The blonde woman trailed off, still coming closer. "Me… you're me…"

"Yes…" Vessa said simply, still tired, still holding out her hand. "Come…"

Her words hit me harder than any of the cage drake's blows. I staggered away from the two women… who had just claimed to be one woman…

It didn't make sense. But the banging in the distance reminded me that there were many things in this place that did not make sense, and we did not have time to wait for them too. Nova's head tilted slightly as she heard the sound.

"That's them," she announced, finally stepping up to Vessa's capsule. "They want to eat us."

"They won't stop with just us," Vessa answered her. "If they eat us, they'll be able to eat everything else, and the night sky will grow dark…"

"But we can't let that happen," Nova answered, her hesitation leaving. "It's not who we are."

"It's our sky to keep bright," Vessa nodded. "But I can't do it without your help. I need back what I gave you."

"You have it," Nova said firmly. "All of it. But I get all of you in return. And he gets to be safe," the blonde woman demanded. "He can't just be our tool."

"Then you better never point a weapon at him again," Vessa said back. "I don't care what our excuse is."

"We didn't have one," Nova admitted. "I'll do better too, then. Now let me quit hesitating and do this."

Without another word, the two bodies reached out and clasped hands, and then my entire world went white.

For a brief moment, the two women melted and merged together. Golden-tan skin met pale-gray skin, as bright-blonde hair met jet-black, as bright-blue eyes met cloudy-gray, all in a bright pool of blue light that spilled out into every device in the room. The ship hummed with power, as more lights that I had never noticed flickered on to chase shadows away.

My Soulscape started spinning, hungrily sucking in the blue light. The spiritual world grew, to almost double its old size, and Nova's comment suddenly drifted into my mind

You knew the world was rotten, so you tried to build a better one…

The little planet pulled at the spinning women, Drawing Source energy from the air as it did so. I felt my qi condense again, as a second drop began to form, halting though, as if it had a question I needed to answer. The same thing happened to the mana and essence in my soul, wanting to form another wisp, and another crack, but needing an answer to a question I didn't even know I had.

But my inner planet kept pulling at the two dissolving women in front of me, and when they didn't move, I found myself walking toward them. Finally, I had stepped into the pool of light covering their bodies, and once again, the planet opened my soul to vent spiritual atmosphere around them.

Protect, I heard it say. *Protect… protect…*

The distant banging quieted, as if our hidden lurker had suddenly lost the scent of its prey.

Then the melting figures suddenly separated into two gold and silver pools, rearing up and forming themselves into two feminine bodies, distinct from each other, yet similar in such a way that I couldn't help but think of the other even if I only saw one of them. They threw back their long-haired heads and cried out with liquid mouths, creating two notes that somehow blended in harmony.

The two bodies let go of each other. The golden pool backed away, panting as it became Nova again. She looked at me with her bright-blue eyes, now glowing unmistakably, but with equal parts pain and gratitude.

"Blast it, Jas," she said, without revealing why. "After every promise I just made you…"

"What?" I asked, completely baffled.

I turned and saw Vessa, sitting upright in her capsule, taking deep, strong breaths, and staring at me with eyes that drowned her cloud-colored cheeks in rain.

"You… hypocrite," the ship-woman breathed, shuddering as she spoke. "You kind… clueless… brave… hypocrite… how dare you never stop… thank you."

I backed away helplessly from both bodies of the ship-woman. I couldn't begin to figure out how to respond. But the world inside my soul spun joyfully, as if it had gained something precious.

"They're going to find us soon," Nova spoke up in a serious tone. "We can be mad and happy at him later. But for now, it's time we left."

"Agreed," Vessa said as she turned her attention to the new lights within her capsule bed. "Stand by for an additional jump. This one will be a longer one."

"Standing by," Nova said as she grabbed my hand and led me over to a terminal with handles. "Jas and I will wait right here. This will be a bigger jump, Jas, so you'll need to be more careful for this one."

I nodded dumbly, distracted by the two new objects that were floating around my Soulscape.

"Activating now," Vessa said, reaching and touching the new light on her capsule. "Hold on tight, in case something goes wrong. And Nova?" The gray, dark-haired woman turned to look at the tanned, blonde one. "I'm glad I got to meet me."

"I'm glad I got to meet me, too," Nova said as she grinned back. "Even if Mr. Hero here is unaware of how much trouble he's in."

"Not making any sense, by the way," I said distractedly as I stared into my soul.

"We know," Vessa said as the blue light spilled from her capsule. "But don't worry. We'll find a way to fix this. So that you can be happy we're so mad."

"What?" I asked, completely confused. But neither of the woman's bodies gave me anything resembling an answer.

Shield her, the planet inside me said. *Help her… we need all of her to light up our night sky.*

I looked inside myself again, but the two new objects were still there. Off in the distance, a constantly exploding light was sending waves of radiance out over my spiritual planet. Sailing through that light was a tiny spectral boat, sail catching the light as if it were wind that could power the vessel across the invisible seas in my soul.

Another drop of qi suddenly coalesced inside of me. A crack in the image widened and completed. And a wisp of gray joined the tin deposit inside my mind.

Then the floor beneath my feet rocked violently, as the Soulship took me and her other two bodies off to some new place under the night sky.

End of Book One.

Afterword

Hello everyone! I hope you enjoyed my book and I really appreciate you reading up to this point. This is my fifth published work, so I would love for you to leave feedback on a review on Amazon, especially if you liked it. Reviews are the lifeblood of indie authors like me, helping our books get the exposure readers need to find them. If they can't find our books, they can't buy them, and then we authors starve and die, instead of continuing to write. Is my writing still good enough that I should keep going? Please leave a review and let me know what you think!

You can also join my facebook page, Armies of Avalon, for more information on dates for my work and also meet other people who read my stories. It will be my primary method of communication, so that no one gets lots of email spam. Barring that, you can also follow me on Amazon. I can also be contacted at the email addres nathan.thompson.writer.email@gmail.com.

Thanks to all the people that helped me polish my book: Dantas Neto, Ezben Gerardo, Adam Shook, Regina Benton, Sean Bradley, Brock Daniel, Denny Johnson, Antonio Nelson, and Odhinn Crosson. I greatly appreciate both your feedback and time spent reading my drafts. Special thanks also to my editors, Celestian Rince and Stephanie King, who have both worked figurative and probably literal magic on this story. Finally, thank you Antti Hakosaari for your phenomenal cover art, and May Dawney Designs for your excellent typography.

This is a work of fiction. Names, characters, businesses, places, events, locales, and incidents are either the products of the author's imagination or used in a fictitious manner. Any resemblance to actual persons, living or dead, or actual events is purely coincidental.